ROUND

CW00482641

Frederick Louis MacNeice was ~~~~~~~~~~ up in Carrickfergus, Co. Antrim and educated in England. He studied Classics and Philosophy at Oxford and was known as a translator, literary critic, playwright, autobiographer, BBC producer and feature writer as well as a poet. He died in London in 1963, and was buried in Carrowdore churchyard in County Down, with his mother.

Jon Stallworthy, FBA FRSL is Professor Emeritus of English at the University of Oxford. He is also a Fellow and (twice) Acting President of Wolfson College, a poet, and literary critic. Stallworthy's biography of Louis MacNeice was published in 1996.

Roundabout Way

Roundabout Way

Louis MacNeice

writing as Louis Malone

FOREWORD BY JON STALLWORTHY

CAPUCHIN CLASSICS

CAPUCHIN CLASSICS
LONDON

Roundabout Way

© The Estate of Louis MacNeice 1932

This edition published by Capuchin Classics 2012

Foreword © Jon Stallworthy 2012

2 4 6 8 0 9 7 5 3 1

Capuchin Classics
128 Kensington Church Street, London W8 4BH
Telephone: +44 (0)20 7221 7166
Fax: +44 (0)20 7792 9288
E-mail: info@capuchin-classics.co.uk
www.capuchin-classics.co.uk

Châtelaine of Capuchin Classics : Emma Howard

ISBN: 978-1-907429-38-5

Printed and bound by CPI Group (UK) Ltd, Croydon CR0 4YY.

To my Wife
who has the gift of
enjoying and so will
(I hope) enjoy this
unheroic story

Contents

Foreword	11
Chapter One	15
Chapter Two	26
Chapter Three	36
Chapter Four	50
Chapter Five	61
Chapter Six	73
Chapter Seven	88
Chapter Eight	102
Chapter Nine	117
Chapter Ten	133
Chapter Eleven	143
Chapter Twelve	155
Chapter Thirteen	170
Chapter Fourteen	188
Chapter Fifteen	201
Chapter Sixteen	215
Chapter Seventeen	234
Chapter Eighteen	247
Chapter Nineteen	257
Chapter Twenty	265

FOREWORD

Louis MacNeice embarked on his second novel in the autumn of 1930, when a newly appointed Assistant Lecturer in Classics at Birmingham University. He was encouraged to do so by his Head of Department, the poet and distinguished scholar of ancient Greek, Professor E.R. Dodds, who would become a lifelong friend and, later, his Literary Executor. The novel was drafted by May 1931, when MacNeice wrote to Anthony Blunt that it contained 'someone vaguely like you . . . Only no one will think he's you because he's a) of medium stature and b) well-tailored.' He went on: 'If you think of a good *nom de plume* for me, do let me know. It seems reviewers blackball one if they know one's an academic. I want to keep my Christian name though.' At some point he settled – probably not at Blunt's suggestion – on 'Louis Malone', a name with a good Irish pedigree ('Sweet Molly Malone') and just a hint of himself as the Romantic Solitary (Louis M[.]alone).

He sent a copy to Rupert Hart-Davis, who had written encouragingly about his previous (unpublished) novel when he had sent it to the then junior reader for William Heinemann a couple of years previously. Hart-Davis found its successor 'readable'; offered to send it to Heinemann; and generously volunteered to read the proofs if it were accepted. His praise of a minor villain of the book, the Revd John Bilbatrox, produced an interesting response from the novelist: 'By the way (as you say you like Bilbatrox) I hope to write a novel about North of Ireland clergymen (one of the few subjects I know something about) – mainly hypocrites but one, at least, hopelessly sincere.'

Despite Hart-Davis's good offices, Heinemann did not accept the book. In January 1932, MacNeice told Blunt he was revising it and, in March, wrote triumphantly: 'my second novel, *Roundabout Way*, which I had given to an agent, has just got itself accepted by Puttenham's* (all along with Marie Stopes)'. In October, he sent Blunt a parcel with a letter saying, less euphorically: 'Herewith my unhappy novel in its goddammed wrapper and full of other people's punctuation. I wrote it 2 years ago and am not now very interested in it, especially . . . seeing that it was a negative experiment, an attempt to write a novel according to popular standards 'coherent'.' This is probably an honest statement, but MacNeice's coolness may also owe something to embarrassment at the portrait of Blunt that his friend would find in the book. Hogley is unmistakable: a brilliant, cynical and witty young don, he dislikes women, has strong views on architecture, and is consistently described as the serpent in the garden: 'his head poised like a cobra' with a 'snaky smile'.

Roundabout Way is a light-hearted romantic novel (containing many references to romance and its cognates), in which Boy meets Girl, loses Girl, recovers Girl and, at the last, seems likely to live with her happily ever after. It is almost certainly a sequel to the earlier public-school novel, and chapters 8 and 9 describe a return to Hillbury/Marlborough (where MacNeice was famously at school) that may well be a recycling of material from the first book. *Roundabout Way* is unashamedly autobiographical. Devlin Urquhart, its orphan hero, has abandoned his course in philosophy at Oxford and been diagnosed, *in absentia*, by 'England's leading neurologist', Sir Randal Belcher, as suffering

---

* A misspelling of Putnams.

from '*Acute* psychosis . . . bound to end in suicide' – a diagnosis based on the subject's alleged wild behaviour and a paper glorifying intolerance 'and full of remarks about courtesans', delivered to an Oxford college society. Devlin runs off to disguise himself as a gardener, saying to the father of a friend (recognizable as his own friend John Hilton): 'SEX and LIFE are the two great things to avoid . . . that's why I'm going to be a gardener. I imagine you don't get either if you're a gardener.' His phoney Northumberland accent is recognized as such, and his cover blown, by Sir Randal's spirited and rebellious daughter Janet. She looks like MacNeice's wife Mary: has a roundish face, 'like a rather mischievous moon', white skin, dark hair, and 'a ballet dancer's figure'. She, too, 'dances like perfection' and wears chypre. More interesting are Devlin's resemblances to his creator: 'Thought of being taken to church when wan and little. . . . The smell of pew varnish, the marble skull opposite belonging to John Hogarth, the frightening intonations about *sin, hell, death*.' Devlin 'wished his mother was alive. Not his father though.'

Roundabout Way is a young's man's novel, but the exuberant work of a young man who would become a major poet. This, his only surviving novel, is a revealing introduction to the author of such twentieth-century masterpieces as *The Sunlight on the Garden* and *Autumn Journal*.

Jon Stallworthy

CHAPTER ONE

'That's that,' said Sir Randal.

There was silence. From this room there was no escape; the door was hidden by a heavy curtain. Just such another curtain hung over a cupboard and four more such over the windows. The pattern on the curtains was both heavy and straggly.

In the middle of the room was the table, a vast pile, product of fine fancy and many men's labour. On the right side of Sir Randal was the fireplace, huge as a mausoleum, hidden in which was a cold, funereal fire. On his left side was a vast mirror, well trained to reflect the impressive home-life of England's leading neurologist. (It had ample opportunity to learn its part, everyday's cues being nearly exactly the same as those of the year before yesterday.)

The whole family was at dinner except Aileen, his second daughter. At the head was Sir Randal, on his right Janet, his third, on his left Elaine, his fourth, at the foot Maude, his eldest daughter. All separated by several yards of table.

Sir Randal looked angry, but at the same time pleased. He had just been blowing up Janet about her new young man, Garfield, to whom he had been so successfully rude this afternoon. Janet had asked him to tea. Whereas Sir Randal saw at once that he was not, or hardly, a gentleman – why, his only amusements seemed to be dancing and socialism, as Sir Randal had now triumphantly explained – in spite of Janet's arguing. Janet was the one who demurred most but none of them ever succeeded. The great unrippled mirror remembered their defeats.

The silence sat like a mist on the Family Table, on the Family Plate, on the Family Glass, on the Family.

'Not another word,' said Sir Randal suddenly. Janet's small white hand flashed from under the table and seizing by its neck the heavy port decanter, whizzed it over Elaine's head crash into the mirror – right in the middle, starred from corner to corner.

There was a second silence.

Janet, gone quite green, pushed back her chair and stood up. 'I've always wanted to do that,' she said and forced a laugh; walked to the curtained door and pushing the cumbrous revenge-laden curtain forced her way outside.

Sir Randal gazed at the mirror; it had been very expensive (to his father, that was); what was far more, it had been a permanent symbol. But now something new had come and broken it. Elaine, who was still a schoolgirl, was crying, Maude was indignantly flustered. Whereas himself felt not so much angry as brought down with a bump and very tired after his day's work.

Had got up at seven this morning, an hour's revising proofs before breakfast; had, after breakfast, answered eight letters; had after that rung up Griffiths and arranged about the amendment to be put to the Association; had then rung up George and promised to preside at the Committee Thursday next; had then driven over to the Burfield Mental Home, and examined three new cases; then lunch; hard on lunch had taken the train to town (having promised Maude the car to see Lady Spinder) and in his consulting room in town had had half an hour's interview with that stupid fellow Grayling.

Not that there was any doubt that Grayling's ward was a case; but after all. After all he (Sir Randal) had other things to do. Though he did think young men who were obviously wrong should be kept a careful eye on. It was they who corrupted the next generation's morals, who ate into the nation.

And this boy Devlin Urquhart sounded a bad case. Clear case of psychosis. Yes, he was unfair to poor Grayling; he was right to come to him. They might sound petty, the boy's misdeeds, so far (bad manners, eccentric, undependable), but remember the Bolshevik Government. It was the work of just such runaway boys. And it was against this type in our youth, mentally unsound and dangerously assertive, that he and Bilbatrox had started their campaign – the campaign the newspapers were full of, campaign for a new sanity and purity in England.

He must remember to read that essay of the Urquhart boy which Grayling had left him as a sample.

Sir Randal stared at the mirror – he was a hard worker, struggling with national evils, but at the same time he had always been a father. A good one. But look now, children could not be calculated. His mind zigged and zagged between anger and merely being upset. In anger one knew where one was; otherwise one was merely upset.

Meanwhile the Graylings were upset too. In their dining-room Mr. Grayling was telling his wife all about the interview – 'Really an astonishing man – such insight; I'd quite forgotten how he struck one – it's quite three years since I've met him personally; almost more striking than when he's on the platform.' 'He's certainly a very striking speaker,' said Mrs. Grayling. 'Yes, very striking indeed. Puts it all so plainly and at the same time powerfully. That's what I like in a speaker——'

'So he actually said Devlin was not quite?'

'Oh, I wouldn't quite say that, dear——'

'Well, he obviously is. I shall never forgive him for this. I've hardly slept the last two nights, you know I've not.'

'No, darling, it's very hard on you. Sir Randal thought that was the worst point about it. He says there's obviously something wrong about a boy who can't show gratitude.'

'He never *has* shown any. Never in his life. Look how he behaved at Hillbury.'

'Yes, he's behaved very badly. Very badly indeed. I can't understand it at all.'

'And then when we pay money to send him to Oxford, then he goes and runs away. It's astonishing.'

'Yes, it's astonishing.'

'Rupert and John now——'

'No, of course, Devlin was never like *them*,'

The. Graylings became silent. Mrs. Grayling slowly drew back her lips in a fanged and thoughtful smile – rather like that of the fanged tiger kippered on the wall behind her.

Meanwhile Devlin at his refuge in Yorkshire, the home of his friend Gunter, was showing off to the Gunters. Perhaps it was the April spirit for the rooks were showing off like mad outside. Bragging about their prospects.

'SEX and LIFE are the two great things to avoid,' said Devlin; 'that's why I'm going to be a gardener. I imagine you don't get either if you're a gardener.'

'I'm afraid you're a *poseur*, Devlin,' said little Dr. Gunter, twinkling his eyes; he expected young men to aim at effects.

'No, no, I'm not,' said Devlin, apparently believing himself, 'I'm not a *poseur* at all. That's just what I'm running away from. LIFE and HAVING TO FACE REALITY – that's where the pose comes in; all just so much claptrap.'

'What do you want to face then?' asked Gunter; he was an ordinary 'intellectual' undergraduate, always heckling among the smoke-rings.

'Oh, nothing much. Flowers, I suppose, and mud.'

'Seriously, Devlin,' said Dr. Gunter, 'you're not really thinking of being a gardener?'

'Yes, I am.'

'But you know, you have to know something about it.'

'I know that, but one must start somewhere. As a sort of apprentice or gardener's boy or something.'

'Awful low pay, you know; besides, do you think you're strong enough?'

'Oh, I'm strong enough, aren't I, John?'

'Yes,' said Gunter, 'he's a lot stronger than you'd think.'

For Devlin was short and thin but wiry, a little monkey-like; his eyes were brown and rather sad like a monkey's. When he was excited in talking he hunched his shoulders.

The trouble about him was, Gunter thought, he was too much brain and not enough – well not human enough. Of course he could be as enthusiastic as hell, but somehow one felt it was a display commanded by the Government; at the back of the bunting and mob fervour of the body was a cold man in an office or cabinet of ideas. When he knocked down Harvey for instance. An ordinary man knocks another down on the impulse, but not Devlin; it was a put-up impulse. And this breakaway to be a gardener, it was surely all pose.

Still he was rather delightful, Devlin. One never felt one knew him, but he was good to look at as a spectacle or performance of masked figures. And *poseur* though he was, he at any rate posed vigorous; refreshing after the Oxford languids. But chucking up Oxford in the middle of one's second year was a bit quixotic; he would never go through with being a gardener. Or, if he did, it would just be damned perverseness.

Dr. Gunter went on talking; he was satisfied with his life, but that young men should be discontented seemed to him natural. He liked an iconoclast. He went fishing for icono-clasm in his spare half-hours.

'What, do you think of Bilbatrox' lecture-tour?' he asked. And Devlin rose like a young and arrogant fish.

'I think it's muck,' he said.

At that very moment Bilbatrox stood on the platform of one of the largest halls in the midlands.

'Our mission is not one peculiar to either clergy or laity. Our campaign is a campaign of universal importance. We stand not for the aims of sect or party, but for the redemption of the country at large. When two of the most prominent men in the country, the Bishop of Veir and Sir Randal Belcher, came to me one wintry day in November and suggested the creation of this magnificent league, a league which should conduct a campaign through the length and breadth of Britain, a campaign with the double object of a moral regeneration and a physical revival, *mens sana in corpore sano,* a pure mind in a pure body, on receiving this proposal I was struck first by the proposal itself, secondly by fact that I should be invited to a leading place on its executive. I cannot tell you how honoured I felt by their selection of me as their colleague. (Loud clapping.) I felt at first like St. Paul on a similar occasion. I thought I was but a weak vessel, a vessel unfitted to hold the priceless wine committed to it. Never the less I prayed for strength. . . .

'And now I stand before you and in the name of all that is pure, of all that is noble, and of all that is holy, I ask you, I implore you, I challenge you, to be on our side in the great combat of today, to grapple with today's problems and crying evils. What are those problems and evils? Look anywhere, around you, look at the back streets of your own city.'

And he told them many home-truths about their negligence, which, considering they were soulful and sensible people, was really extremely culpable. After which he went home to the comfortable house of his host (the Lord Mayor), much flattered by his reception. While his audience too went home, much flattered by the thought of their soulfulness and sense and even slightly moved by that of their negligence. For they were now sharers in the work of the future, the backbone of the country, the kernel of the nation. There were many evils in the country – oh, dreadful evils; think of all children in the slums, the children who should never have been born . . . he was broad-minded, the Rev. Bilbatrox; like Dean Inge, but a much more telling speaker . . . but it was only right to be broad-minded, one must move with the time; we are all on the move now . . . that great man is devoted to action, so are we all . . . action, devotion, social regeneration . . . it is We who shall make the future. . . .

And so they fell asleep; on hair or flock mattress, and, underneath that, box spring, vi-spring or something else comfortable.

Though the best mattresses in the country were owned not by a Christian at all but by Herzheimer, the aluminium king, now sharing them illicitly but according to his custom with Mella, the lady 'whose life was like a book.' He too had heard Bilbatrox – on the wireless – and had burst into loud laughter (he had a vast chest with black hair on it).

'Do listen, Mella,' he said, 'this is that puritanical rogue who came pestering me last week.'

'What? The pig who wanted a subscription?'

'Yes, he is a rogue, that man. He bluffs die public!'

'They call it a campaign, no?'

'Yes.' Herzheimer like all good Jews and Jesuits, was omniscient; he explained to Mella how the English love philandiropists.

'What a swine!' said Mella, 'and who is the other fellow? A doctor you say. I thought doctors had more sense. Famous ones, I mean.'

'He is a poor chap,' said Herzheimer, 'he is carried away by publicity. I dare say he has a good heart.'

'Well, for God's sake let's go to bed,' said Mella; her nerves were bad after their row that afternoon. It was their first row since they came to England three weeks ago. Paul had begun it so abruptly while she thought he was reading.

'Now we are in England,' he had said, 'what do you think about looking for your son?'

'Gabriel you mean?' The idea splashed over her like cold water and for a few minutes she let him talk, then she argued.

She had left her husband before that crash, it was all so long ago, Gabriel had been so young, he must be all right now, enough money to get on with, she could do him no good blurting out of the past, why, what good on earth could she do him?

So Herzheimer gave in; if he had had a son alive, his nature would have goaded him to find him but Mella was different, rather a tigress.

'Let's go to bed,' said Mella, and putting his arm round her he led her upstairs to the gentleness of their bedroom where the lights were hidden in the cornice.

Just as they turned on the lights, a taxi drove past their house. In it was Devlin Urquhart's friend and patron, Cyril Hogley (a don at Devlin's college). He and the two young men in the taxi had just left a riotous party and all smelled of spirits. They were looking for Gabriel Crash, who had escaped from the party a little earlier and much more drunk.

'Merde,' said Hogley, 'there's absolutely no chance of finding him.'

It struck a quarter to eleven. Gabriel was standing in the alley way beside a cinema which had closed down ten minutes earlier. Twenty minutes earlier he had bought a ticket to the astonishment of the girl, and staggered in to see the final embrace. Coming out in the crowd he had retired for quiet into the alley which was used for queues. But it was not reposeful. A huge female sprawled on the wall before him. She had very little on. Gabriel found her repulsive.

Bits of old records kept humming in his mind (he never went to dances or revues, but he was always buying records), humming like telephone wires, then suddenly vanishing as if the wires had been cut. Humming and oozing, sexually arrogant, snakily slimy ; saxophones, Americans, negroes; Jack Smith, Sophie Tucker, Nick Lucas. Nothing but romance – wedding-rings and cradles and a sky the colour of rhubarb.

Like the sky behind that female there. Gabriel prodded her with his stick.

'Hullo!' he said. 'What's the point, anyway?'

But it seemed there was no point.

'Good-bye,' said Gabriel and waving his stick at her, he went off. He felt on the whole happy; the records, though, had a nasty taste; too much jam.

As he reached Hyde Park Corner, it struck eleven. The sound galvanised him. Beating time with his stick he began to sing:

'Here we go round the Marble Arch,
The Marble Arch,
The Marble Arch;
Here we go round the Marble Arch, at five o'clock in the
morning.'

A policeman's face appeared – hanging in the sky like the moon. Even though he had a helmet he was much shorter than Gabriel. Gabriel had nothing but his hair which was wild and red.

'Here,' said the face, 'what do you think you're doing?'

'Why,' said Gabriel, 'I'm singing.'

'What are you singing about?'

'About the Marble Arch. This is it, isn't it?'

'No it's not. What I'd like to know is——'

'Bum,' said Gabriel (as Hogley said, Gabriel when drunk had only three moods – vulgar, sentimental or dangerous).

'Here,' said the policeman, 'stop it. You've been drinking, haven't you?'

'I don't know. How do you mean drinking?' Gabriel stood swaying, tall against the night.

'Need a bit of looking after, you do. Just you come with me.'

The policeman's arm took him by the elbow. A taxi appeared, driven by a face with a huge moustache. As they were getting in, Gabriel dropped his stick, which the policeman picked up. 'I'll look after this,' he said.

'I say,' said Gabriel, sprawling in the taxi, 'ever heard the story of the three little birds?'

'What I want to know is,' said the policeman, 'how you young fellows can afford it. Always on the drunk or the randy.'

'Three little birds,' said Gabriel sleepily. How comfortable taxis were——'

But the policeman made him get out again; the cold air splashed in his face, nearby a slowly moving car was pushing the shine of its lights along the wet of the road. The policeman pushed him forward.

Everywhere there were policemen – one of them jovial, one of them gruff with a moustache. After that he was again able to sleep.

He had a very good and cosy sleep, but when he woke up his head ached. He wanted fruit, a grape-fruit or an orange. There was a dim light in wherever he was. It was all tiles. High up in the tiles was an aperture with bars – a 'drain-strainer' Gabriel thought and then proudly realised he had coined a word.

He began to sing – the room was pleasantly resonant like a bathroom. Incidentally there was a lavabo in it. That was very odd. Gabriel stared and stared at it. He went to sleep again.

When he again woke, his limbs were stiff and it was dawn. He took in that he was in gaol. He felt full of the world's wisdom as he stared cynically round the walls. He could hear clankings, bangs, laughs inside the building – and outside, through the bars of the drain-strainer the sound of early hustle, horse traffic; a car being cranked, refusing to start, at last starting. Then another car drawing up, the engine left running, then going away again.

There were all those nasty grand phrases in Freud; that last one was a good one, 'anal erotism'; very suitable, very suitable.

Theories. Excrement. Barks. Clatter.

Russian novels and Russian plays. Hogley had said to him: 'The only place you'd feel at home, Gabriel, is a Russian novel.' Bloody bogus rot.

Outside the dogs barked. It was dawn in England. They were barking under Herzheimer's window too. Herzheimer woke;

living on his nerves he was not a good sleeper. Mella woke too by instinct, turned over towards him and stroked his forehead and his hair which was greyed and curly. The dogs stopped barking.

But the dogs outside the gaol went on. Gabriel took off his shoes and loosened his socks from his feet. His tongue was rough, and he was wildly thirsty. 'I almost wish I'd taken that tutorship,' he thought.

'Though there can't be any worse hell than teaching the piano. And the brat's father talked too much. Everyone talks too much. Still, I don't know where I'm going to get any money. One can't live on tick for ever. If one's an orphan one ought to have the knack of getting on. I. don't suppose there's many grown-up orphans so bad at getting on as I am. Perhaps it's because I talk too much. Everyone talks too much. Everyone thinks he's got an axe to grind, and it's only his own bloody teeth – or like hyenas who eat their hind legs out of spite.

All theories are just spite – like, those dogs out there. The only decent thing is to compose or play music. No message, no moral, no point.

Gabriel sat gloomily thinking on the great wooden bench of the cell. Outside the dogs continued to yap.

CHAPTER TWO

Gunter came into Devlin's room as he was shaving. Devlin's face, always pale, looked macabre under the lather. 'Damn you, John,' he said, 'that record you would play yesterday made me have a nightmare.'

'Nonsense. What was your nightmare?'

But Devlin would not tell him.

'You mean 'The Rosy Road'?'

'Yes.'

'But how on earth could *that* give you a nightmare?'

Devlin would not explain. Gunter was all right but he had something missing. He would find his dream an interesting conceit but nothing more.

Whereas it had been to Devlin purely tragic. He had gone to bed tired and found it hard to get to sleep. Kept hearing his ear ticking in the pillow. Had felt suddenly discouraged about his garden scheme. Saw himself as a fraud, a pocket pseudo-Tolstoy. Had thought of even Hogley as rather a fraud too. And Hogley was the one person he allowed himself to imitate. He was the 'free man,' unalloyed by prejudice.

But as he lay in bed he felt lonely – Hogley was no comfort. He wished his mother was alive.

Not his father though. His father was another of the people who were so fine and yet impossible – impossible to get any sympathy from. And he fell asleep repeating to himself: 'My father was governor of Madras.'

He dreamed he was straightway in the middle of a vast garden with tall threatening yew trees and an unending series of terraced lawns, of the smoothest possible grass, dotted with stone vases of flowers. Suddenly he was slipping into the house which had appeared from nowhere, and gliding through doors to the tune of Gunter's record, and pushing back Victorian curtains and slipping between screens, there at last in a room where there was a table with a pot of tulips on it, he found a girl standing; and it flooded his mind at once that this was his own life's lady. Before anything could be said she vanished and he was running through the corridors crying. Coming out through the french windows he saw her whitely slipping down the long darkening lawn; and he himself felt himself flying, skimming only a foot or so above the ground, and occasionally dipping, like a gull, to touch it with his toes. Black clouds hung on the yew trees and the whole garden seethed like water before a storm; he felt the animals were creeping to their holes and nests. But that white flake in the distance inspired him till she disappeared round a great clump of yews. And he, flying round it in a rush of following wind, came to a dead stop. For there she was but she was stone. She was beautiful and white but only a stone statue.

This dream he would not tell anyone.

At breakfast, in order to forget the dream, he was very merry.

'So you're really leaving us today?' Mrs. Gunter said.

'I'm afraid so,' said Devlin, 'I must really start my vocation some time.'

'But will they take you on if they see you're a gentleman?'

'It's quite a serious point,' said Dr. Gunter. 'In this country they like a man to keep his place.'

'Never mind,' said Devlin, 'I'll be a yokel. I'll have a dialect,'

'The other gardeners will soon see through that,'

'Oh no, they won't. I shan't be a local yokel you see, I shall have come from somewhere distant.'

'Scotch?'

'No, no. I refuse to be Scotch or Irish. Far too romantical. But Westmorland would be quite nice, I think.'

'And what about the dialect? Ever been in Westmorland?'

'Not me. All the more fun inventing it. A dialect's merely a matter of rote. You merely go to the other extreme from high-class pronunciation. If you want to talk high-class you say: 'At Flaahz in the Azaahs Sir Richard Grenville lay,' and if you want to talk dialect, you say. 'At Vloots in the Azoors,' and when you want to write it, you put some dots on the top.'

'You've been reading William Barnes,' said Dr. Gunter, and Devlin laughed; he knew where he was with Dr. Gunter, who was essentially fair and sane; whereas the creatures at Oxford must be either one thing or the other – to them Devlin was either a genius or a bleeder.

'Well, I'll give you a pound if you get away with it,' said Dr. Gunter, 'but: hadn't we better lend you some clothes? You're too respectable as you are.'

So they chose some clothes, Devlin strictly banning anything 'romantical,' especially John Gunter's suggestions for neckwear.

'You don't understand,' he said; 'I'm not doing this for a spree. I don't want to go about like a nature-poet.'

At half past two he left the house, respectable English household – clockwork maid, faded mistress, twinkling Dr. Gunter, and walked with Gunter to the station, respectable English station plastered with notices of trips – the word PLEASURE flaming everywhere. Of course – it was nearly Easter. Time for awakening. Devlin wondered if he could ever get away from the torpor of this everyday world.

The bell went and he leaned out of die window as the wheels revolved, and said good-bye to Gunter, respectable English undergraduate – tussore tie, restrained voice, neither shockable nor shocking, very charming but in no way vital.

'That is the end of all that,' thought Devlin, settling down in the thick atmosphere of his third smoker. Beside him were two soldiers with beefsteak faces; opposite were a fat, frightened clergyman, a working-class girl in grand stockings and an old maid reading a shocker. Devlin began to smoke. He didn't know why but smoking seemed to get him somewhere; probably a schoolboy illusion.

Looking at the other people in the carriage he remembered his onslaught on 'realism' at the Sedley Society last term (beginning 'Intolerance is the salt of Life'). 'Zola,' he had said, 'is superannuated and as for all these middle-aged English novelists – anyone can sit in a railway-carriage and put down in detail the features and remarks of the passengers. And slosh on a bit of ordure and when you have done three hundred pages cut it off slap like a slab of butter or cheese, and there you have your divine work of genius, so sublimely natural, so takingly realistic, so throbbing and unashamed with all the incoherence and slap-dash hotch-potch of the most living life of the most natural nature.' He remembered with some pride what scorn he had poured on chunk-of-life literature. And how his audience had sat round mokishly smoking, occasionally reaching forward to take a chocolate biscuit. And what a boring discussion afterwards – everyone going off at tangents. Only Hogley was very amusing, had picked quite a number of holes in his paper while saying he agreed with its tenor. He was very sharp, Hogley.

'But the point is,' thought Devlin, looking sideways at the beef-faced soldiers, 'that chaps as they are are just rather dull; what they want is writing up. Not that I mean putting them in fancy dress. No, I imagine that what I mean is giving them beginnings and endings in the right places. Make life grammatical (nature and life are so bloody anacoluthic). In life, you see, everyone is just born at random and then has a series of accidents – ending in some sort of casual extinction. In fact the whole thing is untrue – according to a coherence theory anyhow.

'But to return to these people here, this clergyman and that old maid and these beef-faced soldiers, how incredibly boring they are. They are, in fact, untrue. They started untruly (lor, I've been and started another) and they will almost certainly end untruly – dying of fever on the 21st of January when they might just as well die of mumps on the 25th of October.'

Devlin felt very indignant with them. Just compare the Elizabethan Tragedy of Blood. That was really dying – one died according to one's cue and one's death gabled imposingly a whole structure of intrigue and balanced passions. But 'real life' was not written by an Elizabethan.

At any rate one thing about being a gardener was it would save him for a bit from the bores he was used to. Think of all the men at the Sedley. They never realised his paper was all against themselves. Green, who worked and worked and worked, besides going for a run before breakfast, who drank little and did not smoke, who wore great owl-like glasses and a prim old maid's mouth, who had no particular likes or dislikes and would never become anything interesting – God! how untrue he was.

And Butterley, who went about with friends whom he called 'the lads,' but: belonged to the Sedley because of his passion for Shaw, who did nothing wild except on Bump Supper night, and occasionally went to the Union when there was anything on Free Trade or Mining – God! what a bore; how untrue.

And Robinson, always powdered and usually scented, with his thousandth-hand drawl and his at first winning flattery ('You're such a relief, my dear, everyone here's in such a rut').

All the under-world, too, the mangy little men with accents and bad complexions who spoke of Noel Coward in tones of triumph and with the glint of self-made intellect coming sideways off their eyes.

All untrue.

But after all 'Truth' was a nasty word and flat on the tongue. Let it go into the rag-bag along with 'Sex.' Devlin found himself staring into the clergyman's eyes. The clergyman, like so many clergymen, terrified of being caught out, blinked and dropped his eyes quickly. Devlin remembered the bishop at Hillbury talking about the Threshold of Life in his sermon to the leavers. At the same time he thought of the harlot in the book of Proverbs. He looked again at the clergyman who was self-consciously filling his pipe and had a sudden delightful vision of the Threshold of Life (he must be getting sleepy for it was very vivid).

In front of him rose a colossal Woolworth's building, only instead of Woolworth's there was written there in the familiar red and gold, LIFE LIMITED. The windows were crammed with toys. In the sky floated instead of clouds innumerable toy balloons, red, pink and yellow, while at every doorway street walkers were lounging with real roses on their breasts and (for some unknown reason) batons in their hands. Then Gunter's tune, 'The Rosy Road,' began inside on a gramophone and the street girls began to Charleston, at the same time winking and laughing.

Hearing himself breathing heavily Devlin sat up suddenly, took out his wooden cigarette-case and lit another cigarette; that would keep him awake. He made a show of his wooden case; it was his profession that silver ones were vulgar.

His tongue was quite sore by the time he reached Wytt, which looked a dull place from the train. 'I suppose it's a mistake,' he thought, 'to choose places by their names.'

He had found it on the map yesterday and promptly decided to go there to look for a gardening job. 'Even though, it's in the South,' he said, 'my guardians will never smell me out.'

He walked from the station down the Station Road, which was a blind alley fifteen yards long, and into the only street, which was called High Street. Here there was quite a nice looking pub called the Silver Swan. 'This is where I turn on the dialect,' he thought,

'Rwawms?' he said to the barmaid.

'What?'

'Got any rwawms?'

'What sort of talk is that?' said the barmaid to one of the customers.

'Rwawms?' repeated Devlin; he was still nervous. He shook the kit-bag at the barmaid, which Gunter had given him instead of his suitcase.

"E wants to put up 'ere,' said the man at the bar.

'Oh, you want to put up, do you?' said the barmaid. 'Now, look here, young fellow, can't you talk straight?'

'Oo aa,' said Devlin.

'Well, if he aint a ninny,' said the barmaid, impatiently. 'Four and six bed and breakfast.'

'Well, and if that ain't a durrible ard proyce,' said Devlin, 'never do they jarge such a durrible lawt in Vessmawrlaan.'

'In where?'

'Vessmawrlaan.'

'What kind of a place is that?'

'Whoy, whoy, whoy, never heard of Vessmawrlaan. Hast never read thy joggeraffy book – Northoomberland, Coomberland, Vessmoarlaan, Durrm?'

'Why 'e comes from Westmorland,' said the man at the bar, 'that's it, to be sure it is.'

'You've got it, Ned,' said another man sitting by the door.

'You come from Westmorland, do you?' said the barmaid.

'Oo aa.'

'It wouldn't seem to be much of a place,' said the barmaid; the men laughed heartily. Devlin felt inglorious; there was no point in making a pretence unless one did it with gusto. He offered the men drinks; then he got on better. He took a room for the night.

Later he asked if there were any gardening jobs going. They were all eager to make suggestions – 'There might be a place up at Mrs. Lane's.'

'Aw, Mrs. Lane's isn't much of a place. The young fellow should try the Colonel.'

'What about Granfield 'Ouse?'

'I 'ear as Mrs. Berkeley's wantin' an odd job man.'

Devlin thanked them, made a list, and went out to look round the village. He was rather pleased with his acting, though he had spoken as little as possible.

It was a soft evening. Devlin felt: like hallooing to the sky. He walked up to the churchyard. The church was small and old with a dumpy owl-like tower. He went into the graveyard and looked at the very varied monuments. A great number of plain square slabs, more or less greened with moss; a rough granite cross, pretentiously Lutheran – '*Da stehe ich, ich kann nicht anders*'; some polished marble nineteenth century monsters, shining like brawn – draped urns and gold lettering, truncated pillars; plaster doves and flowers under glass domes, all the usual junk. Then in one portion of the ground some really distinguished tombs, which stood up like altars with barrel-tops and details of scallop-shell and cross-bones. All belonging to the name of Hardle. Devlin remembered one of the places recommended belonged to a Colonel Hardle, and decided he would try there first.

He returned to the Silver Swan, had a meal in the parlour of boiled eggs, bread and soapy cheese, and went up to his bedroom with its mauve-flowered wall and rusty gasbracket.

The flowers on the wall were the colour of Michaelmas daisies but turned out to be roses.

He sat for two hours on the bed reading a ninepenny paper-backed thriller, much crumpled from the kit-bag. He loved thrillers.

He had scored well over Robinson once – Robinson came up drooping and pawing with his 'I *adore* Aldous Huxley' (or someone equivalent); to which Devlin answered: 'Never read him but I *adore* Edgar Wallace.'

'I can't stand books,' thought Devlin, 'which are always scoring off someone, whose authors have no real slant of their own – never beget but carp at other people's babies. Now I'm

talking clever. Always the mark of the beast. Damn cleverness.'
He plunged in the kit-bag and took out his flame-coloured
pyjamas, all wrinkles and smelling of the train. The sight of them
held him for a moment. There you are again, you see. Bought
them because he liked the colour and then found the very fact
of buying them placed him in a set, lumped him in with a lot of
other people who would buy them for order reasons – in order
to be dashing or because they were 'so' or as a reaction from
their Quakerish parents. 'Not but what I too,' thought Devlin,
'have often acted from reaction.

'Still, I'm not going to stop buying my things at Felrnore's just
because a number of bloodies buy theirs there.

'Though, by the way, I won't be able to buy anything, now I'm
a gardener. Well, never mind, damn money. Though I fear it's
romantical to say that. Never mind.'

Sitting up in bed he went on reading, while the gas popped
and muttered. 'Thank God for melodrama,' he thought; 'thank
God for full-blooded slush which doesn't give itself airs and try
to be real by making lavatory jokes. Damn Beverley Nichols,
damn Noel Coward, damn Aldous Huxley. Thank God for——
Is there a cinema here, I wonder? I suppose not.' He went to
sleep in a grump.

He had rather a vivid dream (it was the excitement made him
have all these dreams).

He was walking along the tow-path by the Port Meadow stretch
of the Isis. It was rather chilly; in fact there was a frost. He could
see on the flooded part of Port Meadow skaters gliding serenely
and thought what a relief it was from walking – all push and
pistons. He thought at some length about the contrast. Hogley,
who turned out to be walking beside him, made epigram after
epigram. 'Skaters always remind me of Sir Francis Drake,' he
said; Devlin thought this amazingly funny. And when he had
finished laughing himself, he heard other laughter coming from
up-stream.

There came sailing down the stream two swans (only he called them 'drakes' in his dream), their heads held high like snakes about to strike, and shaking with metallic cackles. It was very frightening. Hogley took a revolver from his pocket and shot at them. He missed and both the creatures swerved out of their course and made for the towpath. At this horrible point Devlin woke up.

It was very dark in his little room and he felt lonely just as he had last, night; this loneliness was new to him. The room was stuffy and the pillow hard. Devlin took it up, shook it out plump and turned it over. When he looked at the darkness he saw shapes on it, so he shut his eyes and tried to think of something comfortable. He visualised a pretty little Fête Champêtre like the Giorgione in the Louvre. Fruits on salvers. Brown eyes laughing.

But he was haunted by swans. Swimming, walking or flying. It must be the name of the pub which had set him off. He could not bear their cruel women's eyes. What should he think of now?

For example, what should he do tomorrow? Walk up to Colonel Hardle's – odierwise the Manor House – walk up there and, remembering to talk Westmorland, ask for a job as assistant gardener; admit his ignorance but show he was strong and willing.

It would be great fun digging. When he was a little boy he used to dig potatoes, with a great spade too big for him. Shouting with joy at a cluster of small purples or with chagrin, yet mixed with delight, when a potato came up divided – sliced in two, the severed halves shining. He was asleep again on lumpy bed, under the mauve roses which were black now in the night.

CHAPTER THREE

On the same morning that Devlin left the Gunters, breakfast occurred as usual in Sir Randal Belcher's house. When one first wakes up one feels yesterday's row must have been a dream – or at any rate nothing much. But as soon as Maude and Elaine pushed their way through the curtain, there was the broken mirror; a baleful star shining disaster on the plates and silver toast-rack.

'Good morning, dear,' said Sir Randal to each of them, kissing Maude on the cheek and Elaine on the forehead. Then they sat down. Sir Randal said nothing more but began to eat fast like a man preoccupied with reality.

Besides, he had said quite enough last night. Janet had not reappeared but he had, for the benefit of the others and himself, first accused and then defended her – explaining as a neurologist how she could have come to be so silly while putting, as a moralist, the blame on her generation. 'You can't expect to keep your nerves,' he said, 'if your life is haphazard. It's as true today as it ever was that one's life must be organised in order to be sound. It's not enough to avoid what is definitely wrong – I should never expect any of you to be troubled by that; it's the border ground that is dangerous, the indifferent possibilities.

'What one wants is a criterion. One wants something positive, a positive principle. And none of you today seem to have that.' And his heavy eyebrows seemed to shadow the whole table.

So he managed to explain it to his daughters; they were surprised he took it so mildly – he was really rather a dear, and Janet had gone a bit far.

But to himself he could not fully explain it. He had been as good a father as he could. Surely sometimes a father must be a wall against his children? Davies, for example, would let his daughter do anything, go off with a dustman. He could never subscribe to that sort of thing.

Besides, it was only Janet who was so difficult. Maude and Elaine had turned out perfectly well. They and he had had their little disagreements but nothing of the nature of a rupture. Whereas Janet – and at the same time she had something special, was somehow finer than the others; it was difficult to pin down, on the face of it she did nothing; both Maude and Elaine sketched (very well, too), but Janet did nothing; nothing but go dancing with shallow young men or sit in the garden reading.

For all this, last night was unique. Quite new and sudden; there must be something wrong.

And no one knew better than he did that one should not upbraid where one ought to be curing. Violent spurts like that often preceded a breakdown.

But looking at the mirror he felt sore and angry. If her nerves were bad, it was her own fault. Idling and dancing naturally strain a girl. He must make her see it was serious. He could not let it pass. The cracks in the mirror, the splinters on the floor cut him – behind the bulwarks of his chest in the shrinking softness of his heart.

Really it was brutal of Janet. He had never been prepared for it. It was so unfair. If only he could forget it.

And now where was she? Why wasn't she down? He wasn't like a Victorian father who *ordered* his daughters to be punctual; the fact was they always *were.* Punctuality is not a mere formality, it's a matter of health and morals.

She would apologise but he would not accept it till she had seen what she had done, taken in all the implications, realised that she had attacked more than the mere mirror. Realised that it may have been just bad temper and nerves on her part but that for him it was an attack on his happiness and the whole happiness of the family.

He took another piece of cold toast from the wedding present toast-rack. Lady Valor gave them that, but Cécile had never liked it much, had said it was more the sort of thing for a male club; it was odd the things she liked and disliked.

Why could he never *see* her in his memory? Only glimpses – cut short, as it were, by a door closing in his mind. It made it so much more lonely never being able to see her. Though sometimes Janet looked like her.

Perhaps this loneliness was why he worked so hard. It was noisy work, too; too much publicity. But still it was a good cause. Someone must get up and rouse people from their apathy.

He smoothed his eyebrows with his forefinger. 'Have you seen Janet?' he asked, frowning.

'No, Dads.'

'Well, will you go and call her, Elaine?'

'Right you are, Dads,' said Elaine, pretending an everyday levity and trying not to look at the mirror while Sir Randal watched her.

'Janet!' Elaine called, as she went along the passage (dead white paint – doors like in an hotel). No answer. 'Hullo, Janet,' she shouted through the door; then opened it. To her great surprise Janet was asleep. Sleeping with a frown and with her face propped on her hand.

'I say, Janet, wake up. It's breakfast.'

Janet grunted and sat up, wrinkling her face and stretching her arms. With her arms out in a cross and one eye still shut she stared at Elaine with the other.

'Oh, hell!' she said; 'why did you wake me up? I'm so beastly stiff I can hardly move.'

'Do hurry up, Janet. It's breakfast and Dads is chafing rather. What are you stiff for?'

'I don't know. Slept all wrong. Besides, I only went to sleep a short time ago. Did you say breakfast was in?'

'Yes, it's been in ages. Do hurry up, Janet. You don't want a row, do you?'

'I don't mind,' said Janet wearily. 'Tell them I'm not coming down yet, and ask Margery to keep my breakfast hot. Or you needn't do that, I don't mind it being cold.'

'Oh, Janet!'

'Stop it, Elaine. I tell you I'm damned tired.' Janet turned over and pulled the bed-clothes up to her face. Elaine went downstairs.

'I say, Dads, Janet says she feels very tired. She says she doesn't feel like getting up yet.'

'Why? Is she ill?'

'No, no, I don't think she's ill. At least, I don't know. But she seems awfully tired.'

'She'll be more tired if she stays in bed. I'm tired too, but I don't stay in bed. It's mere childishness. Tell her to come down at once.'

Elaine, almost crying, went upstairs again.

'I say, Janet.'

'Oh, damn you, Elaine. What do you keep coming for?'

'No, really, Janet. Do wake up and dress. Dads seems rather fed up and besides – don't you remember about the mirror?'

'That's a good one,' said Janet; 'of course I remember about the wretched mirror. I suppose they'll have to get a new one.' She suddenly sat up in bed and stared at Elaine in a childlike way, her eyes very big with the lashes standing out round them. She began to laugh.

'Janet, what is wrong with you? It's so late.'

'Is it? Never mind. This isn't a boarding school, Elaine dear. Look here: you go and tell them that I'm tired and that I'm not getting up till I want to – they know very well that there's nothing for me to do if I do get up – and you can say that as for that mirror affair I'm sorry if it's an *objet d'art* or anything, but that I had to smash somediing just to show them, and it was the biggest target going. By the way, I suppose the decanter broke too?'

'I don't know. Oh dear.'

'Well, don't start crying about it. What's the good of being sloppy? I feel perfectly sick but crying's no good. I tell you, Elaine, Dads is all right but he's spoilt; he's got out of hand. Autocrating us about and then being rude to our friends. What right had he to speak to Robert like that yesterday?'

'I don't know.'

'Well, go and tell him what said.'

'All right.'

'I know you won't tell it straight. What you've got to say is that I'm not staying in bed to avoid him. Say I especially want to talk to him when I come down, but I'll choose my own time. Go on.'

Elaine went down again.

'Well,' said Sir Randal, 'is she dressed?'

'She's just going to dress, I think.'

'Oh. Good. It's ridiculous sulking up there like that. I suppose she's frightened. Did you tell her what I said last night – that I understand exactly how it happened, though I regard it as very serious?'

'Oh, no, I don't think I did. She says she'd like to see you when she comes down.'

'Of course she'll see me. Isn't she just coming down?'

'You see, you've nearly finished breakfast.'

'Never mind. I'll wait here till she comes,' he took up his paper.

Maude and Elaine finished breakfast. Sir Randal told them to run off and see to things.

He waited for half an hour and Janet did not come. 'Funking it,' he thought, and went angrily to his study where he sat behind his desk, drumming on the glass sheet which covered it.

'Men go queer without wives,' Janet thought, as she lay in bed; 'if mother hadn't died he'd never have got like this. What does he mean by going for one as he does? He likes one a lot and then he goes and mucks one up. Got no imagination, men haven't.

'If mother hadn't died,' she thought, and her mind strolled away, into the parks of memory – parks with no placards, no keep-off-the-grasses. Little girls in swings dandled, white sails on the pond dawdling, she herself little like a doll in a little peasant-like dress, that seemed to be cut out of paper. And she had a big sun-bonnet. She held a balloon on a string (always terrified of it popping), flaunting and bobbing on the end of a string. And at mid-day when the others had lunch, she looked forward to her soup-plate of pure cream and sugar – everyone, Dads especially, had been horrified when she started this habit, but her mother had said it was all to the good if she liked it.

All to the good if one liked it. That was how her mother looked at things. Whereas Dads would ten to one say it was all to the bad.

Like the time he said swinging was bad for the stomach.

And then there was Piffoon, Dads *would* have him killed. And it turned out he was curable after all.

He never seemed to gather children could be really sad.

God! couldn't one be sad? Not only the nightmares – those one had still – but the sudden feeling one got of absolute loneliness. And then that air-raid – it had seemed not worth living.

But Dads had just strode through – especially after mother's death.

'Damn! what a headache I've got.' She got out of bed and went to her dressing-table. 'I don't half look washed-out,' she thought. She took a clean handkerchief and, without unfolding it, put some eau-de-cologne on it from a big bottle given her by Jim Haig for her last birthday. She then opened out the handkerchief full, showing sixteen dark little circles dominoed neatly over it (in the same way as window-panes are marked in a newly built house). She smiled at her simple little pattern.

'Now I'd better form a plan of action,' she thought. She walked over to the long mirror and looked at herself. Being slim and athletic and in canary-yellow pyjamas she looked like a boy except for the cascade of her hair, almost black now but shot with red in the sun. She gathered it up and made a rough bun of it.

Through the window a huge crow flew across the sky; his jagged wings went up and down, up and down; he said nothing but seemed to have a purpose. 'Well, well,' thought Janet, 'better get on with it.'

She looked about her for her fleecy slippers; here was one under the bed but where the hell was the other? 'I can't be bothered to dress,' she had suddenly decided. 'I'll go down as I am. Where the hell is that slipper?'

Meanwhile Sir Randal had taken a wad of foolscap from a long envelope. It was the essay of Mr. Grayling's ward which Grayling had given him yesterday. 'May as well look at it,' Sir Randal thought; 'one can't put much on what a young man writes, still – one gets indications. Bilbatrox told me that before preaching at Oxford he looked up the latest numbers of all the undergraduate journals. Doubt if it was worth it but it showed him, I suppose, how their minds worked.'

Sir Randal did not wear glasses; he started to read without any preliminary fuss – no smoothing out of the manuscript with his hand, no wrinkling of the face.

'Intolerance is the salt of life,' said the paper.

'What? What's this? A silly epigram?'

Sir Randal read on, taking it very seriously.

What's this now? What's the point of it? Has he got his tongue in his cheek or does he mean it? In either case it's rubbish. Decadent rubbish at that.

And callous, too. Bilbatrox is quite right – they don't care what they say because they don't care what they do, except that they're frightened of the law and public opinion.

He connected it closely with Janet's outburst – both symptoms of the evils of the time. Only that Janet was a victim whereas this young man was one of the originators of the evil, the devil's missionaries. What young men say at Oxford affects the country at large. Moral – let us see to our young men; if they are mentally unsound like this one, someone must put a stop to them. 'That's what I told Grayling – he *must* put his foot down. (Where on earth's Janet?) I don't know how people at Oxford put up with it; indecency on one page, blasphemy on the next.

'Like Nietzsche, but worse. There's no excuse for it. Son of Urquhart of Madras, educated at Hillbury and Oxford – no excuse whatever. I expect he ran away from Oxford because they made it too hot for him; I hope so.'

At this point Janet came in and stood before him in canary pyjamas and bedroom slippers, having rouged her lips (as was her custom) in proportion to her weariness; they were very red. She looked very small in this high, heavy study.

'Janet!'

'Good morning, Dads.'

'What are you doing? Why aren't you dressed?'

'It's quite warm in the house. I haven't had time to dress yet.'

'What do you mean? You've not been walking about the house like that?'

'I have. But don't you bother about that, Dads; let's get on to business.'

'That's for me to say, I think. I have several things to say to you, Janet. I hope you're sorry for last night.'

'I'm sorry about the mirror. At least I'm sorry I had to break it.'

'*Had* to break it? What do you mean?'

'Now listen to me for a little. I don't really hold with smashing things, but sometimes if people won't understand one, if they keep over-riding one——'

'Over-riding you?'

'No, please don't interrupt. If people keep brow-beating one and won't listen to what one says, then if one can't defend oneself by talking, what is one to do? You'd done it so often, I'd got the feeling a long time ago I'd have to smash something in the end – just as a symbol or something. Just to show I'm not completely flattened.'

'But Janet——'

'No, I haven't finished yet. I'll pay for that mirror out of Aunt Edith's money——'

'You'll do no such thing. It was sheer bad temper your breaking it, but I can——'

'Nonsense, Dads; it was not sheer bad temper and I *am* going to pay for it. It was well worth it. And it wasn't, as you seem to think, just temper or impulse. I may have to break something else unless you see my point.'

'For heaven's sake, Janet, what *is* your point? I don't believe you have a point——' Sir Randal was not angry, merely grieved and puzzled; tracing with his fingers on the glass top of the desk.

'You don't believe I have a point? Well, it's the first time you've ever given me a chance to explain it. My point is I've got a perfect right to have my own likes and dislikes, my own pleasures, my own friends; especially my own friends. Yesterday you talked to Robert as if he was dirt; well, I'm damned if I'll have you talking like that again.'

'Janet.'

'Don't interrupt. It's no good your saying——'

'Now look here, Janet——'

'It's no good your saying, 'Don't swear at me, I'm your father.' What I say is, don't be rude to my friends, I'm your daughter.'

'Now listen, Janet; I'm your father. I've got a perfect right——'

'You've got a right to behave like a father, which is as nicely as possible – ' she suddenly smiled at him – 'but you've got no right at all to treat one as if one was five. Why, I'm of an age to be a wife and mother. And another thing I'll tell you is that any girl as soon as she's grown up knows about twice as much as any man of any age. And what's more, she has a much harder time. Look at the hell I have every month; if you or any other man had that you'd make such martyrs of yourselves we'd never hear the end of it. Don't look so shocked; what are you a doctor for if you can't hear plain facts? To go on——'

'Don't go on.'

'Well, shortly Dads, I know you're no end of a worker and have all sorts of public things to attend to, but what I say is you don't know much about a family or *the* way to manage them——'

'Perhaps not,' said Sir Randal wearily.

'The way to manage them,' said Janet, putting her hands on her yellow hips and looking him straight in the eyes, 'is not to be always putting their backs up about trifles, losing your temper and talking like a schoolmaster. Why can't you recognise they've got characters just as you have and let them follow out their characters in the way that comes natural? Don't you know that if you stopped me marrying someone I wanted, I'd ten to one go off with the next chimney sweep?'

'I suppose so,' said Sir Randal. He had surrendered.

'Cheer up,' said Janet. 'It's not every man has as nice daughters as you have. And I tell you I'll pay for that mirror. After all, one pays for coconut shies.'

'No, no, you won't pay for it. Listen Janet dear——'

'Nonsense, I tell you I broke it just to make my point; but I'm going to pay for making my point.'

'No you're not.'

'Yes I am.'

'You're not, Janet.'

'I certainly am, but I can't argue now; I'm off to have a bath.' She tripped out of the room.

'Janet,' he shouted after her, 'what about your breakfast?'

'Oh, that's all right; I don't want any,' she shouted back.

'It's a mistake to cut one's meals,' said Sir Randal aloud, but to no one in particular – in the manner of a Greek chorus, momentously quiet before or after a row.

The bathroom, Janet always said, was the only possible room in the house. White tiles and a hot rail and lots of space. The bath, too, was decently long.

The water made a good noise rushing in and the steam was comforting for someone who had had no food and hardly any sleep. Janet stood on the cork-mat smiling. She never used the over-mat – too much fuss, its continual rucking up. Besides, there were no pretty ones in the house, not like those checks in Valery's windows.

As she lay in the bath the water slid tickling under her knees and between her small breasts. She played balloons in the water with her face-cloth, for she felt quite dazed after her triumph. But disapproving on principle of lying long in a hot bath she broke the spell and began to wash vigorously.

When she got out she felt much better. Having dried she wrapped her towel round her and ran across to her bedroom. There she locked the door and throwing away the towel danced in front of the long mirror. Then she stood and looked at herself. 'Yes, I suppose I have got quite a decent figure. Wish I could say the same of my face.' For her face was too round and doll-like for her own taste.

'It's funny,' she thought, as she began to dress, 'very funny how the world is. On one side there's the nuns who have baths in their chemises and all the old spinsters as well, and the clergymen and schoolmistresses and river conservancy people, all thinking there's something wrong about being naked. And on the other side there's the creatures who always want some sort of peepshow or other, who'd pay pounds to see a girl in her skin – what the point is *I* can't see.

'If one likes someone, if one's in love at least, one likes their body too, I suppose; and if someone's got a fine body, like an athlete, dicn it's worth looking at, but all this feverish crawling and peeping, this falling for someone just because it's of a different sex – that I can't understand at all.

'But as for the nuns in their chemises, good Lord! – that I just can't understand.'

She sat at her dressing-table and gave herself a 'facial' with cold cream. 'So you've got through it now,' she thought, 'the poor old chap's surrendered and now you can do what you like. It's a bore having to spend Aunt Edith on that mirror, but after all it's only decent.

'It always gave me creeps when I was younger seeing the whole family reflected there. All just as they were, munching and squaring their faces. I don't think I hold with mirrors in dining-rooms.

'But wasn't, it a gorgeous smash?'

It was nearly time for lunch when she came down.

She met Maude and said 'Hullo Maude' very cheerily.

'What have you been doing?' said Maude; 'been feeling bad?'

'Not at all. You haven't mislaid that new record of mine?'

'What new record?'

' "The Rosy Road" '

'No, I haven't touched it. Have you seen Dads?'

'Yes, saw him hours ago. Why?'

'Oh, I didn't think you had. He's gone, out now.' Maude looked clumsy, as always when surprised.

'Well,' she said, 'if you're going to play that record, I'll get out of range.' For she knew Janet's habit of playing the same thing over and over.

Janet going into the drawing-room picked 'The Rosy Road' from the top of a tall heap, put it on and wound the little handle furiously. Awfully slushy words but the hell of a good tune. In a moment it was flouncing through the open door out over the house.

'I've had tears – tears,
But you've had stars and roses. . . .'

'Please shut the door,' shouted Maude up the stairs. But Janet was revolving round the room, seeming unaware of the thickly marshalled obstacles – filigree tables, complicated lampstands, revolving bookcases, and a never-used grand piano.

The words were all repetition.

'The rosy road,
The rosy,
The rosy road of love. . . .'

and then the ravishing bit with the saxophone, and then,

'I've had tears – tears,
But you've had stars and roses.'

As it came to an end Janet pounced, started it again. And without changing the needle. For by now she had forgotten all about the row, and her triumph also; now she was one with the record, revolving round a point.

Completely unbothered by theory creed or complex she moved delicately among the room's monsters, her feet flashed defiance to their extinct museum-like hulks. Like a silver fish that zigs and zags its way between portentous wreckage.

Nor could the gold curtains deceive her, bulging to hide the light. She knew there was the country beyond them. She worshipped the country. It made Robert Garfield laugh; he had said she ought to keep a nature notebook when she told him that the tit's change of manners occurred in January. After all, it was the same time as her birthday, just the time to change one's manners; and tits were so plump and delightful, really rather human – the way they sat on a string. She must really get them another coconut; the old one was practically bare.

What a row there had been at school when she hung up all those bits of suet in front of her cubicle window.

The record came to an end and the needle ran round rasping. Janet stopped it, changed the needle, wound it up, started it again.

'I've had tears – tears. . . .'

She was pink and full of life, as full of life as a bird, as she moved like a swallow round the stupid drawing-room; beyond the bounds of which lay the still more stupid world, nothing but platforms and campaigners, missions and fonts and venereal diseases, nuns in their chemises and actresses writing for the papers, rot and trash and finicky nonsense – the prudish, crude, lewd, rude, tampering, tattling, medicating, meddling, fiddling, money-making world; the snippet-collecting, ticket-collecting, poster-plastering, remedy-vendoring, ballot-clattering, stamp-loving, baby-licking, clapper-clawing world; the bad, sad, boring and bawdy, prurient, esurient world.

CHAPTER FOUR

'Where d'ye come from?'
'Vessmawrlaan.'
'Where?'
'Vessmawrlaan.'

'Oh, give over. Wherever it is you can go right back there.' The puritanical gardener of the Manor House gazed at Devlin contemptuously.

'Aw, mister,' said Devlin, 'thou woulds't not toorn one away just because one derivigates from Vessmawrlaan?'

The gardener's sneer changed into a puzzled frown; he snuffed a conspiracy.

'Look here, you,' he said, 'firstly there ain't no job like that going here anyhow, and even if there was I wouldn't give it to *you*——'

'Thou talkst bats,' said Devlin unexpectedly.

'What? Say that again.'

'Thou talkst bats thou owld curmudgeon cop, thou griffin cuss, thou podge-fowks——'

'Now look here' – but at this moment the Colonel came through the gap in the hedge.

The Colonel, from Devlin's first sight of him, struck him as something of a sun-god. Or cross between a sun-god and a leader of Vikings.

'Good morning, Bearley,' he said (pronouncing it Barley), 'what's this boy doing here?'

'This boy, sir? Says he wants a job about the place. And *I've* just been telling him there ain't one.'

'Well,' said the Colonel, 'I'm not sure another worker wouldn't come amiss. You remember what I was telling you, Bearley, about that rockery I'm thinking of?'

'Oh, *I* remember, sir. But, if you'll excuse me, it doesn't look as if this hoy was the sorts——'

'Why not?'

'Impudent, sir.'

'Oh, he's impudent is he?' said the Colonel, with sudden interest; impudence had always attracted him.

'Yes, sir; calls one names one can't even understand. Got no education, sir.'

The Colonel being an antiquarian was now doubly disposed in Devlin's favour.

'Well,' he said to Devlin, 'say something for yourself.'

Devlin hesitated. 'Oo, aa,' he said, exceedingly conscious of the farce.

The Colonel nodded his head gravely, his yellow moustache echoing to the sun. He wanted to prove himself worthy of his friend Wilkins, the authority on everything 'folk'; how he wished he could spot the boy's source for himself.

'So you don't come from these parts?' he said kindly.

'Naw, sir. Vessmawrlaan, that's my hwawm.'

Here the Colonel distinguished himself, being the first person immediately to identify Vessmawrlaan. Having never been there to study its yokelry he was delighted at a chance of doing this at home. Now he would have a tame pet for his distinguished friends – Wilkins and Kammerkopf, and Harrod the flint-digger. He engaged Devlin almost at once.

'I wonder if you're strong enough,' he had said, whereupon Devlin had got down on his hands and done a dozen perfect press-ups. 'Them's what we at hwawm calls the plod-cat,' he said.

'Plod-cat,' thought the Colonel, 'I must remember that,' and he shoved it in among all the litter of his mind, a mind full of rough drafts, jottings, negatives never developed.

Devlin was taken on to do unskilled work and to obey Bearley. The first week was to be probationary. He gave the Colonel his name as 'Urkitt.'

Apart from three fields which were used for grazing the Manor House estate was not large. There was a walled kitchen garden of about an acre and, balancing it, a walled flower-garden somewhat smaller. These were on either side of the house; below the house lay the tennis court which was bounded by a line of yew trees trimmed to the shape of puddings. Beyond these yews was an untended waste with a small stream running through it; this was where the Colonel hoped to build his rockery.

For the Colonel saw all its details in his mind's eye. The only thing was he needed encouragement and Bearley did not hold with rockeries. 'What you wants is good clean flowers,' he said, 'not little creeping weeds and bits of broken gravel you call by grand names.' But now that there was a new hand the Colonel saw hope.

Thus Devlin was favoured by the Colonel but Bearley would not come out to him. He gave him his instructions but otherwise he was closed. Devlin felt lonely. His first few days made him very stiff and tired, and he would have liked to talk with Bearley who struck him as dour, but sound – in no way mean or futile.

But at the end of his trial week he felt master of the situation – a very fine phrase, he thought, as he sat sweating on a log with his wet scythe beside him. He had never scythed before and lo! he had used it perfectly. He began to love it. Really, it was a great success this gardening.

Scything reminded him of how when he was six and seven he used to run among the gone-to-seed cabbages and cauliflowers beheading them with a stick and crying: 'Down thou coward, down thou dastard bastard.' Now too he wanted to shout his triumph, as he conquered the grass by the stream beyond the yew trees. It retreated before him in slow arcs like the tide.

As he stopped honing Bearley came up to him – all the angry puritan. He stood with his hands in his pockets plumb in front of Devlin.

'Look here,' he said, 'seeing as your first week's finished I've got a word to say to you.'

'Oo aa,' Devlin put on his half-wit face and weighed the hone in his hand.

'Now tell me,' said Bearley, 'tell me you; what's the game?'

'What be what game?'

'Oh, drop that talk. What's the game pretending to be a gardener and you obviously a gent?'

Devlin said nothing; the little stream trilled and trolloped; it seemed silly one was not allowed to be a gardener if one wanted.

'Nor you needn't think you've took me in. Not after you was first taken on. Any folks with half an eye could see you was a gent.'

'Nonsense,' said Devlin, in his own voice.

'Why look at your hands. No gardening lad would have hands that soft. So now just you listen to me, and quit letting off that fancy talk of yours. I didn't let on for the week you was on trial for I said to myself: "He'll probably be no good anyhow so what's it matter?" not wanting to let the Colonel see he's been made a fool of if it's all the same as you have to leave anyhow. But seeing now as I can't truly say you're a bad worker, and the Colonel's thinking of keeping you on here, well, before we fixes down for good I'd like to get things a bit straight. I reckon——'

Devlin interrupted: 'Yes, and I reckon too. I reckon it's my own business who I am and how I talk as long as I satisfy my employer.'

'Oh, you want to satisfy your employer, do you? And I guess he'll be satisfied to have somebody like you masquerading in his garden nobody knows what for.'

Bearley stood looking at him with his mouth and whole jowl twisted sideways. Devlin did not answer; he did not know why. A wedge had come into the conversation; they were held up; arguing seemed futile and stray images slid through Devlin's mind – the scalloped tombstones, the sign of the Swan, the pedals of a bicycle in the sun yesterday evening (very odd that was; as the cyclist pedalled up and down, up and down, it looked from behind like a shower of gold falling on each side of the bicycle). Suddenly he realised Bearley was talking again – 'Masquerading . . . monkeying about where you haven't got no right . . . tell the Colonel if you don't face up to it . . . contrary to decency that's what it is.'

'Oh, leave all that out. I've done my work well, haven't I?' 'Yes, yes you've worked passing well.'

'Well isn't that all that matters?'

'All that – no *that* ain't all that . . . my motto is everyone where he belongs; folks is born gents and folks is born gardeners——'

'I don't believe that.'

'No matter what you believes, your believing won't change the face of nature. Why weren't you in church on Sunday?'

'Well, I don't believe in that either.'

'There you are you see. Now listen here. The Colonel, and I'm proud to serve him, is one of the piousessest gentlemen ever walked. And all that works on his place has always been proud to follow him. Men and women. Old and young. Then along comes you talking like a Punch and Judy show, thinking to alter the whole place round. And you with no hair on your face. My motto is gents is born gents, and it's only crooked gents that tries to be anything else. What will you say to that?'

'Well, just listen a moment,' said Devlin, very conscious of his colourless accent, 'and you'll see I'm not really crooked. I suppose it *was* a bit stupid to try and talk like that, but the fact is I wanted to be a gardener just for the fun of it.'

'What was you before then?'

'I was at Oxford University.'

'Oh, Oxford and Cambridge?'

'That's right.'

'Oh, so that's where you hail from?' Bearley was thawing – in his mind was a vague picture of young men in a boat, not properly focussed, but yet quite pretty.

'Well, you see I got tired being up there – just reading books, you know – so I thought I'd like to get into the open air and do a bit of work with my hands.'

'Well, it's a queer idea. . . .'

Devlin had won; Bearley told him for some time that he was making a mistake, that it would never work, that his hands were too white, that *his* job was to work with his mind; but for all that he would not give him away. He shook hands with him.

He watched Bearley's back ponderously, piously receding, and thought what a good old bear he was, even though, a churchwarden. He went back to his lodgings very free, very vital.

He had shifted from the Silver Swan to a little room kept by Mrs. Dudd. Mrs. Dudd, he had written to Gunter, was 'nothing but a moving staircase' or, as she herself put it, 'always up and down, up and down them blooming stairs – slops and pails and whatnots, and then having a basement, it ain't no fit life for a woman of my precedings——'

Up popped Mrs. Dudd like a rabbit and stood before him with her paws curled round her bosom. Rather cosy she was, thought Devlin, remembering the warm scrubbed tiles of her kitchen like a rabbit's sandy parlour – what a pity she was always on the scuttle. 'Good evening, Mr. Urkitt, here's a letter for you from Yorkshire' (for she always scrutinised the postmarks).

'Thankee, mawm, that no doubt be an orfer of a jawb.'

Mrs. Dudd disappeared; in order to save strain on his dialect Devlin had pretended to her that he had strings in his tonsils, so she never expected him to talk much. 'Poor chap,' she would say, 'if it weren't for them strings in his tonsils he would be the makings of a lovely man.'

The letter was from Gunter on lilac tinted notepaper:

'My dear, I have such amusing news for you. My father has just heard from your good guardians who are apparently writing round to all your friends they have heard of. They implore for news of you, but what is so really funny is that they went to Sir Randal Belcher about you and have as good as got you certified by default – or whatever one calls it when the patient is absent. They seem to have told old Belcher all the funny things you have done, like knocking down Harvey and making that scene at the garden party. Also a lurid description of your funny little glooms and pets. Whereupon Sir Randal said you sounded perfectly incurable, in fact it was a case of psychosis. (My father says he is balmy about psychosis.) *Acute* psychosis in your case – bound to end in suicide; I gather he was just going to say you inherited suicide from your father when he remembered that he'd been assassinated and was now in the history books. Well, your guardian swallowed all this and is plotting to rescue you and devote himself to a life of elaborate sacrifice – like an old lady's companion. As soon as they get you back the new regime of quiet restraint will start. Sir R. told them on no account to send you back to Oxford – 'put him in business if yon like, but don't give him any spare time.' These specialists are quite like the Spanish Inquisition. But what I had nearly forgotten, and shows what fools they both are – your guardian raked up somewhere your typescript copy of your paper to the Sedley and gave it to Sir Randal as evidence. Sir Randal finding it to be a glorification of intolerance and full of remarks about courtesans, promptly got really heated instead of merely personal. You've now become one of the items in his great campaign for Purity.

'Well, write and tell me what you're going to do about it. My father has been screaming with laughter ever since.

He has a great contempt, unless it's envy, for most of these big specialists. Personally I think it's damned cheek on old Sir Randal's part. However, I leave that to you. Do write and tell me how you get on with your living Georgic and when you're going to cry off. . . .

'By the way, my father didn't give you away. He admitted you'd stayed the night, but denied knowledge of your present whereabouts; he also added you seemed quite in your right mind. Well, well. Love ever. . . .'

What fun; what a flap; what bloody damned nonsense. Who the hell was Sir Belcher? . . . My God, what a joke! He had a good mind to visit Sir Belcher and try the Dr. Johnson on him, speak straight from the shoulder: 'Yes, sir, what I wish to communicate to you, sir, is that I consider you a damned boob, sir.'

Yes, he could understand the *Graylings* now going to Sir Belcher (who was one of their idols), but *not* Sir Belcher taking any notice of their nonsense. 'I never thought much of these great men but now——'

As Cézanne would say, *'ces b-s de savants.'*

Surely now Hogley had said something funny about him – something about how he had been knighted for translating into a hundred pages of bad English twenty-two pages of precise German by a leading light of Vienna? What sport. 'I'll pay him back sometime; not just at the moment because it's such fun here – life in the present participle, manual labour, sun and shower, plants gradually growing and summer rumbling forwards.'

He almost forgot Sir Randal and his guardians, and even life at Oxford in the daily labour of his body. Bearley was now very friendly, and it was a relief not to have to talk dialect. Bearley talked at length on gardening and life and the helpfulness of religion. 'Look at the Colonel,' he kept saying, 'an old family, a gallant man, a great scholar and a good churchman on top of it. . . .'

'Yes,' said Devlin, 'I don't mind other people going to church. Why can't everyone go where lie wants – into church or into the pub or up on the hill there? I don't say the church service isn't very helpful to you; and the Colonel and lots of others; all I say is, I've never got any help from it, so what's the use of my going?'

'No, no; you're wrong, you can't alter nature. And what's the use of your not going either? What did you do this Sunday it was wet?'

'Oh, I read a book.'

'Read! there you are, you see. Didn't I tell you you're half and half. If you throw up your Oxford why don't you throw up your books too. Be a scholar or be a gardener, but whichever you are be a Christian.'

Bearley slapped his thigh – his sign of Q.E.D.

Devlin was always amazed when he came up against absolute conviction in anyone; it had a pleasantly narcotic, effect on him; he felt like a cat being stroked. He let Bearley talk on piously and made no further defence.

But later, as he was scuffling the drive with his accurate iron rake, the Colonel's great saloon drove in through the gate and changing gear came asthmatically up the slope. Devlin stood aside leaning with his hands on his tall rake-shaft and so had a good view of the world's ugliest clergyman – filthy vulture-face, fleshy and pouched and foul, selfish and sensual, pig pike and serpent.

But of course he did not seem so to the Colonel.

'Who's that lad?' said the clergyman, who was a great noticer, 'I don't remember seeing him before.'

'Oh, he's our new sub-gardener; tell you about him later. Remarkable lad, excellent worker, comes from the north country. Very quaint dialect, the vowels broad you know. And what is more his vocabulary – I'm looking forward to showing him to Wilkins. . . .'

But Devlin was angrily scattering the gravel. 'Silly old Bearley,' he said to himself, 'bowing the knee to swine like that. Silly old

Colonel, too. They trade on good-natured simpletons.' But one must be fair, he thought. Not all parsons were hypocrites – what about the one who gave him birds' eggs when he was little and those old pippin-parsons mellowed between brick walls with a pipe in their mouths and a kind word for everyone?

But the vision in the car shattered his fairness: 'Damn the lot,' he said.

'And damn Spring too,' he said, as a small gust blew a scrap of newspaper over the drive. How ridiculous it was, this ubiquity of newspaper. Useful though; when we light our fires what do we light them with? With yesterday's words and deeds, records in cricket, results of Chinese battles, deaths, births and marriages, records in dancing and can-opening.

And now on his own gravel, neatly raked and loved, this chaste drive smelling of new buds, even here came scampering and rustling these tattered soiled symbols of everyday events of deadly-boring, epoch-making facts.

'Damn them!' he said, pursuing the fluttering paper (fluttering like an old hen) and beating it on the head with his rake. Taking it off the iron teeth he crumpled it up and pushed it down among the rubbish in his barrow.

And yet that scrap after all was comparatively harmless; consisting almost entirely of applications by housemaids for places and of notices of vacancies for housemaids.

But as for Spring, Spring had gone flat by being exposed to that cleric. The daffodils waved in the same little gust which blew along the fortunes of housemaids, but Devlin's heart felt very far from Wordsworth. 'Bloody,' he said; 'bloody, bloody romantical.'

What with Lake Poets (who were all very well, but so limited) and with Bearley, who was much the same, and with the Colonel who was so nice and yet so stupid; what with these on one side and the stinking cheats on the other, with Sir Randal Belcher damning one for a theory and the clergyman in the car gobbling and gloating over his winnings; and what, finally, with the ceaseless vomit of gobbets of printed paper (which like all those marine creatures one reads of in natural histories would rapidly overflow the earth if there were not other creatures to eat them, namely slow and quick combustion stoves, old-fashioned fires and pipe-spill-making maniacs, rubbish-heaps and the lower sort of latrines) what with all this Devlin felt queasy. The clock striking six in the owl-faced tower, he laid the rake and hoe across the barrow and wheeled it away, rumbling sleepily, to the black-felted tool-shed. There he met Bearley.

'I say, Bearley, have you seen that clergyman? Who is he?'

Bearley, standing with his arms hanging and his face lifted like a bear ready for buns, and his eyes full of sincere admiration, spat once to the left and twice to the right, and having spat, said slowly: 'Ah, you've seen *him*, have you? The Colonel's got many fine friends, but you've seen the pick of 'em. That gentleman,' his voice paused momentously, portentously, 'that gentleman you saw was the Reverend John Bilbatrox.'

So that was Bilbatrox.

CHAPTER FIVE

Bilbatrox ranked next to Dean Inge among England's advanced clerics. Not that he had read Plotinus or cared much for the Platonic precedents of Christianity. He prided himself on attending to the things that mattered.

To make a thing matter apply freely the epithet modern – modern science, modern industrial conditions, above all modern marriage. In all these subjects Bilbatrox managed to be at the same time advanced and reverent, chaste and daring. For example he wished to limit the birth rate but solely for the good of the country – you make a mistake if you think it was to give people pleasure. On the contrary the only point of marriage was propagation. He confessed to agreeing with St. Paul that it was better, if possible, not to be married. That he himself had a wife and five children was a series of great sacrifices.

And he had often appeared on the same platform as Dean Inge under the banner of Eugenics: – 'The nation needs its best men for fathers; young men like my audience; men of sound fibre, moral and physical. *Mens sana* – (crash) – *in corpore sano.*' And then reams of statistics, some talk of glands and electrons and a crowning quotation from Shakespeare.

He had been, too, the right-hand man of England's fighting bishop in the recent campaign against the whole host of modern corruptions – unemployment, the kinema, dancing and jazz, modern art, the cocktail habit, sweepstakes. To aid which

Sir Randal Belcher the neurologist had contributed a pamphlet on psychosis which solved the problem of evil.

'Bilbatrox is stupendous,' the Bishop had said when the campaign had drawn to its lucrative close. And it is true that Bilbatrox' voice was so nasal that it hurt the coffered ceiling of the Chapman Auditorium (so Devlin was afterwards told).

Bilbatrox had no ear and no eye. Apart from being colour blind, which would not necessarily have precluded him from the usual pleasures, he was actually above and beyond all such weaknesses, took no delight in shade or shape or distance, and as for sounds – he was not only wholly unmusical but wholly unmoved by any sound whatever: by bees or sea or thunder, by fires being lit, by caws, croaks or trillings, by a silver voice or the tinkle of silver water.

Nor had he any interest in history. Except that which he made. For C. J Harrison in reporting Bilbatrox' speech on Vice in Our Great Cities, said: 'The Rev. John Bilbatrox stands at the very head of the adventure of modern thought; petty old-world prejudices cannot stand up against him. His audience, whatever its constitution, peers or ploughmen or those whom he has most at heart, our great middle class of prosperous, well-intentioned people, whoever they be, they cannot but respond to his stirring great-hearted appeals. It may be said without exaggeration that Bilbatrox is making history daily.'

Literature, however, he studied in his spare time though not for its own sake. 'That is all cant,' he would say. 'Everything must be for the sake of something else. If a writer cannot give you a moral, let him go.' He could produce so many morals from Shakespeare (pocket edition) that he had the reputation of a very well read man who might have gone far in literature or become head of a college, had he not devoted his gifts to the far more arduous but less rewarded task of popular propaganda.

At this moment Bilbatrox sat in the Colonel's study sipping the Colonel's admiration——

'. . . your unflagging sense of duty,' said the Colonel.

'Ah, but I enjoy my labours,' said Bilbatrox.

'I see Inge is taking a holiday,' he added.

The Colonel, being a lonely man, was always delighted to put people up, especially those whom he knew to be cleverer than himself. Still Bilbatrox' accent grew tiring after a week (it was a relic of his native country, a cruel land of basalt, stale whisky and yellow, dirty bricks, Presbyterian nurses and hollow shawled faces).

After a week Bilbatrox was still sitting in the Colonel's study, gathering himself up in his fists, gloating over himself like a coprophil baboon.

'I had a hard fight, I can tell you,' he was saying; 'in one place they organised a protest against me. I have even seen my name written up on a wall in a back street in Sheffield. But thank God I have pulled through.'

Meanwhile Devlin had a week's bad temper. When he was a little boy he had always wanted to hit anyone who was ugly. He had got over that but Bilbatrox was too much. He had even tried to patronise him in the garden but Devlin had slouched off.

Devlin began to have doubts as to whether he could go on gardening. Was it not a blind alley? A pleasant one – especially in the Colonel's garden, but were not the Colonel and his whole tradition and household walled off from life, slowly rotting in the leaves of their past years. Like so many gardens and households and colonels in England.

There was a cackle of old maids' voices and in at the garden gate came the Colonel and Bilbatrox with Miss Euphronia Lylie and Miss Nellie Hardstaff. Miss Lylie wore flowing skirts of grey silk, an arbor of muslin on her head, a moustache, and a cigarette in a long holder. Miss HardstafF wore a short sack round her thighs, a leather belt round her stomach and a red nose on her face. Miss Hardstaff was short, Miss Lylie was very tall; being of independent means they were both extremely cultured and original.

Had gone the pace in Badt and Florence. . . .

Like creatures out of an aquarium they came tentacling and clawing through the garden. 'No, no,' thought Devlin, 'I can't go on with this life.'

As they passed near him on their orbit he could hear what they all said. Miss Lylie's voice rang out:

'The Hauerscheiner collection . . . superb; you should really make a point of. I was shown over it by Dr. Browne. Dr. Browne told me he thought the Watershed vase was really superior in line though perhaps the glazing . . .' Devlin could not think why Dr. Browne bothered.

The group swung away into the far regions of space.

Devlin, as he often did, pictured each person as walking within a sort of bubble. Here now were four bubbles moving in the garden. The Colonel's was quite a pleasant one, golden but not gay, a true pippin or bronze heart among bubbles. Whereas the two old maids walked each in a cobweb gauze hung from angle to angle of their projections, a few flies stuck here and there, a few curios. But Bilbatrox had a sort of butcher's bubble, a transparent oily intestine, his own extrajection.

These were the microcosms which revolved round the garden.

At the next equinox he heard of the Indian Crisis, at the next of Physical Training and how good it was for girls. Like a chorus of carpenters' tools the voices rasped and girded and moved away again under the rustic arch (Britain's triumphal progress).

Then: 'So you know Sir Randal?' (Miss Lylie's voice).

'Know Sir——? Ha, ha, ha! Ask the Colonel. Why, my dear Miss Lylie, Sir Randal and I have often worked together.'

'Oh, of course I knew about the *campaign*——'

'Ah, yes, you mean if I know him personally. Well, I am proud to say I do. It began, of course, in our official collaboration. When I say we worked together I should say that he did the thinking and I did the talking; ha. I was Barnabas to his Paul.

'. . . But it's funny you should ask that question just now. Tomorrow I am going to stay with him at his house at Horsley. . . . Yes, delightful man, isn't he, Colonel?'

'Delightful indeed,' said the Colonel.

'I *don't* think,' said Devlin to himself – poor old Colonel, duped all round the board. Still here was a chance (it's a small world as they say) that if Sir Belcher came along here. 'Come over perhaps to fetch the Reverend Bloody. At any rate I could see the man.'

That evening Mrs. Dudd told him what a great man the Rev. Bilbatrox was. What an odd world he thought – all the dears admiring all the charlatans.

And next morning Bearley said: 'The Rev. Bilbatrox is leaving today; the Colonel'll be sorry to lose him.'

'Yes, where's he going now?'

'I hear he's going to Sir Randal Belcher – you've heard of him? Sir Randal's an old friend of both him and the Colonel. He'll be sending over the car to fetch him. I daresay he might come himself.'

But the first person who came was a retired lawyer, who lived in a comfortable London flat reading an odd assortment of books which he obtained weekly from the London Library. He was brought to see Devlin, as to a museum specimen.

'Well, Urkitt,' said the Colonel, 'how're you getting on with that piece of lawn?'

'Oo, aa. Terrible lot gorzel this morning.'

And so they talked for a time, their bubbles bobbing up and down, touching each other's rims. It made Devlin's mind feel woolly, all this pretence and the way the Colonel swallowed it.

'There,' said the Colonel, as he led his friend away, 'isn't he a find? Now that all that sort of thing has so many opposing influences. Wireless, you know, is rapidly killing all our local characteristics. There is nothing picturesque left. In a few years——'

'Yes, yes, Hardle, but about this boy——'

'Well, what do you think of him?'

'I think, mind you this is only an impromptu conclusion, but *I* think he's either a half-wit or a rogue.'

The lawyer spoke biting off his words in a querulous-jocular manner.

'A half-wit or a rogue?'

'Yes, you don't get intelligent lads nowadays persisting in their backwardness unless there's some reason for it. Either they can't help it or else they find it pays. Like so many natives from Scotland to the Congo they trade on your love of the picturesque. Now what I say, my dear Hardle, is blast the picturesque. Take it away, I say. It has no place either in nature or art. Nature as you know, should be natural and art should be – well art, I suppose, should be artistic; but this damned interloping nondescript, this thing you call the picturesque, why it's neither one thing nor the other. It's not a decent picture and it's not a decent view in the country; no; when you finally find it, it's Ann Hathaway's cottage and surrounded by Americans.

'By Americans,' he repeated, clearing his throat.

The Colonel laughed. 'You were always a cynic,' he said. They moved off; flakes of their conversation were blown back to Devlin.

'. . . Very good worker . . . and Wilkins——'

'. . . I leave all that to Wilkins but what I say . . .'

'. . . After all you don't know the poor lad. . . .'

'. . . What: *I* say is . . .'

'. . . Honest lad . . . shines out in his face. . . .'

'. . . What *I* say is sounds damn fishy. . . .'

And then the Colonel's loud viking laugh.

Like bubbles blown from a pipe they floated far off, iridescent souls ready to burst into nothing.

But souls were the concern of the Rev. Bilbatrox whose suit case was now in the hall. Though it was not till after lunch that the chariot came to fetch him. When a car changed down and roared up the drive, the Colonel intercepted it and a girl got out.

'Good gracious me, Janet, I didn't know *you* were coming?'

'Nor I was but Simms had the varicose veins this morning so I offered to come. Dads was all for dissuading me, he is so fussy you know, but eventually I just seized the car and said to him: 'You don't want Mr. Bilbatrox stranded do you?' and of course he couldn't abide anything to happen to old Bilby – no, I don't think I'm talking loud, am I? – well, I seized the car and Dads insisted on Maude going with me——'

'Maude? Where is she?'

'Oh' – a little trill of laughter like water – 'oh, Maude was sick on the way, she's always feeling sick in cars. I didn't know what to do, so I left her in a pub at Reading——'

'But my dear child——'

'Well, you could almost call it a hotel. She'll be all right there. I'll pick her up on the way back.'

'Well, you don't look very tired after your long drive——'

And at this they got into the car and drove on; it was tea time. Devlin, for whom tea time no longer existed, went on; with his work on the other side of the bushes, wondering what the girl looked like who owned that voice. Because you don't often get a girl who pronounces her words instead of just dropping them.

Devlin thought about women. Women, according to the ancient tradition, had no souls, that was why. Hogley disliked them – or why he said he did. And in theory that's all quite true. They can't ever grasp anything as a whole. Things come to them in driblets. They don't think, they just add bead to bead. Survivals, Hogley said, like the duck-billed platypus.

Still . . . Devlin in his furthest memories had circled about women, had liked their gloves and their voices and the silk lining of their coats. There was his mother, of course, with long white gloves all the way up her arms. And the ruby in her ring like wine.

And when he was a little boy in a train the girl who looked like a half caste – her wild corybanfic eyes.

But he had never come near a woman, and since going to Oxford had even shunned them; that was Hogley of course. You don't want, he had said, to filter away your mind.

To return to this girl, however. She was Sir Randal Belcher's daughter – that is, she was the daughter of the doctor who judged cases without seeing them, the eminent neurologist who had the damnedest cheek in Europe. Though her voice sounded nice. He would like to talk to her and say, 'I'm the man your father says is dotty.'

He asked Bearley: 'That was one of Sir Randal Belcher's daughters?'

'Oh, yes, that will be one of the Miss Belchers. A regular crowd of them there is. Come over here for dinners and parries they used to. Very nice young ladies. Sir Randal Belcher he's a great friend of the Colonel's. They was at school together.'

At school together – on this foundation rests so much of our world. Treaties are scrapped and wars declared merely because you and I come from the same old stink-hole, remember the same old blearers bleating away from their desks and can with effort hum bits of the same old vulgar sentimental songs.

Into Devlin's mind rose the old crooked master of the fifth form dressed in his greenish high-buttoned coat and croaking out: 'Now, me boy, don't go and scribble all over your books. Expensive books . . . parents pay for them . . . after-years . . . nucleus of your library. I knew a boy once, sensible boy . . . glad of it afterwards.' The thin goatish face peered at Devlin suspiciously, gradually fading into a high holly-bush and leaving behind in the sky, like a wisp of smoke from a train, his favourite phrase, 'nucleus of your library.'

Devlin turned. Poised in space behind him was a girl with a ballet dancer's figure. And falling like water came the same clear, clearly defined speech:

'Could you tell me where the violets are?'

'Yes miss, right way down the path just by yon wickery arch.'

'Thank you very much.'

Her small feet carried her away but behind her lay a sunlit pool of scent, bathing Devlin's head.

Devlin watched her picking the violets. She had very dark hair and wore a close-fitting dress of black velvet. 'A very un-English figure,' thought Devlin. 'This is flowing, but English girls are canals. This is the manner of antelopes, black panthers and rivers.'

She came up the path smelling her violets with delight. She was the sort of person who showed her delight. Instead of going past she stopped and looked at Devlin.

'Excuse me,' she said, 'for being frightfully inquisitive, but do you like being a gardener?'

'Being a gardener?' repeated Devlin, forgetting his dialect.

'Because I know I've got no right to ask, but it puzzled me. You see, the Colonel's been telling me all about your dialect, and well – not being a man I can tell a fake dialect from a real one. You will forgive me, won't you? Besides – well, anyhow, do you like it?'

'Yes, I like it very much, but I feel a little bit hurt at your discovering me.'

'Yes, I know that was very wrong of me, but I hate letting people think they've taken me in.'

'So do I. Which reminds me; I hope you don't mind but I've got a grievance against your father.'

'Really?'

'Yes; I'm told be wants to certify me.'

'Rubbish!'

'No, it's a fact. My name's Devlin Urquhart——'

'Oh *you're* Devlin Urquhart, are you?'

'Why? Have you heard about me?'

'Have I not! You're the young man who wrote the essay which made my father write another pamphlet.'

'What?'

'Why, someone or other, a guardian of yours I think——'

'Blarn,' came the horn of the car – 'blarn, blarn, blarn.'

'That means I must go and drive Mr. Bilbatrox.'

'Well, good-bye, and thank you for the violets. I'll try and stop my father putting you in a cell. As a matter of fact his bark's far worse than his bite. Good-bye!'

She rippled into a smile and was gone like foam.

Devlin pulled up some groundsel. 'Very funny that about the pamphlet; wouldn't Hogley laugh? Hogley? . . . Hogley's rather a bore sometimes.

'I like the way she looks at one; I like it well. I like people who've got a bit of life. And I must say, I like . . .'

Slowly a crystal formed in his mind. He worked on.

The clock struck six like six fruits falling. Devlin took his tools to the shed. They were good tools. That spade was a new one to match the one Bearley always used. Devlin felt that his hands had already given it a patina – a friendly shine at the handle. Good tools. A good life. Good——

'I have my fear the game's up,' said Bearley.

'What do you mean?'

'The Colonel wants to see you.'

'What about?'

'About *you* I reckon. He looked fair nettled!'

'Oh, I'll soon settle him.'

Bearley shook his head. 'If you get the sack come round and say ta to me.'

'I won't get the sack.'

'I bet you you will.'

Devlin walked over towards the house feeling like a little boy called up by the master. Had possibly Miss Belcher given him away?

'Come here, Urkitt. Why have you been pretending to me?' The Colonel was just like a more aristocratic house-master.

'Been a-pretending, zur? Nayver.'

'For the Lord's sake stop talking like that. I heard you talking now to Bearley. You are a gentleman and you are pretending to be a yokel.'

The Colonel's moustache seemed to have a sharp edge; he stood with the western sun behind him. The thought of Wilkins flashed in Devlin's mind; that was the real grievance.

'I'm very sorry, sir, if you object——'

'Do you expect me not to object? There are plenty of poor lads that would like your job. If you must compete with them, compete with them as yourself. I consider what you have done thoroughly mean and ridiculous.'

'Well, sir, I think one has a right to act. An actor is himself when he's Hamlet. Why shouldn't I be myself when I'm a yokel.'

'Don't talk nonsense to me. Yourself is what you were born. What your father made you and intended you to be.'

'My father was Sir Arnold Urquhart.'

'What!'

The Colonel's attack seemed to have crumpled.

He rallied. 'Then it is all the more disgrace to you. If he were alive . . . I knew your father once and I know what his feelings would be. . . .'

'We can't all be governors of Madras,' Devlin said carelessly, not meaning to blaspheme. The Colonel came down like a chopper. 'Here's your next week's pay and you will please leave my estate at once.'

Devlin could not decide quickly whether he ought to take the pay or not. He took it and, shrugging up his shoulders——

But the Colonel precluded him. 'Clear out,' he said. Devlin went, feeling that after all he was, perhaps, in the wrong.

As he walked down into Wytt he bought an evening paper at the sweet shop and stood in the street reading it. A gruff, cackling voice interrupted him. 'Good evening, I see you are reading the *Evening*——?'

'Good evening, ma'am.'

It was Miss Hardstaff, her nose glowing with sympathy for the working classes.

'Personally I find the *Evening Follower* a very good paper. But of course we all have our tastes. Now what I was wondering was – we have lately formed in Wytt a Young Men's Reading Club. You might perhaps like to join it. I was going to send my gardener to ask you but here we are——'

'No, we're not,' said Devlin in his own voice. Miss Hardstaff stared after him, not taking in who he was or why he had gone away. She was like Deity; evil was for her merely a misprint.

The Colonel's new gardener's boy would not join her reading club. He was a misprint. Blot him out.

CHAPTER SIX

What to do next, thought Devlin, as he went downstairs to his egg and strong tea. He ate breakfast in the kitchen with Mrs. Dudd and her daughter, Gladys.

'Good morning, Mr. Urkitt. It's awful sudden the way you're leaving us. Gladys here was just saying how you ought really to go to one of them specialists.'

'Oo, aa.'

'I had an uncle once; it was just the same with him——'

But Devlin was opening the letter by his plate.

It was from Hogley, sent via Gunter:

'My dear Devlin, – I hear you have cut yourself off from the civilised world. As these returns to Nature never last long, do come and stay with me for a day or two before term. There are some good shows on and I expect you to help me with my belles-lettres article on Terence. Trusting you have not caught gardener's knee. Love, Cyril Hogley.'

'Very, though insultingly, opportune. And it's quite true, my spirit's left me for gardening. It remains to go up and pyrotek with Hogley – the nine Muses and the tenth, which is Scandal.

'Never heard of this article on Terence. Hogley always invites you to help him. Used to flatter me once.'

But a little highbrow shop would be good. In *that* world things moved on (Surréalisme for instance), but in Colonel Hardle's garden time stood like a pond; Bearley even planted the peas in a way now out of date, making each pea his hole with a sawed-off spade-handle and smoothing them over after with a gentle hand.

'Good-bye, Mr. Urkitt; we do 'ope your operation comes off fine, don't we, Gladys? Many's the man an operation's been the saving of. Why I've often thought of one myself. It's something in my back the doctor says; needs levering or something. Hurts me mountin' them stairs. Up and down, up and down, and me a full bodied woman. I declare I'd sooner be in America and 'ave the use of them lifts, gun-running or no——'

Siren-whistle, bull-mouthed bell, green flag, wheels revolve.

Revolving wheels – dissolving space.

Good-bye to Colonel Hardle and his yellow moustache, rabbity Mrs. Dudd, thin-bosomed Gladys, the stream that flowed by the site of the rockery, the yews cut like puddings, the peas asleep in their holes.

'He'll never get that rockery.

'A great many stations on this train.

'As usual nothing to do but smoke. The quickest possible sequence of taking and giving. For those who're too lazy for any other creation.

'And here we are in London. Hogley'll be surprised. Won't like my clothes, I expect.'

Nor he did – like them that was. 'Yes, yes, my dear Devlin, they're very, very amusing but really——' There was a man coming to lunch; Devlin changed at once.

The man was, after all, only a German. Very good English but no feeling for English. He and Hogley had a long conversation about their mutual acquaintances. But immoral people are boring if you don't know them. Devlin got tired of hearing of their immoralities. The German delivered them with such a sly sort of pomp.

'Ah, but do you know what Karl did the day after?'

'No.'

'It was not a very respectable thing he did.'

'Good; tell us about it.'

'Well, the day after Karl woke up, and he had a headache. He said to himself: 'Here am I, I am a philosopher, I am a great philosopher, and yet I have a headache.' You see the situation.'

'Yes. And then?'

'Then Karl sits up in bed and says to himself: 'How am I to cure my headache?"

'Yes?'

'As Karl says this – he says it aloud for he is not thinking – the man in the bed next door hears him, and he happens to be in the navy.'

'Yes?'

'And this man who is in the navy says to Karl: 'What about a dash up channel, my friend?"

'What did Karl say?'

'Ah. That is where you must have great knowledge of Karl's character, my good Hogley. Karl is not an ordinary man. He has always been accustomed——'

'That's extraordinarily amusing,' said Hogley.

'Yes, but that: is not all.' The German told them a great deal more about Karl. He left about a quarter to four.

'I hope you weren't too bored,' said Hogley. 'I find that man perfectly impossible, but – however, those buildings he spoke of. I've got some rather good photographs of them.'

'Oh; may I see them?' (Devlin still tending to play the intelligent dog).

'But, of course, my dear.'

Looking through his drawers to find the photographs, Hogley produced an old snap of himself. 'This may amuse you,' he said, 'it was when I was just leaving school – child-cult, you know.' Devlin looked——

Hogley, very young and wind-blown fresh, stood holding aloft a wooden spade over a great sandcastle (its turrets were discernible); behind him the breakers made a jagged white line.

'How too sweet,' said Devlin, mockingly; mockingly in order to flatter, but really there was something which had dropped out of Hogley, but which in this photo still was.

He thought of Hogley at Oxford, at his Sunday morning sherry parties or his small cocktail parties before dinner, smiling with his cold eyes, buzzing about like a bee collecting scandal; how he doted on it; his mind must be like a honey-comb packed with golden scandal. While round him sat the half-baked obviously ex-schoolboys and a few more polished because more vicious.

In all he did Hogley was admirably thorough. He was the one man who knew all the versions, recensions and scholia of the scandal on the Radcliffe Camera roof. And now, when he had showed Devlin all these loose photographs, he took down a vast book of architectural plates and turned in rapid succession to pages 16, 31 and 32, 40, 122, 131 and 2 and 3, 270, 508. Then he turned back to page 40 and drew a supplementary diagram. 'You see,' he said, 'you can't see from this photo the real proportions of the nave. . . .'

After tea Hogley told Devlin at length of his recent Baroque tour. Talking of Vienna he suddenly veered. 'Do you know whom I met there? Evelyn Grimbley. He had got into some sort of mess with a prostitute. Which reminds me——'

And for three-quarters of an hour he told Devlin dirty stories, amusing but palling. Devlin was reminded of school-boys; the mantle of intelligent dog began to fall from his shoulders.

Hogley suspected something; he had always suspected Devlin, for, after all, Devlin was not 'so.' You don't know where you are with a man like that. Men like that are so pig-headed; if they don't fall for a female they get some other craze which ruins their social value.

Suddenly Hogley said:

'You're too young, you know, Devlin.'

'Don't you like one to be young?'

'It depends how youth takes one. The way it takes you is not entirely fitting. I mean all this gardener type of thing. One can't do that sort of thing today. In the early nineteenth century perhaps; but now——'

'If you're suggesting I'm a lake-poet——'

'Now, now, Devlin dear, don't be so tetchy. The real trouble with you is you're a puritan. You're just like John Dermot was when he first came up.'

'Well, I'd rather be like that than when he went down. I'd rather have his puritanism than his D.T.'s, not to speak of——'

'My dear Devlin, you know John Dermot never had D.T.'s.'

'Of course he had.'

'Rubbish; but if he had, it doesn't affect the case. What I say is, is that you're dangerously innocent. Or ignorant – it's the same thing. I don't say it doesn't suit some people to be innocent——'

'I don't care a damn how innocent I am.'

'Some people, you see, are born to be monks. But you, in my opinion, would be wasting yourself in a monastery – even a mental one. Besides you are too good-looking.'

It always went to Devlin's heart to be told be was good-looking. (The Graylings, whose ideal was the blonde beast off the cover of the *Tennis Weekly*, had brought him up to consider himself plain.) His growing annoyance with Hogley once more dwindled and he smiled.

'There have been lots of good-looking monks,' he said, 'but don't you worry. Soon enough I shall find my Jeanne Duval——'

Hogley smiled tolerantly. 'To return to facts,' he said, 'it's really sheer nonsense your leaving Oxford. Why don't you go up again when term starts? You can easily soothe your guardians into paying for you again, and, even if you don't, didn't you say you were getting some money when you're twenty-one?'

'Yes, I shall get a bit. Quite soon, too.'

'Well then——'

'No, no, Hogley, it's no good. I'm tired of Oxford.'

'Tired of Oxford! Nonsense.' (Hogley turned on his frivol-tap). 'You can't be tired of the glories of Butterfield and the revelries of Ruskin. . . .'

'I've got postcards of all that.'

'But, seriously, Devlin——'

Devlin saw the ominous, rather sickly, light kindling in Hogley's eyes; with persons like Hogley that meant pawing. Devlin shunted his chair.

Hogley was piqued; he got up and yawned.

'Would you like to go to a little party before dinner?' he said.

'What sort of a party?'

'Oh, only a vulgar little cocktail party in some mews somewhere. I'm not even sure if I remember the address. It's an American art fiend who keeps pestering me for articles for the *Illinois Helicon*——'

'For what?'

'That may not be quite the name. He's got the most—— taste. He's just heard of Van Gogh, Van Gog I mean. He asked me if I didn't just worship that great-souled Dutchman.'

'To which you wittily replied?'

'To which I wittily replied: 'Not at all.' You've no idea, Devlin, what bores these men are. The High Table aren't a patch on it. But as for this American, poor Vincent's just about his high water mark. All jam; no bread.'

'You liked him when you were young, didn't you?'

'Who? Vincent? Yes, I liked a bit of gush then. Had all those dreadful colour-prints. Sheer loss, Devlin dear. Well; are you on for this party?'

'Yes, of course I am. I shall tell your American pal you suffer from megalomania.'

'As you will. All I ask is don't expect to meet anyone possible there. They'll all be just bloody.' Hogley's underlip came out; rather a venom-brewer.

'Especially the women,' he added.

(The only possible women for Hogley were middle-aged married women who knew life and the titles of books and pictures.)

The American's rooms were full of smoke and voices – voices hopping about like loose wire springs. The square face of the American filled the angles of the door.

'Come in, boys,' he said. 'I'm real glad you've come. I say, Hogley, I've been wanting to ask your opinion about the work of a young chap I've just met. It seems to me he's got real grip; he's got real sense of form. When these folk have thinned out a bit I'll be able to show you a canvas of his I got this morning.'

'My God,' murmured Hogley, 'can't you just imagine it?'

Too much absinthe ruined Devlin's cocktail and as for the people, they were all just people; barely real. And it was true, the women were bloody. They sat perched round on corners of the furniture, one or two of them hunched up in positions which showed their thighs; not that they would interest anyone. Neither more nor less interesting than any Mothers' Meeting or committee of old spinsters.

Devlin suddenly noticed wild red hair in a corner. Bunched peony-wise and assertive like a flag. Underneath, a man's face. Rather nice, he thought, till he noticed his black shirt and red tie.

'Who's that bloody Bohemian?' he asked Hogley.

'Who? That? That's the parish fool; lie's not only half dotty, but he's called Gabriel Crash.'

'Why?'

'It's his name. He thinks he's living in the nineties. Go and talk to him if you like. It's like giving buns to a bear. He's probably drunk.'

'It bores me, all that sort of thing.'

'No more eccentric than gardening, dearie. Still, it *is* a little dull here.'

'Yes. This is a rotten drink.'

'Completely. Where shall we go for dinner?'

'I don't really mind; I should vote for an A.B.C.'

'Now, now, Devlin, don't go to extremes. Hullo——'

There was a noise of smashed glass. It was Gabriel Crash explaining about Jewish bridegrooms.

'There you see,' he said (having ground his glass under his heel), 'there. Isn't, it sublime? Isn't, it dynamic?'

'Look here, Gabriel, old man,' said the American, 'that's very interesting, but you won't mind if I say it's not very good for the carpet.'

'Oh, the carpet,' said Gabriel, rising to his great height. 'Every carpet should have glass in it. The element of sorrow, you know. You make glass with sand and potash. You make carpets——'

'Gabriel, you're tight.'

'I'm not tight. You make carpets of red and blue, of red and blue and yellow and black and seagreen and red and——'

'What a bore,' said the woman on Devlin's toe, 'that man always makes a fool of himself.'

'Colour is sublime. Colour is dynamic. None of you people here——'

'You sit down, Gabriel,' said the American pushing him into a chair. 'It's very interesting all what you say, but this is a small room.'

'I say, Hogley,' he said aside, 'you couldn't see him out could you? He's not really very tight, but you know how he is.'

'Oh, certainly, I know his little ways.' Hogley sat down on the arm of Gabriel's chair.

'Gabriel, my dear,' he said in a voice like syrup, 'aren't you bored with being here?'

'Bloody damn bored.'

'So am I. What about a little fresh air?'

'God's own air,' said Gabriel. 'I'm on for it. Full of the true the blushful something or other. What about that girl over there though?'

'What about her? Don't shout so.'

'I like it a lot.'

'Stop it, Gabriel.'

'Not the girl, you damn fool. Her dress of course. Black velvet you know. That's why Manet's so divine. . . .'

Devlin looked round and saw a very plain blonde in what was certainly a good dress; just like the one of that delightful girl in the garden.

'Oh, I do, do wish I was a nigger,' Gabriel was saying. 'It's very unhappy to be me. Do you see that girl's black dress? Oh, isn't it divine? I do wish I could wear something like that.'

'Now, now my dear,' Hogley whispered, 'if you talk so much about her, you know what everyone will think.'

'Ha, ha, ha. That's a good joke; oh, that's a roaring good joke. But I do wish I was a negro, a tall pillow of gloom. I say, Hogley, do you see——'

'No, stop it. There's a wonderful sunset on outside; why not come down and see it?'

'A sunset by God? Come on then. I adore sunsets. Oh, I just adore the damn things.'

Gabriel jumped to his feet and pushed his way to the door. They heard him clatter downstairs and fall over the door-mat at the bottom. His headlong arrival on the cobbles of the mews was announced by someone at the window.

Devlin thought the man a complete fool, but, after all, he liked black velvet. While Hogley was bringing out a remark, Devlin ran downstairs and stood over Gabriel, who was now lying on his back like a starfish, staring at the sky.

'I don't see any bloody sunset,' he said.

'Of course you don't. The sun won't set for several hours yet.'

'What's that?' Gabriel floundered over and rose to his knees.

'No sunset? Then I've been done.'

'Of course you have. One's always done when one's drunk.'

'I'm not drunk.'

'Well, if I were you, I should sit on that packing case and get your breath.'

Gabriel sat on the packing case, put a hand on each knee and stared at Devlin. He screwed his eyes as if trying to keep Devlin in drawing.

Wild red hair over a gash mouth and sad grey eyes – that was all one noticed of him; and, of course, his height.

'I love being drunk,' he said at last.

'You just said you weren't drunk.'

'Ah!' said Gabriel slyly, 'that was just to take you in.'

'Nonsense.'

'It was like this, you see. I said I wasn't drunk, but I was drunk really. It's like what Archimedes did when he said he wasn't in the bath because his weight was in it. I said I wasn't drunk, but I was drunk. I adore being drunk. You know what Victor Hugo said, one must either be an artist or be drunk in this world. I would be an artist only I've got no character. Look at Lionel Johnson now. He hadn't got any character and so he was drunk. And so——'

'Why can't you make yourself a character?' Devlin found himself arguing though he knew it was absurd; 'I don't say don't get drunk, but I do say cut out all this talk about it.'

'That's just what I think,' said Gabriel.

There was laughter from the window; Devlin realised he had an audience and stopped.

'Look at that window,' said Gabriel, 'it's grown a lot of faces.'

The faces laughed. Gabriel shook his fist at them.

'I've got something to say to you faces,' he said. 'You've just been saying I've got no damned character. Well, this is what I say to you. I know I've got no character and who's to blame? Not me. It's not my fault I've got no character. And I know you've all got characters, you faces up there. But what good is it to you? You may have characters, but you've got no souls. You don't appreciate anything. I'd rather have a soul than a character any day. Look at Ernest Dowson. Look at Lionel Johnson. They were better men than you but——'

Some small boys came walking down the mews. Gabriel rose to his feet and pointed indignantly:

'Look at them,' he shouted. 'Look at the damned little insects. All of a piece, all of you. Nothing but faces – bloody foolish faces.'

Feeling this was a climax he stopped and put his hand to his head.

'Where's my hat?' he shouted, his voice rising to a squeak. The faces in the wagging window tilted towards him and laughed. A female voice said: 'I do think Crash is *such* a good name for him.'

Hogley came downstairs, gave Gabriel his hat and took him by the arm. 'Come along,' he said, 'we're going to have some dinner now.'

'Can we manage him,' whispered Devlin.

'I can manage any drunk,' said Hogley. 'Gabriel is easy. He'll amuse you perhaps. Autobiographical you know.'

They took a taxi at a rank round the corner.

'Oh, what fun to be off the ground,' said Gabriel, quite like a small child.

'Isn't it?' said Hogley, in the soothing-governess voice.

'Last time I was in a taxi I was being taken up. That was a long time ago.'

'Oh, you didn't tell us about that.'

'I love being off the ground though. I love swings, don't you? There's the ones in fairs and then there's the ones in the trees, the low gentle sort of ones. I do just adore them.'

He was silent and sat happily in his corner looking out of the window. There flashed past a poster for Colman's mustard.

'Oh, I do love mustard,' Gabriel said. 'It's got such a tang or something. I do wish they hadn't made me read the Waverley Novels when I was young. Otherwise I should have been different. They *are* such swine. I do like mixing mustard – all in a little blue egg-cup. Garlic is fun too, and pepper and ginger. Hogley, couldn't we have some ginger for dinner; Hogley darling.'

'Of course, Gabriel. Anything you like. But you must remember to walk straight?'

'Walk straight? I'm not drunk. I only walk crooked because it's the line of beauty. I do everything for beauty. Mustard is beautiful and pepper is beautiful and ginger and garlic and black velvet. A thing of beauty——'

'You mustn't quote, Gabriel, dear.'

'Why not?'

'Because it's childish. You must grow up you know. Grow up and produce something.'

'Produce? I can't produce anything. It's very unhappy to be me. And it's all because I don't like ladies. I do wish I did. Because I don't like women. They're ladies when they wear black velvet, and they're women when they wear nothing. But I can't like them either way. Oh, it's very hard, it's so hard, Hogley darling.'

'Forget about it, Gabriel. After all——'

'No, no. You're all so crass. It's because you were at good public schools. My public school was only just public. It's because you're gentlemen that you're all so crass. I never had enough money. Oh, it's very unhappy to be me.'

Gabriel's face became a pathetic clown's mask. But luckily it was Soho and the taxi stopped. They went into the restaurant with Gabriel between them.

Through dinner Devlin gradually noticed Hogley's snakiness. He sat there with his head poised like a cobra, now and again bending his brows forward in answer to something. It was a habit which used to flatter Devlin because it always suggested Devlin was very clever to get the point (even if he hadn't) so quickly. But tonight it seemed a snake's trick after all.

And Devlin felt sorry for Gabriel pouring out what he thought was his soul, while Hogley sat by him coaxing him. Like a man who keeps apes in order to gloat in the chapel of his reason over their flat skulls and shambling hopeless bondage.

He must have read quite a lot, Gabriel must. Kept quoting all the stock quotations and some others. Suddenly he said precisely what Devlin was thinking. 'I'm a rag-bag,' he said, 'my mind's a bloody rag-bag.' And then suddenly piqued: 'I'm going to pay for my dinner.' He rose from his chair.

Hogley pulled him down again. 'Now, Gabriel,' he said, 'where are your manners?'

Gabriel, like a little boy, hung his head and said nothing. Coffee came and they smoked a cigarette each. Then Hogley said: 'May we come home with you, Gabriel? Devlin would so much like to see your digs.'

'Of course,' said Gabriel, his face spouting into delight, 'do come and see my digs. They are marvellous, aren't tiny, Hogley dear?'

'They are, as a matter of fact,' said Hogley.

Gabriel's dinner had sobered him, and they got to his digs easily. Devlin found the sitting-room very attractive. Quite why, he didn't know. It may have been that the room, as Gabriel proudly announced, was not truly square. Or it may have been that it had dark Jacobean panelling and yet had the feeling of a very light room. It may have been because there was no attempt to keep in character with the panelling.

And it was surprising that for all Gabriel's talk about colour there was no bright colour in the room. Excepting the fire.

Gabriel suddenly said: 'Would you like to see a dragon?' and threw something into the fire. 'Lovely blue flames,' he said. 'You watch.'

They watched the lovely blue flames. 'That's my old tea-packets,' he said. 'I always keep them for dragons.'

Hogley pushed Gabriel on to the piano stool. 'Play, Gabriel dear,' he said, in his wheedling trainer's voice.

'I won't play,' said Gabriel. 'Mr. Urquhart doesn't like music.'

'But I do,' said Devlin, 'only I'm quite unmusical.'

'Same thing,' said Gabriel.

'Don't be silly,' said Hogley, 'we both want you to play; play this.' He slid a music-sheet on to the rest.

Gabriel threw it on the floor. 'I won't play,' he repeated.

'What a child you are,' said Hogley.

'I may be a child,' said Gabriel. 'I won't play, anyhow.' He went over and sat in an armchair by the fire. His head in the shadow of the fire looked like the top of a tree that had somehow been born a man. 'We'd better leave him,' said Hogley softly. 'He's in one of his sulks. He'll be all right when we've gone. He's nearly sober now; and he usually goes to bed blind.'

As they let themselves out, Hogley said: 'I'm sorry the fool wouldn't play to you; he plays amazingly; it's his only use.'

Hogley's flat looked soulless after that odd room with the panelling. As they had a whisky before going to bed, Devlin found himself thinking quite affectionately of Gabriel – as of a dirty sort of urchin who yet moved in an aura, a joyful bright aura like one of Blake's daemons.

'I think he's not bad,' he said.

'Who?'

'Gabriel.'

'A silly sot,' said Hogley, and out came his underlip.

'There's more to him than that,' said Devlin.

'Is there? Well, I'm going to bed.' Hogley looked at Devlin sharply, and went to his room. 'Huffy,' thought Devlin, 'feels I'm cutting loose.'

Devlin remained for a little time in the sitting-room looking at the gas-fire. Then he turned it out and went through the door to the passage. 'Pop' said the gas-fire behind him; he jumped. Too much to eat and drink had affected his nerves.

For the same reason he found it hard to get to sleep. It was like climbing uphill. Always passing a mile stone and always the same mile stone.

Very clear into his mind came the girl who picked violets. With her wonderful pose and her black velvet dress and the scent of chypre and the way she smiled down into the small bunch of flowers.

And now here he was, back among the inverts with their catty talk and eternal alcohol. Wood and steel they were, and the cocktail girls, too. And Gabriel too, though he had, as he said, a soul, was a bungled affair at best.

Whereas she stood out against this wood and steel world as the one being of flesh. The one being sanely beautiful in a world of snakes and drunkards, of process and progress and so-called experiences – æsthetic, intellectual and sexual experiences. These words, 'sex' and 'experience' and 'beauty,' they meant nothing at all; look how Gabriel bandied them in the mews. 'Meaning' itself meant nothing; it was the putting up one thing to represent another. Words could mean her but they did not reach her. She herself was beyond meaning; she *was*. And that was what one wanted, a pole of one's being, not revolving, but marking revolutions. Everything else went round and so was incidental, just as Gabriel's hair flopped over his face or his words tumbled out of his mouth. These people were to her as bats to a phœnix, squeaky fluttering movements, lapses rather than movements; compared with the steady soar of the queen and only of birds. There was no one real in the world but one, in the world but one, in the world but she.

CHAPTER SEVEN

They had breakfast at half past ten. Hogley had very little appetite; he lit a cigarette long before Devlin had finished eating.

'Don't mind me,' Devlin said, 'it makes one hungry being a gardener.'

'It seems to. I must say I'm glad you've given that up. I knew you would, of course.'

'You don't know why I did.'

'I know you were thrown out. Apart from that I bet you'd soon have resigned. You see, you are obviously not thinking of trying another such job. What I want to know is, what are you going to do?'

'I don't know. I'm not going back to Oxford.'

'Once again, why not?'

'Because I'm tired of the place!'

'Pose,' said Hogley.

'Pose yourself.'

'Don't be childish, Devlin. Though it's hardly worth my saying so; you'll go on being a child for some time yet, I fear. Tiresome people children – in some ways. See in a glass darkly——'

'Well,' said Devlin, 'why not? It's a bore always seeing through things. I'd rather have a dark glass any day? One can see the sun through that.'

'What you really like,' said Hogley, 'is a mirror.'

'Yes, I do.'

'Vain, that's what you are, Vain to the core. You'll have to get over your egotism. No great man can afford to be an egoist!'

'Everyone doesn't want to be a great man. Why do you always assume I do?'

'Because *you*, I suppose, might be great. And certainly everyone *ought* to be ambitious. Don't you remember the code – to be human is to wish to be superhuman. Now if I were not ambitious, I should feel thoroughly ashamed of myself. The point is, you see, to be truly ambitious is just the opposite of being mere egotistical——'

'I don't know what you're talking about. Isn't there any marmalade?'

'Isn't it there? I thought I put it out. Half a moment——'

Hogley got up, produced the marmalade from a cupboard and continued:

'The trouble is you're a puritan. Puritans are always egoists. What we've got to do is to stop you being a puritan. . . .'

And Hogley went on and on about what we've got to do. Awful polypragmatists people like that. Sublimated inversion, the psychologists would say. It's not that so much as their two-faced, their——

('Devlin Urquhart? Yes, I remember how crude he was when he came up. I had my work cut out educating him. . . . No flies on me, you see.')

'What are you staring at me for?' Hogley asked.

Devlin came to.

'Sorry,' he said, 'I'm afraid I was wandering. Is my soul saved yet?'

'No; I give it up. It's your own funeral if you won't come back to Oxford.'

'All right. You can all come to my wake.'

'Thank you. Would you like to go round to the Tundish Galleries today? A lot of bilge but two or three decent things. There's a superb early Matisse; you'll like it, I think. It's such a pity Matisse has sold his soul. He's only fit now for the *Sketch* Summer Number——'

For Hogley did react to pictures; though he sometimes lied about his reactions, even to himself. Devlin knew that Hogley was really sad, and angry too, that Matisse had left the broad meadows of his youth, those joyful slabs of colour.

There was another thing Hogley liked and that was the space and wealth of high gradual contours, downs and big fields which lay open to God. For one needs some better name for the air of open country. As Hogley probably knew. Or knew anyhow when he made castles of sand and held his spade above them.

They went to the Tundish Galleries and Hogley paid his homage. At the same time he showed off a little in front of the other visitors.

In the evening they went to the theatre. Devlin had two double whiskies between the acts. This made him more ready to talk and less ready to listen.

'I like that actor well,' he said, as they came home.

'Yes,' said Hogley, 'he's all right as an actor, but——'

'It's a great pity,' Devlin said, when Hogley bad finished.

'What's a pity?'

'A pity you're such a critic. I hope you don't mind, but I feel you're a born critic.'

'Mind, my dear. Isn't that a compliment?'

'No, it's not. Not as I mean it. A born critic is a dead critic. I mean, any critic as such is essentially dead. He must have good taste and so he can't be vulgar. And if you can't be vulgar, you can't create——'

'But, my dear, I abhor good taste.'

'Oh, no, you don't. You abhor what your dons on the High Table call good taste, but all the same you have your own criterion——'

'But of course I have. You wouldn't have me drift without a rudder?'

'That's just it.' (Devlin felt he was arguing brilliantly.) 'Without a rudder you say? There you are, you see. You're like a man in a boat. A man in a boat trespasses on the water; an artist ought to be a fish. Better still a whale. Spouting up the actual stuff he lives in.'

'Rather a crude notion, I'm inclined to think.'

'Damn it, Hogley, you've got to be crude. That's the fault with *you*; you're not crude at all. You're a critic and a critic has to be neat; his fingers have to taper. He lives in the past tense. Anyone who creates must live in the gush of the present——'

'Don't be so silly, Devlin. One might think you were Gabriel Crash. Do you imagine every artist works just by an amorphous urge? It's the old, old fallacy——'

'No, that's not it at all. I detest Inspiration, if that's what you mean. I detest the sloppy idea of genius falling from heaven, as if genius was something unique. As if every work of art was merely a bloody miracle. My point merely is – there is a difference of some sort: between *you* and an artist.'

'I dare say there is. For example——'

'You see, there are only two possible attitudes towards a work of art – possible to people other than its creator. I don't know what to call them quite. Appreciation, perhaps, and criticism. The point is that appreciation proper can't criticise and criticism proper can't appreciate——'

'Absolute bosh, Devlin dear.'

'I don't think so, and I certainly shouldn't say *you* can't, appreciate. The point is that you're not always, thank God, being critical. For all that, you *are* a critic born.'

'Well, so be it.'

'The point is——'

'Devlin, do stop saying that.'

'The point is, criticism is bound to be concerned with fictions, with things which are fictions because they are real things in the past tense. Beauty, for instance. When Keats said——'

'Yes, I know the quotation.'

'Well, when he said that, he meant something definite. But the very fact that it came to us not in *being* as it came to *him*, but in *meaning* as it came *from* him, the very fact that he meant it has made it for us indefinite. But with you critics, it is much worse, you actually *start* at secondhand. And your criticism is entirely a matter of heads and tails. First it is: 'That aspidistra is too hideous – what taste these Victorians had,' and then it is: 'How too divine that aspidistra is,' just because you know that the people who like it like it for what you call the wrong reasons and the people who dislike it dislike it for still wronger reasons——'

'Yes, yes?'

'So that there you have a whole little field left to yourselves, to show your unique power of liking without committing yourselves.'

'Talking of aspidistras, do you know that they make liqueurs out of them in British Guiana? I heard it the other day from one of the Hellenic Travellers' Society who got on the wrong boat——'

'Yes, but to return to criticism——'

'No, Devlin, I just won't return to criticism. You may be a whale as you say artists ought to be, but I'm damned if I'll be a Jonah. I've heard lots of people talk like that before. Poor dear John Dermot now——'

'Oh, damn John Dermot. Anyone can see he's so utterly deboshed he couldn't——'

'Now, don't be catty.'

' – Couldn't put one idea on top of another.'

'Don't be catty, I say.'

'I'm not. I know all about your John Dermot. He was at Hillbury to begin with——'

'Was he? I didn't remember that. Hillbury seems to produce all the bright young minds of the day. Do you know, I've never been there?'

'Why don't you go then?'

'Why should I? I don't make solitary pilgrimages to public schools to expose myself as a butt to the horrid little boys and their horrider little masters. If you would escort me now?'

'Oh, I'll escort you all right.'

'So be it then. Is that a bargain? Any time I bring a car, say towards the end of term, we'll go down there together. Always presuming you're still alive by then.'

'Right.'

'And the downs are nice, you say?'

'Yes.'

The day ended amicably with talking about the downs, their unperturbed and ever memorable lines.

Next morning they again argued about Devlin's returning to Oxford.

'It's no good,' Devlin said; 'my guardians have cut me off, Sir Belcher has banned me, and finally I myself haven't the least wish to return there. Not enough oxygen in that part of the Thames Valley. Besides——'

The telephone. Hogley answered it. Was much surprised to find that it was Gabriel Crash.

'Hullo, Gabriel.'

'Hullo, Hogley. What was the name of your nice friend the other night?'

'Devlin Urquhart.'

'Oh, of course. I thought he wasn't half nice. I'm afraid I was rather drunk; I hope he didn't mind? I say, Hogley; he liked my rooms, didn't he?'

'Of course, Gabriel. Everyone adores your rooms.'

'Well, you see, didn't he say he wants to live in London?'

'I don't think so!' (Hogley was suspicious.)

'Well, the rooms above mine have just gone vacant and I *am* so alarmed someone will take them like the man before; he was a ghastly man. So I thought perhaps your friend might take them if he has nowhere to put up.'

'That's very delightful of you, Gabriel dear. I don't think, as I said, that he wants rooms in Town; but I'll ask him.'

Hogley asked him, adding that he would be damned silly if he took them. This annoyed Devlin.

'On the contrary,' he said, 'if they're a possible price, I should take them like a shot.'

'Hullo; I say, Gabriel, what price are they?'

'Price. Oh, I don't know that. Not more than mine I suppose. Mine's two guineas a week without food.'

'Two guineas a week,' said Hogley to Devlin, 'but don't take it.'

'As a matter of fact I think I will. Tell him I'll come round and see about it. Say I'm frightfully grateful for his ringing up.'

They went round that afternoon, Hogley saying now and again: 'You'll be a perfect fool, Devlin, if you take it. . . . I tell you he's never sober . . . what's worse, he's got no more brain than a hog.'

'Rather a sweet hog,' said Devlin.

Gabriel was out, but Mrs. Frigate, the landlady, was plump and kind, quite like Mrs. Dudd urbanised. Mrs. Dudd, yes. . . .

'Have you got tiles in your kitchen?' Devlin asked her while being shown round. Hogley looked at him.

'I do all the cooking,' said Mrs. Frigate.

'No, I know that. I'm just interested in kitchens.'

'I have lino,' said Mrs. Frigate.

Devlin engaged the rooms; he would move in the day after tomorrow as the day after that Hogley was going to Oxford. He had no idea how he would pay for them.

His last day with Hogley was depressing. Hogley read aloud the article on Terence, but Devlin could offer no suggestions; how could *he* offer suggestions to *Hogley*? On Terence I mean.

An amazing memory Hogley had. A brain like a porcupine, bristling with dates and quotations, with Greek, Latin, French and Italian poetry, with scandal (lots of it), with phrases prepared against occasions, with little feathered flatteries and little pin-prick hits. The trouble was——

The trouble was, wouldn't he eventually, later, ten years on, be rather a bore then? A sort of crust come on him? What about those other dons, I mean; some of them were bright once, weren't they? And now some of them were buried in their wives; the others (the ones like Hogley) were buried in themselves. How long before Hogley entombed himself?

A little negro stool stood on a table in the corner; Hogley had bought it for ten guineas. The seat of the stool was held by the long fingers of a woman, fingers which came shooting from her palms like long straight tendrils. It was exquisitely finished. The almost metallic wood was almost shockingly glossy, black like something very inner, very away from the sun. The protruding great breasts, great round forehead and great eyes pierced our sophistication; noises rose in the brain like falls of dark water. Like being drummed downwards by the heavy hands of a dream.

'Odd,' said Hogley, 'that negro artists can't survive civilisation. Fall in love with wax models at once.'

Devlin came to with a little stab of irritation. Hogley was just about to make a point.

'They lack the critical faculty,' Hogley said.

But next day Hogley took him round to Gabriel's digs. On the way he again tackled Devlin.

'What, for instance, are you going to do about your clothes? You can't go through life on the contents of a suit case?'

'Oh, I shall go round some day and collect them.'

'But what about your guardian?'

'He can't do anything. If I meet him I shall tell him I've now decided my own career.'

'Oh, well, I hope you don't end in a padded cell.'

Gabriel greeted them effusively. He was quite sober and not at all maudlin.

'Hullo,' he said, 'it's a great thrill your coming here. Mrs. Frigate likes you too. She makes wonderful bloody steaks. How do you like your rooms?'

'I think they're charming.'

Devlin noticed Hogley very slightly sneering.

'I'd rather live here than in your part of the world, Hogley,' he added; 'it's very charming, of course, but there's such an aroma of culture.'

Hogley laughed. He knew 'bohemian' meant something detestable to Devlin. 'I expect you'll have a very jolly bohemian life here,' he said.

So when after having tea they parted, their parting was somewhat hostile. But they reminded each other of their engagement to go to Hillbury.

Devlin then went up to his room and unpacked his suit case. He thought it was about time he changed his pyjamas; he really must go home to his guardians. In the meantime he would foster his self-respect by a visit to the chemist's.

Gabriel led him to a decent chemist's, repeating 'Do buy some scent; I do adore scent.' But all Devlin bought was a bottle of hydrogen peroxide for his teeth, a bowl of Fougère Royale shaving soap, some cream for after his shave, some powder for after his cream, and a small file for his nails. 'What *do* you want all those things for?' said Gabriel. 'Do buy some scent as well.' 'I'll get some eau de cologne if you like,' Devlin said.

He enjoyed himself setting these things out on his wash-stand. Meanwhile Gabriel sat on his bed and said: 'It's all very well being clean to an extent. Take off the dirt but why put other things on?' He said this as if he really wanted to know the reason.

Presently he asked Devlin, rather nervously and tousling his red hair, if he would come out to dinner with him.

During dinner he told Devlin he was an orphan and what a rotten school he'd been to and how he couldn't do anything but play the piano, and that was no way to make a living. He ended by saying: 'What's worst of all is I don't like women. Do *you* like them?'

'More or less,' said Devlin.

'I was afraid you might,' Gabriel said simply. 'You're lucky though. Women keep one sane. I was kicked out of Cambridge, you know.'

'Oh.'

'And it wasn't for that at all, because I really behaved perfectly. It was only for being drunk. But I say – do you like any special woman?'

'Yes.'

'Tell me about her. Or don't if you don't want to. As a matter of fact I think I'd rather you didn't, because I know it would only make me wild.'

Devlin found that Gabriel was at the moment living on £100 which had been left him two months before by an uncle. 'He was dotty, you see,' Gabriel said. 'When that's done I shall have to do something. I can't leave my rooms because that would break my heart, but I really don't know what I shall do. I spent a great chunk of it hiring the piano and men keep coming up to dun me. The last one I wheedled by playing him popular tunes. He was threatening me with gaol and hell and the gallows and I really thought I was done when it occurred to me he was such a gross little man I might be able to get at him somehow. So I sat down and began to play 'Dinah's Got the Tinkles.' He liked that. I asked him if there was any tune he liked specially, and he said 'Poodle Doodle' and also 'Velvet Dreams.' So I played them both. Then I played him lots of others and he lay there basking like a turtle. You could see a little glint in his eyes; it made him feel lustful, I think.'

'I bet it did.'

For the next few weeks Devlin was happy. He had no job. He was going to live by writing. Every morning he had a lovely and leisurely shave.

But in the evenings he felt lonely, in spite of Gabriel. And the picture of his 'special woman' had gone blurred; he had breathed on it too much.

Gabriel improved very much on acquaintance. He was not always autobiographical and only rarely maudlin. He was vivid like a double marigold and shaggy like a sheepdog. He would get up any time from five till lunch time. When he got up at five he played the piano (anything from Da Falla to 'Silver Threads among the Gold'); Mrs. Frigate never objected. 'Folks that has genius,' she would say, 'is different from you and me.' This belief also prevented her from objecting to his coming in drunk; which he did not do as often as Devlin had expected.

'I can't afford it, damn it,' be said.

'Blood and belch!' he added – for he coined his own oaths.

But when he was drunk it wasn't always, as in the mews, self pity and defiant rant. Often he was merry, Falstaff-like, obscene. He contrived to be obscene in the most innocent manner.

Devlin was to live by writing. And he could have lived very easily by writing what people liked; he was a great one at knowing what people liked. But that was not the scheme. Hogley had mentioned his name to the editors of two highbrow papers. Devlin leisurely produced an article for one of these; the editor promptly returned it, saying it was esoteric. Devlin was indignant. He said to Gabriel: 'It may be lots of things but it certainly isn't that.'

'Belching rot,' Gabriel said, 'editors don't know anything.'

Devlin sent it to the other editor and heard no more of it. He thought of being a publisher's reader but what a ghastly bore; never be able to write oneself if day after day one had to read Smith and Jones and old Lord Forget-me-not.

'Any job's a ghastly bore,' Gabriel said; 'you'll never be more free than in your garden. If I were you I should marry your girl, whoever she is, and then, if she's rich, she'll support you.'

One Friday evening Devlin sat very depressed in his room writing another article. It was on Artificial Prose, founded on a comparison of Walter Pater and Sacheverell Sitwell. He remembered that when he went for a gardener he had given up all this sort of thing. There was a prodigious clatter on the stairs and Gabriel came in without knocking.

'Hullo,' he said; 'hullo, hullo, hullo, isn't it fun? I'm going to found a modernity hospital.'

'Look here, Gabriel, I've a good mind to quit here.'

'Quit? Nonsense. You can't quit.'

'I think I must. It's summer now and what's the point of being in London without a job and without any cash?'

'Damn cash. Damn job. Look at me now. I'm four hundred in debt and it doesn't hurt a scrap. Life is real, life is balmy, I tell you. When I say balmy I mean fragrant. From India's icy mountains, from Scotland's balmy shore——'

'Come off it, Gabriel. I expect it's all very nice if one's always drunk.'

'I'm not drunk.'

'You *are* drunk. Sit down, will you. I can't bear you gawking up there like a crazy orang-outang.'

Gabriel sat down like an obedient little boy; he smelt horribly of spirits.

'Listen, Gabriel. Tomorrow I'm taking the train to my guardians to collect some clothes and have a confabulation.'

'Don't do that. I can lend you some clothes.'

'I'm sure you can. Well, I shall remind my guardians that I shall soon be twenty-one, so that it's not much good their raising any flap. I shall also ask them Sir Randal Belcher's address in case I want to see him myself on this question of my lunacy.'

'Old Sir Belcher? He's the man certified you?'

'Yes.'

'Right you are then. I'll come along as well.'

'Then he *would* certify me.'

'Ah, me,' said Gabriel; 'no one ever trusts me. I know why it is. It's not because——'

'Now don't tell me all that about women again.'

'No, I won't. Has Sir Belcher got a wife?'

'I imagine so.'

'He *would* have one. Everyone has wives. And daughters too, I suppose. What a world. And oh, my God, Devlin, did you see the fat lady bathing in the *Sketch*?'

'No. Where've you been this evening?'

'I don't really know, Devlin. I had a dinner somewhere and then there was a lovely sky like falling angels and it went amber after, and God knows where I went then. But I'm perfectly sober now.'

'Perfectly.'

'When I say 'perfectly,' you know what I mean. I had a lovely drink somewhere given me by a young man with a lovely mouth, oh, such a delicate mouth——'

Devlin was irritated. He got up, tore up his article on Artificial Prose, chucked it into the empty fireplace.

'Gabriel, old man,' he said, 'do you mind going away now?'

Gabriel went with a seraphic smile.

Devlin had a tiring night; kept dreaming of putting things into pigeon-holes and taking them out again.

He got up early and had a very careful shave; he was going to see his guardians. He rang for his breakfast and told Mrs. Frigate he would be out for the day. Mrs. Frigate said: 'Yes. Going to the cricket, are you?' Devlin said: 'Not today, I'm afraid.' The telephone rang.

It was Hogley. 'Yes, here I am again. Are you dead yet?'

'No.'

'Good. Well, I'm taking the week-end off, came up to Town yesterday. I thought you might possibly be willing to anticipate and go to Hillbury today. What do you think?'

'I'm on. I'd thought of going to see my guardians, but I'll postpone that.'

'What? Haven't you been yet?'

'If you mean have I anything to wear, I've just had my suit cleaned. I say, Gabriel can come too, can't he?'

'As far as I'm concerned, but don't you have enough of him?'

'Then I'll bring him. Thank you so much, Hogley; you'll like Hillbury, I think. Where shall we meet you?. . .'

'Come on,' said Devlin, walking into Gabriel's bedroom, where he lay like a little boy but rather bleary. Gabriel, waking up, yawned.

'What the hell are you doing?'

'Come on, Gabriel. Get up and dress. You're going to Hillbury.'

'No, I won't go to Hillbury.'

'Oh, yes, you will. We're going in a car, you silly. All across the downs and Hogley drives like the wind.'

'You mean he drives fast?'

'Yes.'

'Oh, well, I'll come. I like going fast.'

He got out of bed half asleep and was still half asleep when they met Hogley at his garage.

CHAPTER EIGHT

Gabriel said he had a headache and sat in the back seat gaping at the suburbs. Devlin sat beside Hogley, who was full of gossip. His gossip was like a little rain of dry pellets.

Would it really be amusing showing these two over Hillbury? Couldn't he send them off on their own and himself do as he liked? But was there any such thing at Hillbury?

When he had been there, the whole point was that one had no freedom: one had all the correlative discomforts and joys of routine; it was fun taking off one's wet flannels and getting into a painfully hot bath; it was even fun enduring the boredom and ill-fitting boots of the Corps, for one knew that parade would end after a few æons and then one would have tea.

But once one had left, the whole thing was unreal. It was a mere makeshift community, quite irrelevant to oneself, like a factory, prison or barracks. When there, one had alternately adored and despised it; but its adorable and despicable featues were merely, he thought, incidental. The limes in the court had nothing to do with the boys, the rooks just happened, the few nice masters were masters essentially, but only nice by accident. Hillbury was not an organic whole, he thought triumphantly.

Though, after all, organisms were not properly wholes – look at the appendix now, not to speak of the rudimentary third eye in the forehead, and the bit of a tail with which one was sometimes born; what, too, was the point of being all over fur in the womb?

Hogley went on talking and Gabriel went on sulking, and the road just went on. Backwards under the wheels, flowing back to London. 'Is there anyone I want to see at Hillbury? No there isn't; no one I want to see.'

There was the porter, of course. He was a dear and almost, perhaps, a whole; his soul was a clear bubble. He had been a scout at an Oxford college, which was full of 'real gentlemen'; snobbery was essential to his harmony. He was small and alive and rat-like, long moustaches waved from his nose like whiskers. He had a tiny bowler which he kept among the eatables. When he told a story he closed the door on you to clinch it. He had bad nine children and a grandchild or two, had been invited to be valet to an Indian prince, had bought a water-colour of a cottage in the Orkneys (because that was a better way of spending your money than in the pub), had offered to fight the cook at his Oxford college, had once won £3 on the Derby and bad seen the moon through an arch at Tintem Abbey.

The road streamed under the wheels. 'We shall be in the forest soon,' Devlin said.

'Oh, there's a forest is there?'

'Wake up, Gabriel, you old ape. Of course there's a forest. I've told you how we used to be sent runs there.'

'I didn't know that. I was never at a proper public school.'

'Come off it. A forest isn't necessary to a public school, you know. It just happens. It was there before the school was.'

'I dare say,' said Gabriel, 'they used to cut off people's hands there for poaching. It's all the same principle.'

'Gabriel has got the cynicals, I see,' said Hogley.

They soared into the forest, lifted among the beeches into a bank of luminous leaves and sky. Even Gabriel noticed its astonishing vital clarity. 'By God,' he said, 'I do like sky through trees. It makes me feel living in a city is bilge.'

'Just what I've been telling you,' Devlin said. Hogley drove on, smiling but cold – he worshipped open country, but trees did not stir him; he had not enough of the fawn in him.

'Christ!' said Gabriel. 'I do love the way the sky is – all meshed and minced. It makes me want to drink its health.'

'Here you are then,' said Hogley, and handed him a brandy flask over his shoulder. Hogley looked at Devlin and smiled with his blue cold eyes. Hogley had a grudge against him for bringing Gabriel, and was, inside himself, in a very bad temper. Devlin knew this. Hogley knew that he knew it.

But Gabriel was happy now. Having taken a gulp of brandy he lay back in his seat with his chin up and his shapeless lips apart.

'I do, do,' he said, 'adore the way the sky is.'

Suddenly they were out of the Forest and descending a very steep hill. Below them was the small town, mottled red and comfortable, with its two church towers and on the left the spike of the School Chapel. This spike had always reminded Devlin of the big penknife he got on his eleventh birthday; it had had a cork-screw and a tin-opener, and a spike for boring conkers.

The smoke from the chimneys went straight upwards. Beyond the town, where the ground rose to the downs, were tiny white figures. 'That's the playing-field,' Devlin said, and next moment thought: 'Why the hell are there people up there at this hour?' It was just about noon.

The next moment they were in the High Street. It was tilted to the left and beautifully broad. The gold arrow on the church tower before them shone dazzling in the sun.

'God and Borgia!' said Gabriel. 'I should like to bowl hoops in this street.'

'Gabriel,' said Hogley wearily, 'do repress your child-cult.'

They left the High Street and swung up towards the school gates. They were to leave the car in the school court and return to the High Street to have lunch in one of the pubs.

To their surprise the court was full of cars. They parked theirs at the end of a row, and turned back to the gates. A little rat-like figure peeped out of the porter's lodge and touched his forehead.

'Good morning, Mr. Urquhart,' it said, 'it's a pleasure to see you again. Come down for the occasion?'

'What occasion?'

'What? Don't you know it was Prize Day yesterday?'

'Good Lord, no. Prize Day's in July.'

'So it was, sir. It's been changed. You see, it was like this . . .'

'What blasted luck,' said Devlin. 'I suppose the whole place is full?'

The porter chuckled like a gnome who knew where the pot of gold was.

'Yes, sir, there's a good crowd this year. They're all up at the cricket match.' He giggled on the word cricket; not really a giggle, a sort of habitual break of the voice.

'You'll be going up to see it?' he added.

'I expect we will, Heal. This gentleman is a don from——College.'

Heal touched his forehead. 'A very fine college, sir,' he said. 'Best college but one.' He chuckled.

'Oxford's a magnificent place,' he went on. 'I wish I was there now. *Beautiful* place. Hillbury's all right, but there's something lacking about the look of it. All this red brick, you know, sir. Now there's some people don't care about the look of a place, but for myself . . . there's two places I like above all others – Oxford and Devonshire. In Devonshire you get the country and in Oxford you get the tradition.'

'Very true,' said Hogley; he talked to Heal for about five minutes and very convincingly. Heal decided he was a real gentleman. But he looked at Gabriel suspiciously.

Heal suddenly switched back to Devlin. 'You remember Dock, sir? He's gone since last you was here.'

Dock was the seedy school postman; Devlin was sorry he was dead. Heal could always talk a lot about deaths.

'His stomach was twisted, they say, sir. Dr. Brown was at him day and night, but he wouldn't pick up. The new man don't nearly know the names yet. Not got no brain, sir. So I told him too.' Another chuckle. But seeing some ladies approaching he backed into his cave. 'Well, gentlemen,' he said, looking up at them coyly, 'looks as if I must go and spruce up a bit now. The coat makes the man, they say.' He vanished into the cave.

From the cupola over the cave a bell would ring in a moment. It was nearly half-past twelve. A bell would ring for Hall, the match would be adjourned, boys and parents would flow over the court. Devlin had always hated these occasions when boxes of flowers were laid on top of the colonnades, stiff collars were worn, and there was nowhere to get any quiet; what with the slack-bosomed females and old gentlemen in old boys' ties talking loudly and pointing with their canes.

'For God's sake let's get out of this.'

'Why Devlin, dear; what's going to happen?'

'Everyone's coming down from the field. We shan't be able to get any lunch.'

'Come on then. But shan't we ever be able to see the school?'

'This is the school.'

'Oh. But can't we go inside it?'

'If you like.'

'You don't seem very enthusiastic. It is your school after all.'

'Bloody hell!' said Devlin.

'To lunch then,' said Hogley softly.

Devlin took them into the Ram. 'It's much too low,' he said, 'for any parent to come.'

'Parents,' said Hogley, 'only go to places where it says luncheon.' He cajoled Devlin back to good humour. He bore him a grudge, but, after all, if they were to have at all a possible day of it, Devlin must be in a moderately good temper.

They had fried eggs and bread and cheese and beer. For all his progress Devlin felt quite a guilty little pleasure at drinking beer in the Ram.

Meanwhile boys and relations and old boys poured down through the entrance to the playing-field opposite the school gates. All the unhappiest types of English life – Types. . . . Capital Letters . . . eternal damned Specimens. English Parenthood, Dowds, Adolescents. The older boys elegantly slouching. The masters showing off to the girls. Two sisters dressed like Christina Georgina Rossetti. A master in an out-of-date coat. Otherwise very few freaks. All damned freakishly ordinary. Not knowing what to do with their hands. Hands fumbling at dresses, hands adjusting ties, hands dropping handkerchiefs, nothing but large hands – not known what to do with.

Sheepish old boys feeling fools. Among them Rupert Grayling doing well in the City (not to be confused with John doing well in the Sahara). Very neatly dressed in double-breasted light grey flannel, cream-coloured silk shirt and chaste tie; perched under his nose a tiny pert moustache. Red in the face either through heat or embarrassment. Though *he* knew what to do with his hands, oh yes; where should he put them now? – say left in his pocket and right half-clenched near his upper coat-button.

Rupert was weary of this show. Not as if there were any pretty girls. Excepting good old Molly and that Miss Belcher. A tiring show. He envied his father who had turned sentimental in yesterday's Chapel – the Commemoration hymn about Fresh Young Life. Perhaps that was why his father was being such a cricket fan. 'Wonderful wrists,' he had kept saying, 'wonderful wrists that boy Brown has. Delightful glide to leg – just you watch now – no, you'll see him in a moment – just you watch.'

But now, thank God, his father had left him for old Belcher. 'Fine chap old Belcher; funny eyebrows he has. By jove! there's that daughter of his.'

Rupert pushed after Janet Belcher. At the same time Mr. Milder-Cogg, the lobster-like and oldest master in Common Room, pushed his way after Rupert, while Mrs. Milder-Cogg, who looked like a charwoman in spite of her summer silks, screeched after her husband to return and meet the Honourable Mrs. Cokey-Duck, whose son was always making him lose his temper.

In the Ram Gabriel was drinking a whole tumbler of whisky, neat. 'You think I can't? Well, look here.' 'But Gabriel, dear, you must behave. You don't want to disgrace poor little Devlin before all his old school chums and kind pastors?'

'Yes, I do. Why shouldn't he be disgraced? I've been disgraced often enough. What does a bleeding school matter? I've been kicked out of Cambridge.'

Gabriel made a pellet out of his bread, kneaded it in spilt whisky, and threw it out of the window, which was too high for them to see through.

It fell at the feet of Sir Randal Belcher, who stepped over it as if it did not exist. 'Yes, Mr. Grayling,' he was saying, 'I noticed Brown myself. Promising, distinctly promising. . . .'

And as they entered the Queen's Hotel he finished his monologue thus: 'A really good athlete will ten to one be a really good fellow. And a true good fellow, in the truest sense of the words, is one who is physically, mentally and morally *sane*.'

'Returning to their vomit,' Gabriel was saying; 'poor old chaps.'

Five minutes later Devlin, while still eating in the Ram, was being damned in the Queen's Hotel – 'No, I can well imagine *he* took no interest in cricket.'

'Funny, because John and Rupert——'

'Not funny at all. They are one type; *he* is, unfortunately, another. Don't think me rude, Mr. Grayling. I speak entirely dispassionately; I know that as a guardian. . . .' Down, down,

down; Sir Randal thrust Devlin into the lowest hell until Janet and Ailen entered with Rupert.

Sir Randal couldn't go on damning Devlin because Janet had told him it wasn't fair to damn someone he had never seen; and, since Janet's strange revolt and his own stranger capitulation, he had never won an argument with her. Janet had not told him she had met this black beast. He only knew that she had stuck up for him as for an unknown victim who should still be given a chance.

Sir Randal returned to cricket. 'Well,' he said to Rupert, 'what did you think of the game? Notice Brown? Very pretty style, don't you think? See his leg-glides? . . .'

Gradually he got back to talking shop. He talked to Mr. Grayling about sanity and modern youth, while they both understood Devlin between the generalisations. Meanwhile Rupert talked to the girls about the shows on in Town, and what a good show this weather was and how the new Turbett Six was not half a bad show.

'Brains they call it,' said Sir Randal. '*Brains!* They can't even concentrate on one topic for a moment. They've got no logic and no ideals. Think themselves clever. Ridiculing old institutions; everything decent or noble. Making a mock of tradition. Writing filthy trash that they call wit. It's not as if I was prejudiced. Haven't I had to deal with all sorts? And I don't say some of them can't help it. That's just the trouble. The generation at large has lost its morals, and it turns for guidance to those who are not mentally sound. Don't ask me why. Sensation-hunting I suppose. For some reason or other there's a cult of the unhealthy. Look at modern art. Models all knock-kneed and faces like half wits. My daughter Elaine brought home a whole book of such stuff; I'm glad to say she didn't own to admiring it. But it shows the situation.

'A man who's degenerate and also self-assertive, he's the man to beware of. The revolution in Russia was led by creatures who ought to have been in asylums. Spread contagion. To stop that contagion we've got to segregate the morally diseased. Practise a moral hygiene. Sanity and sobriety.'

'Bilge and Borgias,' said Gabriel (still only fifty yards off).

'Come on, Gabriel, you've had quite enough. We're going round the school now.'

'All right, Devlin. All right, Hogley. I'm not a spoilsport.'

They went over the school. The school was on show – pots and vases of flowers and the floors roughly swept. The smells, however, were invincible. They sidled octopus-wise from corners and climbed clammily up you. In the prison-like Junior House there was a strong smell of garbage and unwashed flannels; echoes clanged drearily up and down the iron-railed well which ran between the landings. All the little boys were out eating or watching the match – cruel little foul-mouthed boys very like street arabs.

Next door was Hall where six hundred boys ate. All round were dirty plaster busts of historical worthies, including Sir Walter Scott twice over; at the end were large oil portraits of headmasters. All round beneath the busts were varnished lockers full of jam and potted meat. There was a smell of soapy cheese and dish-cloth and the presence of innumerable males who never changed their suits. Hogley sniffed: 'Very remarkable,' he said, 'why did they paint it dark red?'

'Oh, *I* don't know. I suppose the old boys, the really old ones, won't let them change it.'

They went next into the fine mellow brick house at the, end of the court.

'This was where I used to live,' said Devlin, and took them up a comely broad staircase of dark oak. 'We were never allowed to use this staircase, not until we became captains. Captains were what you would call prefects.'

'We called them bloody monitors,' said Gabriel, 'but I expect that was because it wasn't much of a school.'

'Not so loud, Gabriel.'

'Loud yourself,' said Gabriel, without truth.

They poked into a room with meat-coloured panelling covered with the gilt names of people who had won the High Jump. And into a superb long room with fine panelling which had been a ballroom before it was a school; but it now smelt of slops and the monotonous bare beds looked like a reformatory. Finally:

'Here, ladies and gentlemen,' said Devlin, 'you see a fine old-world bathroom.' He opened a low door into a small attic with a concrete floor sloping clown to a gutter. Close together on the concrete were four baths, copper tubs let into white wooden stands. Devlin remembered this room as full of pink bodies, all steaming and swearing and sloshing their baths on the floor.

'Were you a captain, Devlin?'

'Yes. For a year. Only one of the junior ones though. I was rather hampered by an emancipated mind. I made them wash though.'

'Did they obey you?'

'Of course they did'

Hogley sneered; he knew they would have obeyed Devlin but liked to keep up his little myth of Devlin as an ordinary intellectual, i.e. the sort that boys at school would rag and that he, Hogley, could boss.

As they went out of the house, Gabriel lurched against the door-post.

'Look out, Gabriel old man, try and keep sober.'

'Say gender rhymes in your head,' suggested Hogley.

'What are gender rhymes?'

'Don't you know? This place reminded me of them. Strings of Latin words at the end of the grammar. Anything mechanical is a good soberer.'

'Don't talk to me of gender, anyhow,' said Gabriel. 'Besides I don't want to be sober. What's the point of drinking?'

'I vote we take him to the chapel,' said Hogley. 'That will put him right.'

'Oh, I was forgetting chapel. Yes, come on. It's full of Burne-Jones and William Morris.'

'Never mind that. Yon know I think they're rather pets those gentlemen.'

'An easy pose.'

'Look to yourself, Devlin dear. Now Gabriel, you come in the middle.'

Tall and neo-gothic, of cold grey stone, the chapel inside was garnished with gilt and green, and now also with flowers. Insipid angels blew long trumpets under the roof. Below the angels were the windows, a jumble of blue and red. Below the windows was a series of pre-Raphaelite frescoes; in one of them the City of God sat squatly in the air like a slab of stale cake ready to fall on the heads of the elect. Gabriel slipped away from them and rambled up the aisle. Hogley was busy reading the names of the departed Old Hillburians, which were written in gold letters on small panels under the frescoes.

'Dearly beloved brethren——'

'What's that?' said Hogley, as the words crashed through the cavern of the chapel, echoing like foam along its carved and arched emptiness.

'Only Gabriel,' said Devlin. 'He's having his bit of fun.'

Gabriel had ascended the pulpit. He was the first preacher for some years who was not too short for it; the common run projected only from the head up, like impotent little jack-in-the boxes. Gabriel towered against a pillar, shaking back his absurd but dominant hair and bawling for all he was worth:

'Dearly beloved brethren, hoy, listen to me. We are all here today to celebrate the churching of this our school——'

'He *is* a fool,' said Hogley. Devlin was already half-way up the aisle to stop him.

'She has done very well, our school has. Come through, I may say, with flying babies. It was a difficult crisis, brothers, brethren, I mean——'

'Here, Gabriel, come down at once.'

'You remember what Plato said, the maieutic faculty——'

'Drop it, Gabriel.'

'What's that?' Gabriel stopped in his harangue. Devlin ran up the pulpit steps and tugged his arm. 'Gabriel, old man,' he said, 'there's a lovely sunset outside.'

'No.'

'Yes, a lovely one, just like the Union Jack.'

'Glory be! Come on then.'

He jumped down and towed Devlin along the aisle; the feeble angels continued blowing their trumpets. At this moment the door opened and the porter led in two ladies.

'Damn,' whispered Devlin.

But Gabriel, seeing the ladies, became at once good and sulky, and they steered him out safely into the ante-chapel. Looking back into the chapel Devlin suddenly . . . he was not sure, but it looked . . . felt a kick of excitement. . . . Looked remarkably like . . .

'Just a moment,' he said, 'I want to ask Heal something.'

'But you can't ask him now. He's showing those women round.'

'Oh, that, doesn't matter. You go on.'

'But damn it, Devlin. What about Gabriel?'

'Come on, come on,' shouted Gabriel at this moment, 'you're forgetting the——sunset.' He pulled Hogley precipitately out. Devlin slipped back down the aisle.

Heal and the two ladies stood half-way clown the aisle, looking at the one window which was not blue and red. In this window there were two languishing, yellow-haired, pale-faced epicenes in the position of people not quite standing, and not quite sitting; presumably half-way from one to the other, only that there was no seat visible. Behind them were vivid green trees and golden apples.

'That window,' Heal was saying, 'is well worth remembering. That's what's known as the 'Revival of Colour.' A gentleman come here once and he said to me——'

One of the women was a well-built but slightly too heavy blonde, unbecomingly dressed in pink. The other was Devlin's 'Special Woman' (as Gabriel would call her). In spite of having been special for a couple of months, she looked very new and strange and frightening. She had a beautiful wide-brimmed hat and yellow dress; the whole exactly as vivid as remembered.

'That was bow it was,' Heal went on, 'before the time of the man who painted that they couldn't get them pure greens, lost the secret or something. And now he's died they've gone and lost it again. Funny people can't hang on to what's good.' Down the aisle came the inevitable chuckle. Janet Belcher, turning from the hip, caught sight of Devlin, and looked at him intently. Then she said something to the pink woman.

Devlin felt suspended in the artificial air of the chapel, pallid like one of the painted, or stained-glass figures, inept beside this exact compact vitality. His best theory of living was merely a stale slab like Burne-Jones' Heavenly City. Felt suspended as if in a dentist's chair.

While still waiting for some drill to dive at his nerve, there she was on him, coming down like an annunciation, fresh and neat with no unnecessary flourish, only a big hat, shadowy, cool, and under it a smile. Then came the running-water voice and absurdly commonplace words:

'How do you do Mr. Urquhart? How odd meeting you here.'

'Isn't it?' said Devlin, shaking hands; her hand was soft, but very firm. 'Are you here for the day?'

'No such luck,' she said. 'My father *will* stay over the night, so that tomorrow he can go to the services in this dump.'

'And you too?'

'Go to the services? No. My sisters will though. They say they like it.'

'You're rather a black sheep then?' (Once one was started talking it went on easily).

'I suppose I am rather. In my father's eyes. It's really very difficult having a father who's a leader in World Crusades. He's all against all sorts of things as well as real immorality.'

'What sort of things?'

'Oh! Lipstick.' (Devlin looked at her mouth and smiled.) 'He likes the shepherdess sort of girl, picking daisies and dabbling in the dew.'

The porter was still talking hard to Aileen. Devlin felt small, like a bee buried in a flower. Janet's hair, though dark, flowed ruddy in the light from the high windows. Her eyes seemed vast; he tottered in his head, felt himself plunge and flounder. Yet all the time he was standing, perfectly at ease and correctly; explaining he had stopped being a gardener and was now——

'But who was the red-haired man?'

'Oh, he's the man who lives in the digs below me. His name's Gabriel Crash.'

Janet burst into laughter which rippled against the pilasters; Devlin could almost see its foam go silver. And delicate flakes of while flew high, flirting.

'I'm sorry to laugh,' she said, 'it's only his name. Oh, dear.' She laughed again. Aileen was looking at her, shocked.

'What was wrong with him?'

'Oh, he was only a little tight.'

Janet wrinkled her nose very slightly. 'Oh!' she said. 'Why?'

Alas! thought Devlin, women always think there must be a reason for getting drunk. 'Just his *joie de vivre*,' he said. Why, he wondered, had he said tight instead of drunk; he hated the word tight; it was so cheap, the sort of word a fellow or chap uses when trying to pal up with a chap or fellow.

But here was Aileen, being introduced, while Heal stood by waiting to tell them more. It struck Devlin that this was one of those few occasions which would stay in his visual memory. This scene would last as precise as a diagram; four persons under the tall cold roof, confetti of colour falling from the south windows; in front of him large pink Aileen with her tilted nose, full mouth, china blue eyes – but her hands she did not manage very gracefully. While beside her the piquant contrast of Janet, standing quite straight without drooping, her hair full of red gold, interested like a child in meeting him there so oddly. Curious the difference of two sisters: Aileen was not self-conscious or clumsy, but Janet was exactly right, nothing was pre-arranged, but everything happened right, fell like leaves of light inevitably into pattern.

Finally, behind the two sisters, stood the porter. A half wistful, half whimsical rat. As if saying to himself: 'It's Mr. Urquhart what's captured their attention. Never knew he was a one with the ladies. Never mind, it's the right tack when you're young. I was young myself once.'

There he stood with his moustaches drooping, but ready to perk up at the first sign of attention, looking on with his grey kindly eyes and reminding himself with some difficulty (for all his children and grandchildren cluttered the door of memory):

'You was young too, yes you was; a long time ago, mate; but you *was* certainly young.'

CHAPTER NINE

Devlin left the chapel to look for Hogley and Gabriel. Janet and Aileen were going up to the field to join their father. 'Probably see you again there,' Janet had said; 'would you like to be introduced to him?' Devlin said, 'Perhaps, but don't let's have a scene.'

'I can't guarantee that,' Janet had said. 'It was your essay, you see, which drove him so crazy. It's rather a shame because really he's very nice, but once he's got an idea——'

Well, where were Hogley and Gabriel? Nowhere. What a bore they were, they *would* waste one's time with their silly idiosyncrasies, Gabriel always slopping about drunk, and Hogley——

There they were, sitting on a seat which encircled one of the lime-trees. It wasn't done for boys in the school to sit on those seats: they were only for putting books on. Hogley and Gabriel looked very out of place on them; even though Devlin had persuaded Gabriel to dress today in his chastest manner.

'Hullo, Devlin, where have you been?' Keeping it in, Hogley was, but his eyes were snaky.

'I've been talking to a girl I know.'

'How nice for you. We've been quite lost. Where do we go now?'

'Oh, well, I suppose we may as well go up the field.'

'What's up the field?' asked Gabriel, who was sobered but not completely.

'The cricket match, of course.'

'Boys?'

'Yes. What do you expect, elephants?'

'Nice boys I mean.'

'Behave yourself, Gabriel. Put your tie straight.' He did not want to go up the field with Gabriel looking like a stage-artist; his hair was quite enough of a good thing.

'Hullo,' came a new voice, and Rupert Grayling appeared round the tree. 'Hullo, Devlin, what are *you* doing here?'

'Hullo, Rupert. I'm just down for the occasion. Mr. Hogley, Mr. Rupert Grayling.'

Rupert shook hands with Hogley suspiciously; Hogley was well-dressed but his tie was a little – a tie should be either sombre or represent something.

'And this is Mr. Crash.'

Gabriel rose from his seat and stood swaying above Rupert, tall though Rupert was. 'How are you?' he said. 'Come and have a drink.' A powerful smell of spirits spurted from his mouth.

Rupert shrank from it. 'I'm sorry,' he said, glaring at Devlin, 'I can't. I must get back to the match.

'By the way, Devlin,' he said, speaking low; 'I wish I could talk to you for a minute.'

'Oh, rather, but I'm rather rushed at the moment.'

'Well, well, I don't suppose it would be much good. The fact is,' he said, speaking still lower, 'I gather you've been making rather a fool of yourself.'

But unfortunately Gabriel heard him. 'Here,' he said, putting his hand on Rupert's shoulder, 'what are you talking about? Calling Devlin a fool? Fool yourself. Devlin's not a fool; he's superb. He's one of the world's fine fellows; he's a true blue funambulist——'

'Stop it, Gabriel,' said Devlin. 'Never mind, Rupert. My friend's a little excited. We'll talk it out some other time. I shall be round at the old home some day soon——'

Rupert was not listening; he was looking haughty at Gabriel, but, never having seen such a thing before, his haughtiness was spoiled by a gapy and sagging astonishment.

'Well, Devlin,' he said at last and with a feeble frigidity, 'I must be off now. I won't let on to father that you're here.'

But Devlin did not respond to this bit of schoolboy code.

'On the contrary,' he said, 'let on as much as you like. I shall probably join him shortly.'

'Oh, well, good-bye.' He walked away self consciously.

'Trousers too bloody well creased,' said Gabriel.

'For God's sake, Gabriel,' said Devlin, 'do keep yourself to yourself.'

'I meant no harm,' said Gabriel meekly.

'Gabriel never means harm,' said Hogley. 'We *are* having some jolly little contretemps. Gabriel, my boy, you must really learn to be more the pure spectator.'

They climbed up the field towards the First Eleven ground, which was cut out of the hill. The sun was very hot and the chalk under the meagre grass seemed to burn one's feet.

'I don't think I hold with chalk country,' said Gabriel, pointing to a bare patch of white glare.

'Too dry for you,' said Hogley, 'some nice treacly clay is more your style, I think. And you never get really lush grass on chalk, I believe. Do you, Devlin?'

'No. The tennis courts here are terrible. Just excoriate one's feet.'

'Do you play tennis?' asked Gabriel. 'I never knew that. Do you hit it very hard?'

'Very hard indeed. Usually into the net though.'

'But how lovely. Can't you go and play at once and I'll come and cheer?'

'No I can't. Don't be stupid.'

'Oh, yes, Devlin, you must. Why don't you play with that girl you met. She's still about somewhere, isn't she?'

'Don't talk bosh, Gabriel.'

'By the way,' said Hogley, 'I suppose you'll be leaving us presently for another half hour's——'

'It wasn't half an hour. But I certainly shall if I wish to.'

'And what are *we* to do?'

'Watch the match, of course.'

Hogley laughed. 'You are a perfect host, Devlin,' he said.

'I'm not a host. You got up this show.'

'Then *mutatis mutandis* you're a perfect guest.'

Devlin flushed. 'Why need you always be so catty?' he said. 'After all, you can enjoy all this just as well by yourselves. It's an adorable day and an adorable view and——'

'I don't like the view,' said Gabriel. 'Look at that great white hole in the hill over there.'

'That's the railway tunnel; but seriously——'

'Seriously, Devlin,' said Hogley, 'of course you must do what you like. I don't mind playing with Gabriel for a little. I was only having a joke——'

'What about?'

'Oh, nothing; I happen to be amused.'

'You may be, but you're certainly also annoyed. The trouble with you is you want a monopoly of one.'

'You flatter yourself,' said Hogley.

'No, no, I don't mean of me particularly. I mean of anyone you're with. They've got to listen to you every single minute until someone else turns up and you give them the chuck.'

'Quite wrong again. Your psychological——'

'What's the damned trouble?' said Gabriel. 'Why can't everyone do what he likes? If Devlin wants to wanton with the female kind, why can't he? Good luck to him, I say. As for me, I'm going to sit under that tree and go to sleep.'

'Oh, no you're not,' said Devlin quickly, picturing Gabriel sprawling and snoring in full view of everyone.

'Well,' said Gabriel piteously, 'you can't say it's much fun looking at those people playing cricket. Why they never hit the ball into the air. Isn't there a pub on this playing-field?'

'No, there's not. I tell you what. Why don't you both go down and sample the bathing place? You see, apart from your female kind, I'm going to look for my guardian. Whereas there'll be no one at the bathing place, and it ought to be superbly warm.'

'My dear Devlin,' said Hogley, 'I detest bathing places, all cement and smelly and——'

'You don't understand. This is open air and quite unique. It's beneath the druids' mound and the rookery; it used to be part of a moat——'

'A moat? My dear good Devlin. Birds' droppings and dolmens——'

'Oh drop it, Hogley. You'll love it. It has laburnum hanging over it——'

'Laburnum's over.'

'—— and it has grass down to the edge and you needn't wear bathing-dresses.'

'What fun,' said Gabriel. 'I adore the nude.'

'Rotten German youth-cult,' said Hogley. 'You're too much of the Teuton, Gabriel.'

'I don't care; anyhow I'm going to bathe. Tell me the way.'

Devlin told him; he must go back the way they had come, behind the rows of spectators. . . . For they were now standing at an upper corner of the ground by the clump of elms where Gabriel had wished to sleep.

'I'm off,' said Gabriel, and shambled down the slope. They saw him pick up a stick and throw it into the air; the stick twisted in the air and Gabriel trotted after it.

'Quite hopeless,' said Hogley; 'I'd better go and see to him. A bathe after all might be not such a bad thought.'

Left alone in the protection of the clump, Devlin scanned the crowd but found no sign of her hat among all the backs of their heads. Nor yet did he see his guardian; and Sir Randal he did not know. He sat down in a little folding-chair of wood and felt suddenly futile. Enervated and full of self pity.

The heat-devils dance on the tired flags, time like a bored dragon spits blood in his sleep, everything is the same, the same lame drag of uninspired events. Up in her shining tower, far beyond clutching and clasping, grasping, kissing or making really own. To be able to say 'my own' of the one creature desired, that must be happiness. A happiness he could not imagine. He could only imagine beating on a doorless wall, beating and beating, and at last desisting with a broken heart and tired knuckles.

A train passed into the hole on the hill and left its smoke behind it. The batsman snicked a ball into the slips and was caught. There was a pause and then a crash of clapping. Little Belcher from the Junior House jotted it down in his scoring-book. He looked at Elaine and asked her if she had a sharper pencil. 'No, I haven't,' she said; 'why need you write it all down, anyway?' Her brother was chagrined and wished Janet had not disappeared; she was at least sympathetic though she never knew which fieldsman was what.

In the refreshment tent they ate ices and cream-cakes. The Classical Fifth Master considered his digestion. Mrs. Milder-Cogg gobbled and searched the recesses of her dress for a handkerchief to wipe off crumbs. The canvas yawned under the heat. Janet, coming out, oppressed by Rupert Grayling, stopped short of the seated rows and looked to the horizon where the haze hung heavy. A melancholy, she thought, sort of day. It got on one's nerves, too, all these dreadful people.

Looking right she saw Devlin, sitting abstracted in the elm-clump. 'Just a moment,' she said to Rupert, 'I see an old friend of mine over there.' Rupert could not see where she meant – being a little distracted by a drop of tea on his coat. 'Right you are,' he said, 'I'll go back to the others.'

There was clapping as the new batsman walked sheepishly to the wicket. Devlin, looking up out of his moodiness, was horrified to see her coming. Horrified for some reason which he did not know; a reason hanging in the air.

'So here you are,' she said – watercarts on dry streets, 'So here you are. Isn't it hot?'

'Isn't it.' Devlin's terror fell away from him; he brightened and raised his petals. 'Under these trees is the only place possible.'

'Why, it's quite cool here,' she said. 'You *are* clever. I'm going to stay here too now that I've got here.'

'Well, look here, I'm going to get you a better chair.'

'No, thank you. This chair is perfect. Only it was yours, wasn't it?'

'No, no, I always prefer the ground.' He sat down hurriedly.

'Do you still want to meet my father?'

'Well, I feel I ought to, but I ought to meet my guardian too, you know.'

'Yes, of course. It's rather hot for meeting anybody. By the way have you tried the ices in that tent?'

'No, I've not. Are they good?'

'Simply delicious. You should really have one.'

'But I'd rather stay here than go and scrummage——'

'No, no, you must have one. It's the only thing to do when watching cricket matches. If you like, I'll have another and then you can get one for yourself as well.'

'Oh, in that case of course I will.'

'You needn't really, but I'm sure you'll adore them.' Janet smiled, her mouth slowly parting.

When he had fetched the ices, Janet smiled again. 'I can't eat ices fast, can you? I'm not sure I shouldn't have told you to get two for yourself. In order to keep level.'

This was delightful, though only marking time. Think of lots, think quickly of things to say. Otherwise she'll go. How strong that chypre is. Think now——

'My little brother is too sweet. He puts all these matches down in a little book of his in pencil and when he gets home he writes them out ever so elaborately in a big book, all in different coloured inks. I bought him a wonderful new ink from an art-shop my sister knows. He does it very neatly, too. With a mapping pen.'

'What fun,' he said, and thought over and over what fun, what delight she was. So natural (if only that wasn't the word). She interrupted his thoughts.

'Why, here's your guardian,' she said gaily.

'Here's your ward,' she added, to a shape which was blotting out the match.

Mr. Grayling was very red. He stared at them both for a vast epoch of embarrassment. 'Good Lord,' he said at last.

Devlin was on his feet smiling, preparing to shake hands. But Mr. Grayling did not offer his hand. 'What are you doing here, Devlin?' he asked.

'What's he doing anywhere for the matter of that,' said Janet. Mr. Grayling ignored her and opened his mouth. 'Devlin!' he ejected in a military way.

'Me?' said Devlin, 'I'm just down for the occasion.'

'And when, I should like to know, do you intend to return home?'

'Oh, I had thought of coming home today, but I came here instead.'

'Oh, so you thought of coming home, did you. What would you have said if you found the door closed.'

'Which door?'

'Don't fool, Devlin. Damn it all, I believe Sir Randal is right.'

'You needn't believe that,' interrupted Janet. Mr. Grayling was checked; one couldn't be serious with girls about. What was she doing talking to Devlin, anyhow? 'Miss Belcher,' he began.

'No no, *please*, Mr. Grayling, don't tell me to leave you alone with Mr. Urquhart. This is the only cool place in Hillbury.'

Mr. Grayling gathered up his cheeks as if he was going to play a trombone.

'I know,' said Janet. 'Let's all sit down and have a triangular talk. I'll explain everyone's position to everyone else.'

'But my dear Miss Belcher, my dear Miss Belcher, what——'

'Oh, I know lots about it. Amn't I my father's daughter? It's about time you consulted me for a change.' She smiled at Mr. Grayling in her best film-star manner. Mr. Grayling's usually (except for his wife) buoyant good-humour returned to the surface.

'Life,' he said, 'is full of surprises. Please tell us how we stand.' He even began a grin at Devlin but recovered it. Devlin moved round a tree and was back with a chair for Mr. Grayling. Mr. Grayling released his grin after all.

Janet, paying no attention to Devlin, began to talk to Mr. Grayling, having first drawn her chair close to his. 'He is certainly a bad boy,' she said, roguing her eyes; 'he has been telling me how he ran away from you and knows it's not quite cricket——'

'But, good Lord, have you only just met?'

'Of course not. We're old friends. We met at a dance——'

'A dance?' Mr. Grayling opened his eyes.

'Yes, I've improved his dancing quite a little, you don't mind, do you, Mr. Urquhart?'

'I'm glad of that,' said Mr. Grayling sincerely, 'but——'

'To go on——'

'But Miss Belcher, your father——'

'Certified Mr. Urquhart. Yes, I know. That's just why I'm trying to get things straight. . . .'

'Managing Young Girls,' thought Mr. Grayling, 'well, well, very charming, very charming indeed. And what's all this she's saying about Devlin having a job? A job? Most surprising, most surprising indeed.'

'What the hell?' thought Devlin. 'What am I supposed to say? Nothing, I suppose. The poor old fellow's swallowing it, anyhow.'

'So you see, it's not exactly *journalism*. Is it, Mr. Urquhart?'

'No,' said Devlin, very red in the face, very hot in his clothes.

'And what's more it's quite safe. It's not like the jobs you're in one day and out the next. . . .'

'All very well,' thought Devlin, 'all this, but it's bound to turn out tomorrow or the next day that I've got no job. Is she doing it all out of mischief?'

Whatever Janet's motive she won Mr. Grayling. Before Devlin had extricated himself from his puzzle, Mr. Grayling was beating him on the shoulder.

'Well, my boy, can't say you've not upset us greatly, can't say you've not been an ass, can't say a lot of things but what I do say is you've got away with it well. Well done, my boy. Jolly good. Getting a job like that. I tell you I'm delighted——'

'And what about my madness?' asked Devlin.

Mr. Grayling coughed.

'It's not madness,' said Janet, 'it's only psychosis. Mr. Grayling and I know that. Which reminds me, what about introducing you to Dads now while the iron's hot? Mr. Grayling will stand by and see fair play.'

'Oh,' said Mr. Grayling.

'As you will,' said Devlin.

Janet laughed at them. 'You don't seem very eager,' she said. 'Here have I been sticking up for you in your absence and now you don't even want to stick up for yourself. What do you think of that, Mr. Grayling?'

'Well, you see,' said Mr. Grayling, 'it might be a little abrupt. And as far as regards Devlin's madness – ha, ha – of course we don't take any of that seriously.'

'What was the point then?' asked Devlin, for the first time a little bitterly.

'Well, you see. You see. It. wasn't my idea at all, in fact I was rather——'

'Never mind,' said Janet; 'it's a well known fact all young men are mad. You needn't go to Dads to be told that. Well, are you on for an interview? I'll protect you.'

But before Devlin answered she seemed to have a sudden idea and looked at her wrist-watch.

'Good heavens!' she said.

'What?'

'You'll be missing your train.'

'My——'

'Yes, didn't you say you *must* catch that train because you had an appointment? Well, you've only got a quarter of an hour to do it. Hurry up. I'll tell Dads all about you. I'm so glad to have been able to be your angel with the olive leaf——'

'What's all this?' said Mr. Grayling. 'Devlin got to go? Got an appointment? Really important, is it? Well then of course we mustn't keep you. Mind you come home next week-end. Hearty welcome. Bygones be bygones.'

'Off you go,' said Janet, 'you'd almost better run, you know.

The next moment Devlin was hurrying down the hill. She had a devil in her, his 'special woman.' What was the idea of it? Now he'd have to carry on this bluff. But she was rather a divine little devil.

Mr. Grayling remained, looking at Janet in bewilderment. She coaxed him and told him a few more details about Devlin's job. Mr. Grayling began to think Devlin was quite a credit.

'But I tell you what, my dear Miss Belcher, I shouldn't mention to your father that you know my ward. Of course——'

'I'm going to mention it in just five minutes' time, when he comes out of that refreshment tent. Funny he didn't notice us.'

But Sir Randal had noticed them; he came stalking over and towered between them.

'You've been away a long time,' he said. 'I see you picked up a swain.' He said this heavily, without merriment.

'An awfully nice young man,' said Janet.

'Oh, who is he?'

'Mr. Grayling's ward.'

'What?'

'Mr. Grayling's ward. The young man you said was mad.'

Sir Randal fumed to Mr. Grayling. 'You did not tell me *he* was here,' he said.

Janet pulled Sir Randal's elbow and made him again face herself. 'Now don't bully Mr. Grayling,' she said, '*he* didn't know his ward was here. And his ward's not at all mad or bad. He only pulls people's legs.'

'A young man,' began Sir Randal, 'who writes——'

'I've told you before, Dads, people, write anything now. What about the girls at school, all the ones you thought so charming when I brought them to tea. Didn't they write letters that would ...'

Janet argued; Mr. Grayling, when called upon, gave evidence. Sir Randal at last conceded that Devlin Urquhart might be not intrinsically psychotic and evil, but merely infected by corruptions with which he had come in contact.

Unweighted by these corruptions, Devlin hurried down from the field; what bothered him was how to live up to the rôle Janet had imposed on him. The match would be over soon, and, if he hadn't found Hogley and Gabriel, they would all be meeting again – his guardian and old Sir Belcher, and that wouldn't do at all. But she certainly had plenty of go; she was a good devil. Devilina rather.

He followed the sordid path to the bathing place, between the smelly labs and the school coal-house. He walked round the bathing place but there was no one there. Scummy in the heat the water lay perfectly still. He remembered how he had spent whole afternoons, when only sixth-formers were allowed here, lying on the bank naked eating cherries with Gunter (good old amenable Gunter), and the adorable evening dips when he floated on the flood bulged by innumerable divers (splashes echoing crash), not minding how much got into his mouth, nostrils, ears, but staring up at the twilight, losing himself in the green drowning sky. Afterwards he would spend half the night getting the water out of his ears.

The moon reflected in the water used to vanish when one dived on it. One could never grapple with æsthetic beauty. What about Janet? Wasn't she also too delicate to remain part of one's world, *one's* world. Where were these bloody bores?

Devlin went up through the rookery to the court and saw that Hogley's car was still there. He crossed to the porter's lodge and called for Heal.

'Yes, Mr. Urquhart, just coming. Just having a drop of tea with my daughter. Well, sir, how's the match going?'

'Oh, the match? Do you know, Heal, I don't really know. I was only up there a short time.'

'Well, you are a one, Mr. Urquhart. If I'd been up there even five minutes, I'd have the long and short of that game at my fingertips.'

'I say, Heal, you've not seen my friends?'

'What, the don, sir, and the other gentleman? Yes, I saw them just before going into my tea, going out of the gates. Must have been bathing, sir, I think. The other gentleman's hair was sticking out something wild.' Heal laughed in his coy gnome-like way. He did not. know where they had gone.

'Well, I mustn't keep you from your tea, Heal.'

'Not at all, sir, but you're a real toff to think of it. A real toff, sir.'

Devlin walked down to the High Street. He looked into the confectioner's at the corner, then walked along by the church and into the full breadth of the High Street.

From before the Eagle two old boys, whom he remembered, were just driving off in a superb racer – green and cream.

'My God, damn fine,' said the. one who was not driving. His next remarks were lost in the arrogant roar of the engine.

A little breeze was trying to rise, but was tangled and muffled in thick blankets of heat. It, was just enough to make the chimney smokes waver; not that there were many chimneys smoking. A paper bag rustled in the gutter but failed to advance. The vicar of Hillbury, in a light grey flannel suit but clerical collar, hurried across the street to go up to the match by a side-cut. Where the hell were Hogley and Gabriel?

The clock struck the half hour; it was half-past five. Only half an hour's more play and the match might end earlier. Old Grayling might come down that side-cut. Devlin didn't feel like any more acting; gardening had cured him of that. He really wished Janet had not put him in this position. What was he to say when he went home next week-end? And where were——

At the far end of the High Street, where a tributary road flowed down steeply and curving, Devlin saw something emerge rapidly. It looked like a man on one of the first bicycles. As it came nearer be saw it was Gabriel bowling a hoop. This was really too much.

Gabriel coming full tilt caught his foot in the hoop and collapsed about fifty yards off. He was up again before Devlin could reach him and started it again trundling. 'I'm the planet Saturn,' he shouted, 'bowling his bloody rings.' Devlin caught the hoop in one hand and grabbed Gabriel's arm with the other.

'That's enough,' he said. 'Where's Hogley?'

'What fun, Devlin darling. Here we all are again.'

'No we're not. Where's Hogley got to?'

'Hogley? I don't know. I expect he got drowned. We had a bathe, you know. Such a lovely bathe; you ought to have been there.' Gabriel's eyes shone; he stood spraddling like the colossus of Rhodes with his knees all over dust.

'Where've you been? You've got yourself drunk again. I do think——'

'No, no, only a little. I adore getting drunk, you know, but I remembered you had a lady, Devlin clear, so I thought I'd be respectable and I didn't drink anything.'

'Bosh.'

'Well, it was Hogley you see. He took me into a pub, right up there somewhere,' said Gabriel, pointing at the top of St. Mary's church, 'and I said to him, 'Give me something with my eyes shut and I'll guess what it is.' Well, we found that was awful good fun, so we played a sort of game against each other, scoring. It's funny how difficult——'

'Where did you buy that hoop?'

Gabriel roared with laughter. 'Buy it, you old joke? I don't *buy* hoops. I lifted it and I took a tin trumpet too, but I must have lost her somewhere.'

'Thank God for that. But pull yourself together; where's Hogley?'

Gabriel was a little frightened of Devlin when he hunched his shoulders. 'It's Hogley's fault,' he said; 'he must have stayed behind at the bathing place.'

'You said just now he took you to a pub.'

'Yes, so he did. Well, I don't know where he is.'

'Then come along with me.' Devlin leant the hoop against a wall and marched Gabriel off.

'Hey, Devlin.'

'Shut up.'

'My hoop. My hoop, Devlin.'

'Damn your hoop.'

'Oh, Devlin dear.'

But Devlin was stern as a policeman. He didn't want everyone to think they were both drunk or mad; or even got psychosis.

Hogley stood at the school gates, perfectly sober and groomed. He was talking to Heal about the beauties of Oxford and the new cricket ground on the——

'Oh, there you are,' said Devlin.

'There *you* are, my dear. I've had the most tiring afternoon of my life.'

'The school's won,' shouted Heal, suddenly and hoarsely.

They fled to Hogley's car.

This time Devlin got into the back seat and Gabriel next to Hogley. They drove slowly through the gates, Devlin staring up the entrance to the field but seeing nobody. Hogley changed up and rapidly up again. Past St. Peter's and St. Mary's, and up the hill to the forest. Hogley changed down and at last broke the silence.

'Gabriel is incorrigible.'

'Why did you encourage him then?'

'I didn't encourage him.'

'Standing him drinks in the pub!'

'What are you talking about? Why the pubs aren't open yet. Besides, Gabriel ran away when I was half dressed. I'd not seen him since.'

'Gabriel, you're a bloody liar.'

Gabriel was not listening; he was improvising little songs and humming them to himself.

Devlin took in that he was now out of danger. He sighed happily. It had been damned worth while coming; and no one had managed to muck it.

The forest flowed over them and the road under their wheels. Gabriel raised his voice and sang his latest nonsense:

'There was an old man called André Gide;
His hair was full of canary seed.'

Devlin folded his arms, They were poor fellows, Gabriel and Hogley. No salt in their lives. No spice. Nothing. No little lady-devils laughing gold and silver.

CHAPTER TEN

They reached London, had a late meal, and Hogley parted from them at the garage. 'Delightful day,' he said, 'perfectly delightful.' Devlin and Gabriel walked home. Gabriel was sober but dazed. He was in one of his silences.

The streets were full of faces. The number of faces in London terrified Devlin. Like a devil-dance of ever recurring masks. Hillbury was very far away. Janet was far away too. London boomed like a huge bowl-shaped drum. The masks revolved; every mask centring round a mouth; mouths sensual, mouths timorous, mouths tired.

Tired faces are the best; the most properly human. Only apes have faces anything like it. Like that old chimpanzee huddled in the dirty straw, refusing to play with his ball.

Mrs. Frigate opened the door. She, thank God, was something more than a face. She was a presence, a function, a habit. Just as Mrs. Dudd and Bearley were something more than faces. But only a few, one could only know a few as individuals. Outside one's house chains crawled the streets, cog following cog, face face.

Gabriel sat down on the piano stool. 'God!' he said, 'I'm tired.'

'Well, go to bed.'

'Bed? No, bed's no good. I'm going to get a job.'

'You can't get a job now.'

'No. Tomorrow.'

'What sort of a job.'

'I don't care. All jobs are bloody. I must have a job though. It's hopeless being idle. Only geniuses can be idle——'

'Geniuses be damned. There's no such thing as a genius.'

'That's just what I mean.'

'Well, I think it's the hell of a good idea. You'll be much better when you've got a job. I only wish *I* could get on to something regular.'

'Devlin.'

'Yes?'

'Were you ever simple-minded?'

'How do you mean?'

'Used you ever, well, used you ever to rant poetry, for example? I don't mean recite it; rant it. In fields and at the sea and——'

'Of course I did. I used to do it all over that mound you saw today. All among the rooks.'

'Yes, that's the idea. Isn't it a pity one can't do that now?'

'Ah, we're very old,' Devlin said mockingly.

Gabriel took him seriously. 'We are, you know. Our sap's gone practically dry——'

'Nonsense, Gabriel, not yours anyhow. You're full of——'

'No, that's just where, you're wrong. It's all a put-up job – me. Getting drunk for instance. I don't get drunk in the same way Falstaff did; I get drunk out of theory. It's the same reason I love my walking-stick. I'm not strong enough to carry myself, so I put part of me into things I like, things like walking-sticks – extrajection you can call it; that's a good word I got out of a text-book——'

'Go on.'

'It makes you feel cosy you see, carrying yourself in your hand. A sort of Narcissism I suppose.'

Amusing the way Gabriel would use words like 'cosy'; so feminine. 'Well,' Devlin said, 'I don't expect you're unique. Probably all love of property starts from something like that.'

'That's just: it. It starts there, but it goes on. Every normal man ends in a wife and family. That's the logical end of the love of property. But anyone who's like me has to fall back on himself. And that: must be an incomplete self——'

'But, my dear Gabriel, you're talking sheer Aristotle——'

'I don't know anything about that. But why one gets drunk is to forget about oneself, meaning by *one's* self the incomplete self. As it were, to forget about one's clothes. But it's no good; one can only exchange one narrowness for another. Oh, to get really wide – 'cosmic,' the word is. Wouldn't you give your soul to be cosmic?'

'Sounds awful, Gabriel, but I think I know what you mean. My belief is you ought to have gone into a monastery.'

'You're quite right. Either women or hair shirts. All monks are probably Narcissists.'

'But don't you get cosmic when you play?'

'Oh, that's different. Yes, that's different altogether.'

'I suppose so.'

'You see, there's two sorts of gods. One's the Dying God you read about in Frazer, and the other's a good earthy god like Falstaff. That's the sort *I'd* like to be. I'd like to stand this world any amount of laughs.'

Gabriel looked hopelessly into the empty grate. He reminded Devlin of the picture of a clown, vast and melancholy, with frills round his wrists and——

'I do hate fireplaces without fires,' Gabriel said. 'Did you know my father put his head in the gas oven?'

What was Gabriel saying? Had he said something or was that imagination? The picture of the clown——

'I'm just using that because it's a stock phrase. Actually he gassed himself in his office. Suicide while of unsound mind. It always is, isn't it? He was the only nice man I knew for a long time.'

Devlin said nothing.

'He was always on the verge though. Your old friend, Sir Belcher, would have said he had a psychosis. But circumstances helped, I suppose. I had a devilish queer mamma, you know.'

'Oh?'

'She was very handsome, by God she was; but they couldn't blend somehow. So eventually she ran away. Then my father and I lived by ourselves. He said it was only to be expected and that she was too good for him. She went off with some swine to India; I expect she's still there. Well, my father and I lived by ourselves until that happened It wasn't a tragedy though. He must have done it quite naturally, just like anything else. Just like Shelley was always ready to drown, to see what would happen next. He must have forgotten about me for the moment. He was always carried away by his enthusiasms. I saw him once come straight from his bath and start playing the piano all wet and naked; never noticing the cook (she was an awful hag). He was well out of it, I expect. It upset me though; especially all the racket.'

'But, Gabriel, how——'

'No, no, don't start commiserating. Once one's used to it, one's used to it. I expect it would be different if it was you. My father and I, you see, we were wrong to start with. He got a lot of fun and I get a lot of fun. But neither of us has got a proper mainspring. I can't see my living in the light of a duty. If I wanted to quit——'

'That might be all right for yourself. What about everyone else?'

'Oh, they won't mind——'

'Yes they would; I would anyhow.'

Gabriel smiled. 'That's very sweet of you, Devlin.' He went out of the room.

So all those headlines in the papers stood for something live – stood for the death of a life. Death was, after all, not hackneyed. For all that fluster of paper, all the monotonous cries of the newspaper boys with their palms nimble for coins.

The flush roared like a phantom. Gabriel reappeared, smiling. 'Hullo,' he said, 'I'm afraid I've made you feel bad. Did you hear the record I bought yesterday?'

He put on the very same record which Gunter had played in Yorkshire, which had been the motive of Devlin's dream about the lady who turned to stone. The soft sugary phrases terrified Devlin; the ever-recurring saxophone. But he did not ask Gabriel to take it off. When it was finished the needle ran round and round rasping. It was hours before Gabriel took it off.

'That record's as old as the hills,' Devlin said.

'I don't mind that. I only heard it the other day. What are you looking at me for?'

'Nothing.'

There was silence. Gabriel looked through a pile of records. 'My father,' he said suddenly, 'he could really play.'

'Did he teach you?'

'Yes, when I was about four. But I shall never play like him. They wanted him to go round and give concerts and things, but he never would. My mamma used to get wild with him about it. She called it his silly anti-money prejudice.'

'I say, Gabriel, your mother – do you mind me asking——?'

'Oh, ask anything.'

'Did she marry the man she went to India with?'

'She may have now. She couldn't then. She hadn't got a divorce you see. I'm not even sure who the man was; there were quite a number always hanging round. If I ever meet him I'll tell him a few things.'

'You think it was his fault then?'

'No, of course not. It was my father's fault. He was no good as a husband. All the same one can't let the other man go free. It's instinct, not reason.'

'I suppose so. I've never had my instinct tested?'

'Just as well. Have you heard my new Hawaiian guitar?'

'No. Where do you get all these new records from? Won't you go broke?'

'Didn't I tell you I'm going to get a job?' Gabriel wound up the gramophone and started it. 'This is called 'Lonely Sugar', he said over his shoulder.

And when it had finished, 'I haven't tried the back yet; let's try it.'

So instead of going to bed they played records, working back and back to the old out-of-dates which were kept in the dirty hole under the window-seat.

'What does that suggest to you?' Gabriel would say, and Devlin would say: 'Let me see now. Lots of things. Chiefly, I think, a little cocky train, a narrow gauge train with a clanky little engine and a long, long funnel, ricketing along its silly little lines between bright viridian hedges, all its buffers jangling, every now and again letting out a snort. . . .'

'Not bad,' Gabriel would say.

At last, 'I'm dead tired,' said Devlin. 'I think I'm going to bed.'

'You go on then. It will be dawn soon. I find it's no good going to bed after three. One's mind's too bloody active.'

'I used to find that at Oxford. I used to keep awake there by drinking tea; a big pot after hall and another pot. at midnight.'

'Makes you awfully sweaty.'

'I know. Well, I think I'll go. Dawn gives me the creeps.'

'All right.'

Devlin looked at him and had a sudden absurd panic that Gabriel might be going to suicide. 'No,' he said, 'I won't go after all.'

'All right.' Gabriel put on another record.

'What's this? 'Poodle Doodle'?'

''Pweel Dweel?' Yes, it is.'

Devlin kept his eyes fixed on the record. A black sea with a moon behind the clouds.

The yankee voices whined and quavered. The great jowl of the he-man. The sugar-canes, the mocking-birds, the cayman sprawling on the mud. Reptiles taking their pleasure; humming birds; moths. Long pendulous fruits dipping towards the water, where their own roots are clotted with yellow scum.

And a long procession of great stallion niggers, carrying things on their heads, their teeth flashing like foam, the moon and the banjo strumming while small feet danced.

Dance hall after dance hall full of high heels jabbing and sliding. Young men grinning, shaking their cuffs. Young men being dashing, girls being daring. Chinese lanterns, paper pineapples, long tropical twisted many-coloured festoons.

Another record twanged and gurgled and disclosed a new world. One went into it under an arch. On either side of the road were flowering trees in tubs. At the end of the road was a chair. Janet sat in the chair. He would go up to her——

'Garn,' said the needle, rasping round and round.

'Nearly asleep weren't you?' said Gabriel.

'Yes.'

The room had gone queer and unreal, the walls seemed made of nothing. Gabriel, searching for a loud needle, stopped.

'Why, it must be dawn,' he said and pulled back the heavy curtain. There was no more need for the light; he turned the switch and the silly thing went out.

It was grey and cold and terrible and silent. Devlin got up and stood by Gabriel looking out of the window. Not entirely silent, being London, but the feeling was still. The grey bricks opposite were so clear that you could count them. It seemed wrong for them to be so clear before anything began to be jolly. Before any cars hooted. Only heavier traffic rumbled, while there were no cocks at all.

Every second the outlines grew intenser. It was awful this underlining; with the next slightest pressure the pen would tear the paper. It was so much more definite and cruel than ordinary daylight.

'I'd like to stand the world any amount of laughs.' Devlin suddenly saw this written on the bricks, printed in definite type. That was dawn all over; he could not be sure whether Gabriel had said it this minute or some time back or had never said it at all. Anyhow the whole scene was a repeat; he knew it had happened before.

Gabriel cleared his throat, and passed his fingers over his eyelids. 'Let's have some whisky,' he said. Exactly, down to the last T, it had all happened before.

The syphon gave a little hiss. 'Damn,' said Gabriel, 'that's all the soda there is. We'll have to drink it neat.'

Devlin hated whisky. 'I always think,' he said, 'that this stuff tastes like sick.' As he said it, he was uncomfortably aware of his own voice. The words seemed to remain in the air like a caricaturist's label, an obscene sausage-balloon stuck in Devlin's mouth.

'There's not going to be any bloody sunrise,' said Gabriel. 'Look at those clouds. What about going for a walk?'

'A walk? Don't be so romantic, Gabriel. You've been reading 'Walks and Talks in Picturesque Old London'.'

It was always reassuring to have Gabriel to reprove. But he was not as assured as usual. Gabriel was not quite the same as yesterday; Gabriel had a tragic past.

Devlin moved on his chair; in spite of the cushions his buttocks felt thin and hurt. He took his last little drop of whisky; it was loathsome and viperish.

Talking of romance, he thought, I've always been trying to keep clear of it; and yet it's rather silly. It's all reaction. Reactions from the Victorians and the Movies. All those captions about So-and-so went out into a World of Adventure and Passion, of Beauty and Flowers and the Cold Eyes of Hatred. It makes one shun fine writing and try to keep prosy. But Janet is quite another story.

Gabriel suddenly laughed; it was very startling,

'What the hell are you laughing at?'

Gabriel put his hand to his mouth. 'I don't know,' he said. 'I suppose it's because I feel so entirely alone.'

'How do you mean?'

'I hope you don't mind but I really feel just as if you didn't exist or anybody else either. I often feel like that when I'm marking time. Don't you ever feel like that? Marking time and able to look on. It's this time of day gives it one most; before the sun starts flustering and hoyking one about. Making the crops grow and all the bloody rest of it. But before all that rumpus starts, one can feel completely a ghost and able to look on and see it all shallow. I feel most tremendous inside my head and then I look out of it and what do I see? Nothing but four walls and you sitting in the middle.'

Devlin sympathised. Gabriel to him looked just as unimportant; and Janet for a moment seemed unimportant too. Somewhere she was lying in a small single bed, under a cold white bedspread, and there were probably some pictures on the walls, looking extremely silly, caught out after the night, and nothing moved in the room and there was really no reason why Janet should start moving either. Why should people always go slipping the catch of jack-in-the-boxes? Why couldn't we all be Endymions and not care a damn if the moon was full or crescent? Devlin was reminded he had not been to sleep even in his chair, and he would have no sleep till tonight; for he hated going to sleep even after lunch. How odd it would be if he never slept again. Then he would always be as Gabriel was now, thinking nothing real.

'By the way. Did Hogley tell you he knew your friend, Sir Belcher?'

Devlin sat up. 'What's that? Knew him personally? No.'

'Don't get so startled. He's been to his house in the country. Quite a long time ago, I think. He said some funny things about it.'

'Where is his house?'

'Somewhere called Horsley, I think. But you mustn't go going down there and call him out. The house is called 'The Rose Fortress' – isn't it fun? Hogley says it's on the strength of there being one rose in one corner of the estate and a castellated gardeners' lavatory in the other.'

Devlin thought 'The Rose Fortress' a good name. He went red.

'What's wrong with you, Devlin?'

Devlin thought Gabriel might as well know. 'I'm in love with his daughter' he said, and smiled.

Crash went Gabriel's laughter. Crash and clatter and rolling coins of laughter, rolling all over the floor and settling in the corners.

Devlin could see it was funny. 'So it has happened,' he said. 'I thought it would amuse you.'

'My God, that's funny,' said Gabriel several times, 'old Sir Belcher's daughter. She wasn't the girl you met in the chapel?'

'Yes she was.'

'My God! And was she the one you mentioned before?'

'Yes.'

'Well, you *are* a stinker. I say though, the next thing to do is to write to her.'

'Unfortunately no.'

'Nonsense, Devlin. I'll give you the address. What luck old Hogley remembered it. He won't be half wild by the way.'

'Ho!' thought Devlin suddenly, 'why shouldn't I write, anyhow. It's quite natural. In fact it's only decent. To thank her, of course, for helping me out with the old man.'

'Write now,' went on Gabriel, 'and if we post it before breakfast, she may get it this evening. I'll get you the writing-paper.' He went to a drawer and pulled it. 'Damn this bloody drawer, it's always getting stuck.

'Oh! damn this drawer,' he repeated.

Then the knob came off in his hand.

'All right,' said Devlin, 'I'll write.'

CHAPTER ELEVEN

Not going to bed leaves one very open, very bleak and unprotected. No walls remain, whether taboos or comforts. History might never have existed on this bare and cold down. How easy it would be, for example, to shed all formality. To write to Janet not a letter of thanks but what one would like to write, a letter of truth and desire. 'I know life is bloody and people bloody awful, and this being so and death so near, come here to me quickly. I know it may be, I know it is, bound to be a failure; I have no romantic illusions. But come to me, my life, come for only a little and the devil take the rest. . . .'

No, no; one can't write like that. Even Gabriel wouldn't write a letter like that. One must conform.

So he just wrote a witty little tribute to her cleverness, asking at the end if there was any chance of seeing her in town. Because 'after all,' he wrote, 'I shan't know how to keep it up with my guardian. I don't even know what job I'm supposed to have got. . . .'

'Now,' said Gabriel, 'have you finished that letter?'

'Yes, but I'm not. sure——'

'Never mind about that. You give it to me. I'll post it.'

Devlin handed it to him, Gabriel stuck a stamp on crooked and went out singing:

'The best of all possible worlds, by God,
The best of all possible worlds.'

He did not come back to breakfast. Devlin first swore, later became worried, then panic-stricken.

At half-past twelve Gabriel's voice roared up from the hall. 'Hey, Devlin, I've got a job.'

Devlin leaned over the banisters and saw Gabriel ascending like a St. Michael in triumph; he carried a great paper cone of roses.

'Roses, roses all the way,' he said. 'I'm a made man.'

'I thought you were dead. What've you got?'

'Job in a cinema.'

'A commissionaire?'

'Not quite. Playing their damned piano.'

'Oh, good show. Where?'

'Up north. Miles away. Smelly as hell. It's called the Regal.'

'How original. But you aren't half lucky, Gabriel. Will they pay you well?'

'No.'

'Do you have someone to relieve you?'

'No.'

'Won't that be tiring?'

'Of course it will. That's the point. God-damned Katharsis.'

So Gabriel was on duty from two-thirty till eleven at night. He would slouch home about midnight swearing because he couldn't get a drink. After a few days he laid in three bottles of whisky and three of gin. 'Now I'll have something to look forward to,' he said.

'Your sobriety doesn't worry me,' said Devlin, 'but what about these ghastly long hours. And isn't it very soul-destroying?'

'Soul your grandmother. I'm enjoying it like hell. Just playing trash and trash and trash. I haven't half woken up that orchestra.'

Gabriel was lucky, thought Devlin. For himself he was in a stupid dither. Hadn't gone to his guardian's after all. Hadn't begun another article. Hadn't done anything but wait for Janet's answer. He never realised she had nowhere to reply to, as he had not put his address.

He went several times to the Regal. They had some good comedies there. It may be vulgar, but it's at any rate alive. No offence meant to our elegant essayists; 'Belles Lettres,' thought Devlin, 'made up to order. But this Comic Hero, he's our old friend Boots or Dusty jack all over again. He's the poor third son whom everyone laughs at and who conquers (eventually) everyone. Slap-dash, bum-fun, bottle-fizz, pop. There you are, you see. He can't even take a cork out of a bottle, but before he's done he'll beat the ogre, climb the castle, win the lady. The vindicated nitwit, boob triumphant.'

But people liked weeping better than laughing. Lots of people wept over Buster Keaton. 'Did you 'ave a good cry, dear?' 'Yes, dear, I 'ad a lovely cry.'

Devlin's *bête noire*, Romance, paraded unashamed. Not so much even in the dramas as in the blurbs of the Pathé Gazette – 'A Country where the Maidens hang their lamps in the Banyans and No-one grows to feel Old.' 'And so, as the World goes Spinning through Space, Men go out to Venture over the Remorseless Deep.'

Crimson curtains, gilt medallions, the smell of a Turkish cigarette; Gabriel's orchestra washing about their heads – he certainly gave them go: or was that imagination? – in front of Devlin a woman snivelling over the last film; to her right a girl's head lying as if truncated on the shoulder of a natty blue suit. The arm of the blue suit curled round her neck like an evil but listless snake.

'So one can't go being a Tamburlaine or Manfred or even a Blonde Beast. Anything the crowd adores, that is not for me. Even if they don't see it straight and I see it straight, I don't know. What's Gabriel playing now? I see; it's to work up for the rencontre of Bill and Nicolette.

'No wonder Bilbatrox calls jazz an evil narcotic, and says it saps clean thinking. He's wrong, but he's got hold of the right stick. By the wrong end, of course. Poor old, filthy old Bilbatrox. But it *is* pernicious all the same. Lotus, lotus, lotus.

'Perhaps I can't cut off from the crowd. All of us are, after all, human; which means we have an upright posture, forefeet which, like monkeys, are hands, and hind-hands which, unlike monkeys, are feet; all of us——

'But who do all of us consist of? Why of young Elbowe Jerks in his striped collar and breast-pocket handkerchief and oily, erotic leer; and of the typists whose pulses keep bounding at the close-ups; and don't forget the broad-minded sporting parson and the humorous undergraduates and the butcher who gapes at the film star's underclothes; and last of all Hogley, indebted to the film for livening a stale hour, but maintaining all the time his vast superiority, his scathing——

'It's all damp it is, like cake not kept in a tin. If they can't have bread, give them cake. That's the stage we're at now; post-war decadence. Sodden confectionery. Picking out the cherries.

'Harold Lloyd is divine though. Wish I could have his abandon, go straight ahead and be myself. But perhaps to be an ego is much harder than to be an actor.

'Take novels written in the first person. You can never admire their hero. It gets too sludgy, you can't keep it crisp. You find that his course, which looks dead straight abextra, is really horrible, deviating, spidery, full of false starts, staggerings, stoppages.

'Wrong ends of the right sticks. Same with Sir Randal probably. He must be a good man to be Janet's father and yet see what he does – acts like another Bilbatrox. The people who can't handle theories always *will* get on the platform. Janet wouldn't go wrong there, perhaps because she is a girl. No, it can't be because of that. For what about the schoolgirls who get religion and the young women who get art and the old women who get committees?'

'God's on the platform,
All's well with the world.'

People have a lust for beating about the bush. Yet you can't cook your dinner in a megaphone.

Janet would never go roundabout or talk when she ought to be acting. Perhaps she was unique but he knew it for certain that she would never require sanctions for her likes or dislikes, would never cringe to taboos or red tape. She lived like a picture, not like a text book.

That was true romance – or try some other word – that was at the back of all lyricism. No, damn it, lyrics. At all costs keep out the isms.

False romance is doing a picture on text-book lines. The romance of the *Geographical Magazine* and the Pathé Gazette. Commercialised, wholesale. The whore of Babylon.

There was Gabriel's head showing up through the well where the orchestra sat. The light danced like sand on the screen. The heroine opened her mouth hugely and gulped the spectators down.

It was very barren her inside. There was little warmth in her inside. Not even a double bed and, as for the decorations, nothing but photos of her outside. Or perhaps a water-colour, a cottage in the Hebrides. For we all have our little sentiments.

Drought in his mouth, his neighbour's eternal Turkish tobacco, the sight of Gabriel chained to this tawdry treadmill; all this irritated Devlin. Besides, he had had no letter.

'Aren't you tired?' he asked Gabriel, when the cinema closed.

'Not me. Thirsty, yes; thirsty as hell but tired—— . What do you take me for? Eight hours is nothing. You know I can play the same record for hours on end. Well, I can do this just as easy.'

'But it's such *slush*.'

'Slush be damned. The stuff with the blue lights is a bit much, but the pink lights is superb. And apart from the overture, the actual stuff while the films are showing, it has lots of possibilities. It's awful sport if you enter into it. Coo, I don't half enter into it. I don't even notice the spittle from the wind-instruments. I tell you I just soak myself with the right sort of feelings and then I give it all back to the audience. Three times as hot as I got it. I make my context. When I get home, first I'm going to have a little gin and then I'm going to play lots and lots of Bach.'

'God and Mammon,' muttered Devlin.

'Oh, go to hell. You're just a snob. You think I can't play Bach because I've been playing this other stuff. Well, I can. I'm not a snob.' Gabriel laughed gleefully and, though quite sober, took off his hat to a lamp-post. 'I worship all forms of light,' he said, 'and I worship all forms of music, and I'm not going to give that up for all the snobs in the world.'

Devlin thought Gabriel's nerves seemed bad; he said no more. Gabriel sat up half the night and got up just in time for lunch. He would do this two days out of three.

No letter came for Devlin. He felt as if he had been jilted. Since his return from Hillbury things had taken on a new life. His chair, his bed, his toothmug, had looked to him as he thought they must look to an artist. Gradually this life disappeared. They became even deader than formerly. And so silly, so helplessly expected, the river always flowing the same way, oneself hanging one's coat on the same peg.

He decided to go over to his guardian's. But what was he to do about that job? Even though Janet had not answered, he would not let her down. He must first get some job somewhere.

Hogley had said to him: 'I know of a job I could probably get you, but it's the dreariest job in the world.' That was all. Devlin had not been interested. Now he sent a card to Hogley: 'I want that dreary job of yours. Can you get it for me?' Within a week he was on the staff of a leading weekly illustrated. And it was indeed dreary.

The next week-end he went over to his guardian's. With a first-class ticket. (That was for show.)

The antelopes in the hall held their heads high, the tiger gnashed its teeth, but Mrs. Grayling herself was all welcome to the prodigal. The prodigal did not weep. He said: 'Hullo, the place looks nice. Sorry I've been too busy to come before.' He said: 'Hope you've not let the moth get into my tails.' He said: 'I'm awfully well off you know,' and dropped his first-class ticket on the hearthrug. He said: 'By the way, I'm of age in about a month, amn't I?' Thus he precluded the prepared sarcasms and sorrowful generalisations which Mrs. Grayling was going to let fall by accident.

He told them he was on the illustrated – and thereby impressed them; he did not detail his salary. To show their forgiveness they promised him a twenty-firster feast. Before going he said: 'You needn't worry about my madness. His daughter tells me Sir Randal can't judge a man till he's seen him.'

'You know one of his daughters?'

'Oh, casually. Met her at a dance. I'm always going to dances, you know.'

Mrs. Grayling looked suspicious. 'My dear Devlin, what did you go in?'

'Clothes, you mean? Oh, I hired them.'

'Devlin!'

'It's all right. I haven't caught anything as yet.'

He returned to London triumphant, but feeling slightly cheap. He had been a great one at baiting schoolmasters, but, after all, it's an underdog's game.

Life now was all routine. Up early; not time to dawdle, as he loved, over his shave; rest of the day dazed in the smoke-filled office writing captions for photos; referring to works of reference; tacking labels to the latest type of airship, a new

Van Dyck, an insectivorous plant just discovered in the Congo. Being very laboriously careful not to contradict what we said in our June number for B.C. 72. Looking up dictionaries for the spelling of foreign tags. Smoking and sitting about. Playing with the super-typewriter.

Oh, yes, and listening to Holmes. Holmes was very young but a great womaniser and cosmopolitan. 'Good Lord,' he would say; 'good Lord, Urquhart. I don't understand you. Haven't you got *any* interest in women?'

'Oh, they interest me all right.'

'I don't mean that. Don't you ever want to go back with a woman?'

'No.'

'I don't believe it. I met a chap talked just like you first time I was in Vienna. English chap though; these foreigners know better than that. Well, a fortnight later I met him again. . . . Knowledge, you see; that's all one wants.'

'It all depends what you call knowledge,' Devlin smiled. He was not at all abashed by Holmes's lecture. He used to hear it about twice a week, in some of the long gaps when work was suspended in the office. He soon knew all about Holmes's life.

Time lapsed along. Devlin had his twenty-firster and came in for a comfortable sum per annum; but he stuck to the office. As winter came, the atmosphere in the office grew denser and denser with smoke. The girls in the office all developed catarrh and looked drawn under the eyes.

All over the world people were getting older, even those who had joined Bilbatrox' Youth and Purity League. Sir Randal Belcher, having given a last address at the same League's headquarters, went abroad for the winter with his three elder daughters. Elaine the youngest had suddenly passed out of a schoolgirl into an art-student. For Sir Randal no longer was the man he was. The world did not notice it but his daughters knew he was vulnerable. Even though a new sheet of glass filled the dining-room mirror. So Elaine set up on her own with much advertisement and a blare of sophistication. Sir Randal fled abroad. So did Bilbatrox.

The other Y.P.L.'s mainly stayed at home, being poor middle class people who thought England was best, but would one day take a trip to Switzerland. Just one trip and ever afterwards an alpenstock in the hall. Gabriel and Devlin stuck to their jobs. Gabriel had a continuous sore throat and Devlin felt sadly devitalised. He would sit in his chair for half an hour before managing to cross the room for a book or a matchbox. The week became distorted and strangely proportioned. From Monday to Thursday counted as nonexistent, as mere blank dough; he lived for the week-ends. Though in each day there were little bits definite and coloured, his morning shave, lunch-time, and above all the evening.

His shave and his lunch he managed like an artist, and any little thing which gave a feeling of definiteness and purpose, he would do well and neatly. Sharpening a pencil for instance. But the office itself, amorphous, fuggy, pointless; he wiped it out from his world. As he told Gabriel, 'I only hang on out of sheer cussed Masochism.'

Holmes's face had suffered from the weather but his buoyancy remained. With his forefinger he shot his cigarette ash far across the room and said: 'Urquhart, old man, you look a bit off colour.'

'Yes,' said Devlin unwarily, 'everything's so boring.'

'Boring, eh? Tell you what, you need a bit of life.'

'How do you mean life,' said Devlin irritably.

Holmes told him. Life to him meant at the moment Pansy. Pansy was a nice girl. She was more or less Holmes's monopoly. A refined sort of girl. A milliner by day. Very amusing, too. Devlin should come along and see her.

'Why?'

'Why? She's a nice girl, I tell you. You'll like her.' Holmes beamed over the office his benevolent omniscience.

'She really is the goods,' he added.

'Well?' said Devlin.

'Well what?'

'I'd quite like to see what your idea of the goods is.'

'Fine. You're coming along?'

'Yes.'

'Good man. You'll like her, Urquhart, you'll like her.'

'I'm not committed to anything, am I?'

'Oh, no,' said Holmes tolerantly.

They took a bus to Pansy's. They sat opposite an old lady who said to the conductor: 'Can you let me down at St. Andrew's Assembly Hall?'

The next moment they were climbing a steep awkward staircase. An ugly plaster frieze seemed to be climbing it with them. From a door at the top oozed a slow, syrupy waltz.

'Oh, Jimmy,' said Pansy, with a sugared emphasis on the 'Jimmy.' 'Come on in Jimmy. Well, Jimmy, I thought you were never coming.'

Holmes introduced Devlin. She slid a little smile at him, really quite fashionable. Devlin who had felt a little queasy, began to feel exhilarated.

'Well, my dear,' said Holmes. 'What've you been doing?' He sat down on the sofa, crossing his legs in a lordly way. Pansy drew her fingers genteelly over her forehead. Over her head the light was a dull crystal pear.

Pansy told some stories about her work in the shop. Her gusto amused Devlin. Whenever he laughed, Pansy looked quickly at him and smiled. Presently she said: 'Won't you boys have a drink? I've only got a drop of Scotch, but I hope you won't object. Jimmy loves Scotch, don't you, Jimmy?'

The way she said 'Jimmy' seemed to sum up Holmes completely. Devlin stared at the bubbles rising in his glass while she put a tune on the gramophone. The tune too was spirituous; its bubbles rose and stuck on the ceiling, wobbling a little round the ridges of the moulding. Something inside him would like to follow those bubbles, a little flutterer beating in the cage of his brain. 'I can understand well,' he thought, 'why chaps go off with women. All the same Holmes can't call it knowledge.'

Not it. He leaned back on the cushions and listened peacefully to Pansy's tattle. Only Holmes's rejoinders annoyed him. Holmes was so sure of himself, like a cock wagging his wattles. But listening to Pansy gave him a woolly feeling. As listening to anyone does who is unconcerned and sure of themselves and yet quite apart from the auditor. Like listening to commercial travellers. Or watching animals. Hypnotic, woolly, perfectly contented.

Suddenly Pansy laughed. Artificially. She and Holmes were going away. 'You'll excuse us, I'm sure,' she said.

Devlin remained alone with the clock's loud but irregular ticking; sometimes it spurted, sometimes it dragged. Pansy's handbag was lying on the floor. He looked at it for five minutes and then put it on the table. The feel of it gave him a sensation.

On the wall was a gay little art-shop broad-sheet. And a large framed photo of St. Peter's Cathedral. A demure room except for the swirls of scent and the whisky bottle and syphon. Poor old Sir Randal, thought Devlin.

Then he thought of Janet. It was funny to think of her that way round, with Sir Randal first. The thought of her was alarming. She herself had gone, but she had left behind her a wake of disillusions. Disillusions by contrast. Devlin could never now be a simple fellow like Holmes.

'I can understand though why men go off with women; irrespective of which. The fascination of woman *qua* woman. And Pansy now is quite a good specimen. Nothing more of course. No mind, no soul, nothing, but a heap of physical attractions and a certain yielding, beckoning——'

Snap went the door again and there were Pansy and Holmes, fresh and smiling. They seemed like conspirators; they began to tease Devlin, unsuccessfully. Then they talked again about Pansy's work and the evil ways of the manageress. Eventually she asked Jimmy if his friend would like to see her roof-garden. 'I bet he would,' said Holmes.

She came over to Devlin and stood in front of him, girlish, pathetic, and said: 'Well, would you like to see my roof-garden?' Devlin knew this was a gambit, a rubicon. And he knew too that the pathos was not real; it was something which she suggested and he supplied – she consciously he unconsciously. He faltered and said: 'As a matter of fact——'

'You don't want to,' she said; 'right you are. It's not very much to look at.' She went back to Holmes. Neither of them paid Devlin any more attention. At last Holmes said: 'If you're bored, Urquhart, please don't wait for me.' Devlin went down into the grey unending street.

The street was full of women walking in couples. Devlin felt terribly bored and wise. 'The true sirens,' he thought, 'are nothing so tangible. The idea is the real harlot; *'Sirenes usque in exitium dulces.'* '

CHAPTER TWELVE

Sir randal and Bilbatrox returned with Spring, for a great meeting was due on Easter Monday. The Misses Maude, Aileen and Janet Belcher returned to the house in the country. Birds were already nesting and the vicaress was cadging for cuttings from the Rose Fortress garden. Janet filled her bedroom with daffodils and was very happy for a week. After a week she decided she had had enough of the family.

For it had been a trying winter. It might be called going abroad, but she knew better. And the very fact that she had subdued her father did not make her comfortable. His eyes were always reproaching her, like those of a puzzled dog. She found it hard to imagine what it was like before she made that outburst.

She wrote to Elaine and said: 'Can you put me up for a day or two?' Elaine did not answer for four days and then sent a wire, telling her to come.

Elaine was now typically unconventional. She had entirely sloughed the schoolgirl. No one would believe she had ever been such a thing. No one would believe she had ever been cowed by her father. She did not enlighten them.

On one side her hair was drawn back, revealing a rather peaked ear; on the other side it gambolled carefully forward in a natty and alluring curl. Her ear-rings were artistic. Her dress was symbolic. Her hat was dashing. Her finger-tips were yellow. She lived in comfortable rooms with an American girl called Jean Kipper. Sir Randal paid the rent and gave her an allowance.

'Jean,' said Elaine, speaking with her cigarette in her mouth, 'here's Janet wanting to come and stay. What are we going to do about it?'

'Give her a party, I suppose.'

'I suppose so.'

Jean was very good at arranging parties; the only thing was they were always the same people.

'The only thing is,' said Elaine, 'don't you get tired of having the same people?'

'Who do you want then? Blokes like old Herzheimer?'

'I don't know about *him,* but someone a bit different. Janet, you see, well, you know what she's like——'

'I know. Doesn't like to talk unless it's about nothing. She'd go down well in the States. Not that I don't say——'

'Look here,' said Elaine, 'I'm damned if I'm going to rack my brains for nothing. Let's wait till she comes and let her choose 'em herself. Plenty of time to ask 'em if we have the show on Sunday.'

'You're a bright girl, Elaine,' said Jean.

Janet, when she came, was only too willing to suggest people. 'First of all,' she said, 'you must have that old dear, Herzheimer.'

'We thought of him,' said Elaine, 'but we decided——'

'Never mind,' said Janet. 'He'll do well.'

'He's an amusing bloke,' said Jean Kipper.

'He's a dear,' repeated Janet. She went on to suggest several gay young men. Elaine was depressed. 'Isn't there anyone,' she said, 'well, a bit more distinguished?'

'Distinguished?'

'You know,' said Jean Kipper, 'with a bit more of the mentals.'

'Oh!' said Janet, 'well, *they're* your look out. I'm only choosing *my* share.'

'Damn,' said Elaine to herself.

'What's biting you?' asked Jean.

'I'm trying to remember the man's name. Your talking of the 'mentals' reminded me. You know, Janet – the poor young man who ran away from Oxford and Dads tried to certify. You said you'd met him several times.'

'Oh! Devlin Urquhart. Yes, he's sweet.'

'Let's have him. He must have something to him if——'

'Urquhart you said?' said Jean.

'Yes, know him?'

'You bet I do,' said Jean. 'Not that I've met the bloke before. He's in the same job as that silly fellow Holmes, and he lives in the same house as a crazy bloke called Crash——'

'Complete detective bureau,' said Elaine.

'We get that way in the States,' said Jean. 'I know this fellow Crash, you see. Met him once at old Van Buren's. I can track his address easily. We won't have *him* though, only the other bloke. Did you say he was certified?'

'Yes,' said Elaine.

'Not quite,' said Janet. 'It was only that his guardian consulted my father about him. . . .'

'How interesting,' said Jean. 'Now that really is interesting. You know, *I* wouldn't mind having a father a neurologist. Well, we'd better send out for some drinks before the Sabbath catches us.'

That afternoon Jean Kipper strolled into Gabriel's room, having walked into the house without knocking or ringing. Finding no one there she scribbled on a card, laid it on the keys of the piano and went away again. Mrs. Frigate found it while dusting, and gave it to Devlin when he came in. He was much surprised at such an invitation; especially as he imagined he had in some way offended Janet.

He found the party in a small room full, according to schedule, of smoke. He stood in the doorway looking silly in a dripping mackintosh. 'Here,' said Jean Kipper, 'who are you?'

'Devlin Urquhart.'

'Oh, yes! So you got that note? Do take off your raincoat, and put it somewhere. On the floor's about the only place I'm afraid.'

'Oh, that's all right,' said Devlin, 'It's very wet out.'

'I only wish it was as wet in,' said Jean Kipper. 'Put that raincoat down and come and have a cocktail. Do you know Sally Green?'

Devlin knew where he was. One hadn't got to dress, but some of the people were dressed. It was all guardedly nondescript and rigorously informal. You could drink anything you liked. Jean Kipper forced on him a vivid green drink. 'Cute isn't it?' she said.

'Yes,' said Devlin. It tasted like a strong cough-mixture.

'Well, introduce yourself where you like,' said Jean, and slid away. Devlin looked round for somewhere to put his glass though it was only half emptied. A big man loomed over him.

'Give it to me,' he said, 'I'll smuggle it away for you.'

Devlin looked up at the sweeping nose and ferocious eyebrows. 'Thank you very much,' he said.

'Not at all,' said Herzheimer. 'One should never eat or drink anything that one does not like. What do you say?' He looked fiercely at Devlin as if he was searching his soul. Jean Kipper's little wax face appeared under his arm. 'Hullo,' she said. 'You ask Mr. Herzheimer all about his looney palace.' She went all teeth in a grin and was gone.

Devlin was embarrassed. 'Well,' said Herzheimer, 'want to hear about it?'

'I should love to. I've never been over an asylum, and I've always——'

'Quite. Quite so, my dear young friend. As a matter of fact mine was not an asylum. It was a glass factory.'

'Oh!'

'But you see why, my good young man? Because lunatics are the most patient people in the world. And glass-blowers and factory workers of every sort must be supremely, and above all, patient. So when I was a young man, I had not much money in order to start my factory. So what did I do? I collected a dozen lunatics (of a certain type of course), and I put them down at their places in the factory, and I said to each of them: 'Look here, my good man, this is your vocation; this is what God means you to do.' Then I set them down each at his own little table with his own special appliances, and what happened? Each of those poor men began to work like the very devil. Of course at the start they made some blunders. But in the end they became highly skilled. And you see the point? I never paid them more than enough!'

'It sounds like a fairy tale,' said Devlin.

'Ah, they were very amusing,' said Herzheimer. 'But perhaps, my dear young man, you don't believe my story. Well, anyhow, and as I said, they were very amusing. One of them could imitate a parrot. So whenever you asked him a question, he would answer you twice over – first like himself and then like the parrot. And there was another one who all the time he was working kept saying to himself: 'Coffin . . . coffin . . . coffin. . . .?'

'Not very cheerful,' interrupted a fat young man, looking at Herzheimer unbelievingly.

'So we all thought,' said Herzheimer, 'but in the end what did it turn out to be? It was the name of his best girl.'

'Did he marry her?' asked the fat young man.

'My God, no! She didn't exist. Ah! they were very quaint.' Herzheimer gave a rich confident laugh, and smacked his hand on his hip. Devlin noticed a signet ring on his rather fat little finger.

Herzheimer went on talking. A ring of listeners gathered. Devlin could not see Janet anywhere in the room. He wondered if there was another room. All the time he heard Herzheimer's voice beating like a bell in his ears:

'I tell you, commerce is great fun. It is only the outside of it which is so vulgar, so repellent to people who have taste. The very names of the things themselves are not, well, all they might be. Chemivests, digestive biscuits——'

Devlin looked round. Elaine and Janet had come into the room. Elaine was pale; Janet: had been giving her aspirins.

'I'm too dreadfully sorry,' said Elaine to the world. 'It must have been that Cuban jam I had for tea.'

This made a hit with the world. 'Cuban jam?' they all said. 'Cuban *jam?*'

'When I was in Cuba,' said Herzheimer, 'no one ate jam. I fear the Cubans cannot be what they were.'

'It's got a very remarkable taste,' said Jean Kipper. 'Rather like the novels of D. H. Lawrence.'

But the world did not think this very clever, except Elaine, who said: 'Why I never thought of that.'

Devlin was not interested in these verbal triumphs. He happened into Janet's way. She suddenly saw him and smiled. Again he felt her hand soft but firm. 'Now,' she said, 'I've got an apology to make. It's about that letter you wrote me about a whole year ago. You see, you didn't put any address——'

'Good Lord!'

'So you see. And then we went abroad. I've had a dreadful conscience about it. Because it was awfully nice of you to write and I'd been thinking afterwards perhaps I got you into a mess with those fibs I told. . . .'

Janet was as startlingly real as he remembered. She wore a simple dress which followed the curve of her waist; stars winked upwards from her small round-toed shoes. Talking to her was like tasting a fresh apple. Devlin asked if he could get her a drink.

'No, thanks awfully. They say it's very nice, and I know it's very wicked but I can't like anything with alcohol. It makes me feel like choking. It's all so hot.'

'Don't you even like——'

'No. I'm incurable. Elaine, now, she's very good at it; she can drink anything. By the way, do look at the girl she's talking to.'

The girl was dressed in an evening dress of flowered georgette; she had a face like a cod.

'I don't like that sort of dress,' said Devlin, politely

'Nor do I. By the way, do you like this sort of party?'

'Yes. It's——'

'You needn't be polite, you know. It's not my party. You and Mr. Herzheimer are the only two people *I* suggested. At least they blackballed the others. Elaine doesn't hold with frivolous people.'

'But they all look pretty frivolous——'

'Ah! that's only appearance. They're as deep as the sea inside. I'm no good at their sort of talk. I'm terrified they'll ask me what museums I've been to abroad——'

'Why? Didn't you go to any?'

'That's just the trouble. Dads took us to thousands. I can't stand museums. I expect you think that's awful?'

'I find it a vast relief.'

'That sounds sinister. But what I say is that girls aren't cut out for art. Except a few of course. But here's Hertzy.'

The great bulk of Herzheimer was delicately poised before them. He looked at them very gravely like a judge. 'I find it is very hot here. What do you say?'

'I say let's get out of here,' said Janet. 'Elaine says the room downstairs is meant for an overflow room.'

'For myself,' said Herzheimer, 'I think of overflowing out of this window on to the roof. You see it is flat. If you have good heads I should advise you to follow me.'

'Well, you go first and see if it bears you.'

Herzheimer slipped easily through the window and stamped his foot on the leads. 'Come along my children,' he cried, 'you can't hurt yourselves here unless you get astrophobia. Look at the wonderful electric signs. Look at Ranklin's Toothpaste. And look at the fountains of rubies; that's meant to represent a healthy circulation. Ah! this is life up here; it is even better than reading the *Financial Times*.' He began to whistle, very powerfully and sweetly.

Behind him Janet stood on tiptoe, suspended by the night's tantalisation. 'What stars,' she said. 'Doesn't Hertzy whistle like a dream?' She stepped daintily over the leads, her feet winking in the parapet's shadow. In front of her Herzheimer climbed up on to the parapet and stood tall as a chimney, beckoning to the city. He still whistled, like a man lost.

Devlin felt a little dizzy. He was cut off from the other two. They were absorbed; he was still self-conscious. He despised himself thoroughly. The stars made him shiver. They had no use for him.

He thought so hard that he said aloud, 'Janet,' without knowing it. The word fell from him like a spark from a chimney. No one caught it. 'It was the nearest,' he thought, 'approach he would ever make; and yet a vain one.' Herzheimer swivelled on his heels, and, still on the parapet, took a cigar from one pocket and a patent lighter from the other. The glow lit up his swarthy many-passioned face. From the parapet he lectured them as from a pulpit:

'So no one else has followed us? I thought they wouldn't. Very few people nowadays can face the night. (Puff.) Our young cocktail friends over there; it is too primæval for them. It would either bore them or panic them. I am very glad that there are still other people like me. People in England have mostly no feelings.' He held his cigar out over the abyss. He went on solemnly: 'When it comes to stars I take after Abraham and the Prophets. When I was three or four I used to cry when I saw them; they seemed to me so terribly beautiful – (puff) – I still think them that, but I no longer cry. No one can be selfish while he looks at the stars.'

He stopped and plugged his cigar tightly in his mouth. Eighty feet below him a taxi drew up. He looked down and smiled.

'The stars,' said Janet, 'always make me want to dance.'

Herzheimer clapped his hands. 'Then for God's sake, dance,' he said.

'I can't dance out here.'

'Yes you can. The leads are not slippery. And besides you have a genuine impulse. You are a good girl, you see; you don't need sex or drink to make you dance. You just dance because you are part of the world.'

'I dance because I like it.'

'Go on then.'

Janet began to do the old Charleston to the music from the window. In a minute she had wholly forgotten Herzheimer and Devlin.

'Perfect,' said Herzheimer, when she stopped. 'Do more.'

'I'm exhausted. The stars take it out of one.'

Herzheimer stepped down from the parapet and put his arm around her. 'Mella would have liked that,' he said. 'You must come and dance on *our* roof. It is such a relief after that Isadora Duncan stuff. What is the idea of doing a goose-step round the Acropolis all dressed up in a sheet? There you have another abuse of the word 'classical.' The poor old classic!'

Elaine's attractive but commonplace voice rang from the wind: 'Janet! Hey! What are you doing? Remember you're the guest of honour.'

'I must go,' said Janet and retreated.

'Thank you very much,' said Herzheimer. 'Thank you.' He began to walk up and down the leads like a sentry. Devlin walked beside him.

'All rhythm – Janet,' said Herzheimer.

'Yes,' said Devlin in an odd voice.

'It is very odd you know.'

'What? Why?'

'Because of her father. He has no rhythm, alas! He is a fool, I fear. Another of your great Englishmen who stand like rocks and never know their own minds. They do so much harm that I have to dislike them even though in their studies they may be perfectly charming.' Herzheimer spat; the large clot of spittle stuck gleaming on a raised piece of leadwork. The wind did not favour his aim and prevented it clearing the parapet.

'It is the same,' he went on, 'with many of your jolly good fellows, your philanthropists and parsons and professors. There are so many of what I may call unconscious hypocrites. But to go back to Belcher, you have heard perhaps of his campaigns and crusades?'

'I should think I have. I suffered from them myself.'

'You suffered, eh?'

'He told my guardian I was dangerously mad. That I had a psychosis and was sure to commit suicide.'

'Oh! He did? So you deny that?'

'Yes.'

Herzheimer laughed. 'It is a brave man who says he is not mad,' he said, 'but what did you do to the old Belcher?'

'Nothing.'

'Ah! I suppose there is not much to do. Unless he put it in writing and then you could sue him. I am tired of talking of him now; tell me more about yourself.'

Devlin told him of his quixotic escape from Oxford; his setting up as a gardener——

'Silly boy,' said Herzheimer, 'you were only shirking the question. A gardener? What good could that do you? Young men are all the same. When I was a young man I had just the same neuroses, just the same disgust at conditions as they were; the 'Slough of Despond' I called them. It gave me a nausea to see yesterday's meals always served up lukewarm; all the churches and sciences and arts labouring away to produce vast meaningless *rechauffés*. But what did I do? Did I run away and hide my head in a cloud? No. I went to meet my enemy. I plunged right into the thick of the materialism I detested. I took humanity to my bosom and began to manufacture chamberpots.'

'Was that in the glass factory?' asked Devlin innocently.

'No, it was a sister industry. But perhaps you do not believe me. Well, I can tell you, my good young man, I made an excellent job of it. There are great possibilities everywhere. It is astonishing how no one uses them.'

He dropped his cigar-butt on the leads and crushed it with his foot. 'Never throw anything out of a window or off a roof,' he said, 'or even over a cliff. I knew a little boy who was given concussion by an apple-core thrown from a cliff. Mella and I had a time looking after him. So never do it, my dear young man.'

They walked another turn in silence, lifting their feet automatically over the leads. Every time Herzheimer looked outwards Devlin looked inwards to the window.

'Whom are you looking for?' asked Herzheimer. 'I fear I have bored you. I do not blame you. An old man always bores a young one. Let me think now what I can do to make up for it.' He thought, but seemed to find nothing; he reverted to apology. 'For me, you see, young men are full of interest. One can learn from a young man. A good young man always knows his subject, but even a middle-aged man has half forgotten his; his knowledge is gone blurred. Only yesterday I met a young man who keeps carrier pigeons——'

'How exciting. I've always wanted to do that.'

'Yes. It is great fun. I did it myself when I was a boy. I used to enter them for races. But now, alas, I have forgotten nearly everything. I dare say I could no longer distinguish a pigeon's sex. And this young man was so full of his enthusiasm, I felt very ashamed. I decided to breed pigeons again at once; let everything else go hang and breed beautiful pigeons. They are so dainty in their ways. But now tell me what you do?'

'You mean my job?'

'Yes. Perhaps you have not got one. The best young men, they say, turn to tramps.'

'I have a job on the *Illustrated*——'

'Oh! That is a pity.'

'Yes, it's a dim sort of job.'

'I mean it is a pity because I had just thought of offering you a different job.'

Devlin clapped his bands; one forgot one's reserve with Herzheimer. 'Can't I have it then?' he asked.

'But, my good young man, you don't know what it is. And besides why should you leave your present job?'

'My present job is awful. I've been on the point of leaving it for months——'

'Tastes like cinders, eh? Well, *my* job would be something rather unusual; I'm not quite sure what as yet. You see, I run all sorts of businesses. You could be a traveller for me——'

'I should love to do that. I've always admired travellers like anything; they've got such a nice habit of a sort of contented grumbling.'

'That is a true phrase. But I don't think you will be a traveller. Again you might do broadcasting; you have a clear voice. In fact, there is one little job I could get you straightaway as the old man has resigned. That would be giving Uncle Everett's Friday Talks to Tinies.'

'I don't know that I could face that.'

'Nonsense. You're becoming sentimental again. Haven't I told you the moral of my life? You can't keep clear by backing out. Just because a job is stereotyped and deadly is no reason to refuse it. Go into it, my dear young man, go in and make it something different'

'If there is any opportunity.'

'There you are again. Hustling you see. You must wait your time. At first there will be nothing. Then a little. Then a little.'

'One must have a lot of vitality.'

'Vitality? Bosh! Vitality is a mere word. If you keep talking about it, you'll never have it. Look here, my good young man, you come to lunch with me tomorrow, and we'll fix you up a job.'

'Thank you so———'

'Just a moment. It's not for your sake at all, It's for mine. A young man, I tell you, is a gold mine. Provided he's properly worked. So tomorrow———'

'But tomorrow's Monday. It's the busy day at the office.'

'Damn the office. Aren't we agreed that you're leaving it? Tell them you're lunching with me. Don't let them sack you because that would never do. At half-past one then, here's my address, and don't expect a miracle. Mella and I will fix you up a job but it won't be anything great. It will merely have possibilities. Now, let's go in; it becomes cold here.'

The room was now unintelligible with fumes. Devlin found Janet in a corner being bored by Sally Green, the girl in the slime-green dress. 'Hullo,' he said; 'Herzheimer's going to give me a job.'

'He's not?'

'He is.'

'Don't you believe old Herzheimer,' said Sally Green.

'Nonsense,' said Janet. 'Hertzy never lets one down. What sort of a job is it?'

'I don't know.'

'There you are,' said Sally Green, who was a little tipsy, and could not hold her figure together. Janet took Devlin by the arm and led him away. 'Now,' she said, 'I want the facts of this. After all I was the first person to give you a job, even though it didn't exist.'

Devlin told her. 'But it's magnificent,' she said. 'You'll like being under Hertzy. He's always lucky. . . .' She had the gift of enthusiasm. Presently Herzheimer came up and offered Devlin a lift home.

'But it's out of your way.'

'Never mind.' Herzheimer, like a flood, carried one away. Through the rising water Devlin cried to Janet: 'Good-bye;

thank you so, so much' (forgetting she was not the hostess); and Janet replied: 'Good-bye. Remember you're coming to see us soon,' Then in a car which glided like a swan, and the lights flashing past like continuous yellow ribbons, Herzheimer told him stories of an old friend of his, a Chinese mandarin.

The car stopped dead from forty miles an hour without a shock or shiver. Herzheimer was gone. Mrs. Frigate opened the door; he noticed her face was worried. 'Good evening, sir,' she said. 'Mr. Crash has been playing that stuff all evening.' It was the first time Devlin had heard her say anything critical.

For downstairs there rolled and crashed a barbarous fiendish music. 'Spanish he calls it,' said Mrs. Frigate; her nerves were obviously afflicted. 'And he's not going back to his job.'

'What?'

'No.'

Devlin marched upstairs, full of revived self-righteousness, 'What's all this?' he said.

'What's all what?' asked Gabriel, swivelling round on the piano stool. 'What are you looking so bloody elated for?'

'You've lost your job.'

'Lost it? I bleeding well haven't. I've chucked the Goddamn blasted thing.'

'Why the hell?'

'Why the hell not? I've had enough *work* as it's called. As the Americans say: 'I'm back on the blasted bum".'

'Well, you *are* a fool.'

'That's where you're wrong; I'm not a fool. I just couldn't stand it any longer. And it's no good looking at me like that; I'm not going to argue. I'm sick to death of talking. And so every one ought to be in this generation. No one's stopped talking since the war. Theories are just like soda water; they don't improve anything. Did I tell you my good resolution? No more whisky unless I drink it neat. But anyhow seeing the same bleeding film every day for a week – that was bad enough. But it's not that, it's the prostituting oneself, it's the God-awful——'

'Look here, Gabriel. You must go straight back tomorrow and say——'

'Straight? Back? Tomorrow?' Gabriel was almost foaming at the mouth. 'What the red hell do you mean? I'll tell you what's wrong with you, you've been drinking.'

'No, I've not. I've got a job.'

'You've got one already.'

'A new job, A man called Herzheimer. I'm going to lunch with him tomorrow.'

'Well, *I'm* not.' Gabriel glared at him. Then, with a great effort he said: 'But have you really got a new job? Tell me all about it.'

CHAPTER THIRTEEN

As Herzheimer's door closed Devlin again faced the sunlight, and, turning towards Kensington Gardens, felt suddenly free. He had got his new job. If job it could be called. For all he had to do was to write weekly blurbs for aluminium ware; little essays, appearing week by week in various respectable papers, tempered with wit and not overdone. 'You must *not* overdo them,' Herzheimer had said.

After all, aluminium kettles were well worth boosting, not like some of the fibula bones of mammoths and wretched bronze pigs dug up at Tusculum. No more sitting in the office listening to Holmes's confidences and the older men's yawny humour.

For a moment he wondered why he needed a job at all; he could get along (just) without one. But to be idle was for some reason unthinkable. Anyhow, Herzheimer's job came pretty near it.

Herzheimer was incredible. So benevolent, so powerful, and, at the same time, so childlike – in a way. But Mella was a little much. . . . So made up and such sardonic eyes. And she had, unless it was the shadow, a moustache. But she evidently adored Herzheimer.

Wonderful velvet brandy out of deep domy glasses. Still vibrant through his frame as he walked towards the Round Pond. The sun shone, little boats ran, shouts echoed clearly. A cheerful Siamese grinned like a widening ripple. A plump baby beamed out of its pram. In spite of the sun the air was surprisingly cold (or, rather, streaked with cold), but in its pram the baby was warm in wool.

Wool was a truly divine product. As Herzheimer had said at lunch, one had merely to put on wool and all one's sorrows left one. The Homeric kings were wise to love it and dye it scarlet. And if your puppy was restless, give him an old woollen – that would soon make him settle. Mella had a Sealyham called Karl. He too seemed rather sardonic.

Devlin sat on a seat and watched a squirrel loping over the ground under its enormous tail. He was a pestilence, according to the papers, a tree-climbing rat. To Devlin he seemed a fine flourish of nature, precise, delicate and wary. 'Tree-climbing rat,' was unfair. Rats waddled. Some Jews were like rats, rather obscene, broad in the hips, and short. Herzheimer was not like that. He stood like a great pine, scenting the fields, altering the climate. There were black hairs on the back of his great hands but the fingers were fine like forceps. And he kept his nails well.

Mella's nails were painted, just as her eyebrows were pencilled. Whereas Herzheimer was just slightly shaggy; his hair curled roughly and his tie was a little loose and pulled to one side, rucking his elegant collar.

He was the only elderly man Devlin had yet admired. Excepting his father, who was only a memory. Rather a grim memory, laden with the horror of India as with heavy damp odour. There was no horror about Herzheimer. Herzheimer was not a hero or martyr, merely a vital personality. He gave one jobs and a strong shake of the hand and wonderful brandy out of vast glasses.

Devlin went into the Underground and stood on the escalator. Contrary to his custom he let it carry him standing. People passed him, he watched them hurry down before him and felt delightfully arrogant. Then he gazed at the people passing upwards on his left. Two rather pretty girls; he wondered what he would do if one of them had been Janet. Exultant thoughts rose and kicked in his brain, swirls as of fulgent seaweed dragging loose from the rocks. He was on top of the world; he was going to tea with her soon; he would subdue her father, everyone would admire him, her father would admire him, and she herself——

A grotesque sight arrested him. A little old man from the country jumping off the escalator. Carefully lifting in his left hand his bowler hat high from the head, he jumped high sideways, frisking up his legs like a goat, while on either side of his head immense moustaches waved outwards and upwards. Devlin broke into laughter, as did a porter, two shop girls and a stout man with shining cheekbones.

Devlin sat in the train looking with infinite scorn and pity at the row of dolts opposite. He heard two old women planning a party. Their remarks surprised him – he could only catch phrases:

'. . . Cider. . . . You get the cider and I'll get the wine . . . you get the cider . . . yes, dear, and them pretty strawberry cakes . . . and take that rug down out of Egbert's room . . . look at Phillips' counter . . . cider, you're to get that . . . champagne, dear, good quality wine.' The woman who talked wore a coat veneered with moleskin (veneer was the impression it gave). The other woman had a fresh scar on her forehead and watery eyes. Devlin imagined her saying to herself all the way home: 'Cider, I'm to get that.'

'Champagne? Sensation-hunters all,' thought Devlin. 'Everyone who wants 'Life' goes straight off to alcohol. More of a draw than sex even. Holmes says the taste of alcohol greatly adds to sexual enjoyment – and, in a lesser degree, cigarettes. Though a good cigar was best perhaps.

'Must be funny to regard sex as a commodity like that. *I* don't want a commodity, I want Janet. Poor fools all.'

He pitied the two old women planning their society crush. And he pitied, though more coldly, Jean Kipper and Elaine, and all their unnumbered duplicates, barging round with their friends, talking about significance.

As he walked up the sloping tunnel he had a relapse, his confidence left him. Like a cat he wanted to get his claws into something and work both hands alternately, pulling out the stuffing.

'Don't say Gin and It, say Gin and Cin,' said a poster. All the way home he wondered how 'Cin' should be pronounced.

He found Gabriel asleep and woke him. 'Well, I've got my job,' he said. Gabriel was delighted. 'By God, you're hot stuff,' he kept saying. Devlin regained his confidence.

'You know,' said Gabriel. 'I've changed my mind. I wish I had a job again.'

'I thought you would. Never mind; you go round to old Herzheimer.'

'No, no. I won't go round to him. I've got a monition about him——'

'Rats. How do you mean a monition?'

'I feel I've met him before or perhaps I've dreamt about him. Is he a little weedy man——?'

Devlin burst into laughter.

'Well,' said Gabriel, 'whatever he is, I tell you I've got a feeling about him. I don't want to meet him.'

'My dear good Gabriel, you can't go psychic like this. . . .'

But Gabriel was obstinate.

Three days later Devlin sent his first aluminium blurb to Herzheimer. It came back next morning covered with crosses and comments in red ink. 'Too subtle,' was Herzheimer's summary, 'and, of course, you don't know your subject. Come round to dinner with me tomorrow and I will tell you all about it.'

Devlin went to dinner and met a Professor Shawes and a lady film-star. Professor Shawes was a mediævalist and had the disillusioned expression of a monkey; all the time he was not eating he would do balancing tricks with his knives and forks. Occasionally he would say, 'Good, very good' (at some remark of Herzheimer's). Very occasionally he would smile like a thought-weary seraph. It was he who had discovered the Castabellan manuscript of Pocuccio.

The film star had dyed hair and no conversation. She had learnt to say 'Isn't that clever? Isn't that pretty?' Herzheimer invited her merely to look at her hands. In spite of this Mella was jealous of her to the point of being rude. Mella's own hands were slightly clumsy, in spite of the painted nails.

They talked about literature. Herzheimer was sceptical just where Devlin was not sceptical. Herzheimer said there was nothing wrong in prettiness; 'But cynicism I suspect. There is no need to be cynical. Try manufacturing chamberpots and you will see that everywhere there is ground for faith and still more for enjoyment. As for your friend Joyce, he is very funny, but still . . .' He explained that James Joyce had intellectual worms. Owing to internal disease he could not be controlled, limited or dieted. He always had to go on, on, on, gobbling up refuse, biting the furniture, chasing his own tail.

After dinner Herzheimer took Devlin into a large attic stocked and shining with aluminium. 'Here are my specimens,' he said. 'You ought to get an enthusiasm for them and then you will write well about them. Do you realise the qualities of aluminium; do you know that it is the most god-like stuff there is? Come here and I will show you.'

Devlin went home with a new creed. Complete sanity combined with vast enthusiasm – that was happiness. And it was a possible ideal because you found it in Herzheimer. A true man existed; there was no need to look further, to go digging for gold in Hogley or in other dubious countries.

On the table in his room he found a small letter. He saw it from the door and knew it was from Janet. Whereas all it said was:

'Dear Mr. Urquhart, – Can you come to tea here on Friday of next week? I shall be too delighted; and don't be frightened of my father – we won't let him bite you. Elaine will be there too, and we have both told him of your sanity. If you come by train, there is a good train at 3.5. Please come. Yours sincerely, Janet Belcher.'

That was eight days off. Never mind. He must set himself in order so that nothing might go wrong.

Gabriel came in in his pyjamas, looking ill and haggard. 'Hullo,' he said, 'had a good dinner?'

'Yes, but what's much more important, I'm going to tea with her Friday next.'

'Good,' said Gabriel dreamily, 'That must be round about my birthday.'

Devlin looked at him. Gabriel sounded old; the spirit had gone out of him. Since his blaze the night he chucked his job, he had not touched the piano.

'Gabriel, you don't feel ill, do you?'

'Ill your—— I only can't sleep.'

Devlin got the panics. 'Can't *sleep*, Gabriel?'

'What do you think I said?'

Devlin collected himself. 'Now,' he said, 'we're going right down to put you to bed. Come along.' He walked downstairs, and Gabriel followed. He made Gabriel get into bed. Then he moved about the bedroom and made it tidy. 'You can't sleep in this mess,' he said. 'Let me feel your pulse.'

'Bloody hell take you,' said Gabriel.

'Now, now. Hand it over.'

Gabriel put out his wrist.

'You've got a temperatute,' said Devlin.

'Temperature yourself.'

'Don't be silly. Wait a moment.' Devlin went upstairs, put eau-de-Cologne on a clean handkerchief and brought down a volume of Grimm. 'Here you are,' he said, and gave Gabriel the handkerchief.

'Ah,' said Gabriel, 'now you're being some use.'

'Well, now you must go to sleep. Lie quite still and I'll read you a story. 'Once upon a time there was a poor man'...'

In twenty minutes Gabriel was asleep. Devlin went up to his own room and re-read Janet's letter. 'Poor old Gabriel,' he thought, 'but isn't life fun?'

Next morning Gabriel was better. Devlin spent the morning writing about aluminium. That completed his work for the week. 'What a job,' he thought, 'though, of course, I don't get much for it.' He sent his compositions to Herzheimer; it was rather like competing for the essay-prize at school.

Two days later came Herzheimer's reply: 'That's better, though not perfect. I take them, however. Will you like to come to dinner on Thursday next?'

On Thursday next Devlin was only too glad to go to dinner; the next day, he felt, was decisive. It was good to distract oneself with food and wine and cigars.

The film star was there again and a little cockney painter. The film star was there because two days before Mella had had an outburst; Herzheimer had said, 'Why, my dear, how can you be so foolish? If you cannot see how much finer you are than she is, I shall have to bring her round and we can compare you.' Mella would not stop seething, so Herzheimer rang up the film star. Devlin did not know this story, but was conscious of a tension as if a rope crossed the table between the two women. Herzheimer, however, was as usual.

' ... self-expression ... ' said the little cockney painter.

'Self-expression,' said Herzheimer, 'is not, I think, what you mean. Self-expression, as they call it, is merely an affliction, a bad mental catarrh. ... The Jews, you know, have a saying that ...' He then talked about the Jews.

'I long ago decided I needed Christian company. One must have a background of contrast; Jews are too specialised. So when I was a little boy, I said to myself: 'Dear me, I *must* have a change from all these inbred people; they are very amusing but, oh! how they do shriek.' And at first I thought I would take up with negroes. My father at that time had a negro coachman with a very fine voice (I often dream about that voice), so I asked to be allowed to live in the coachman's little lodge and not see my family except on the Sabbath. But they did not approve of that. And then our negro coachman was sent away for stealing whisky and I was very sad. I was so sad I ran out of handkerchiefs. So at last I had to forgo the ideas of negroes and take up with Christians. And now I have become so broadminded, or perhaps so weak-minded (I cannot really decide) that there are only two Jewish characteristics about which I am really snobbish. And the first of these is that like all good Jews I worship bread (just as the good Greeks did also) and if I see anyone wasting bread it hurts me more than if I see them forging a cheque. And the other thing on which I pride myself is that I always wash in running water. Ever since I began to wash myself, I never remember using a plug in the hand basin.'

'You were lucky,' said the painter, 'they used to slap me if ever I let the water run.'

'That is your lamentable tradition. They would say, of course, that it wastes the water. What blasphemy. There is nothing so revolting as a hand-basin full of standing water and suds.'

'Well, that *is* interesting,' said the film star, 'I'm afraid *I* should never have thought about it.'

'It is very odd,' said Mella, 'how some people never think about things. And then other people always think of the same things which most people never think of. I have always, since I was a child, washed under the tap.'

'Ah,' said Herzheimer, 'but there are different reasons for doing the same thing——'

'My reason was the same as yours,' said Mella jealously. Devlin looked at her and wondered how she could be so queer. You'd think she'd see she was embarrassing people, taking remarks so seriously. And you'd think someone, who'd seen the world and had that sardonic expression, wouldn't reveal herself so easily.

He was surprised after dinner when she said to him suddenly: 'Have you had many adventures?'

'None at all, I'm afraid.'

'Oh, you needn't be afraid,' she drawled the word 'afraid' and left it hanging in the air.

Herzheimer came up. 'Well, my dear young man,' he said, 'how do you amuse yourself with your so abundant spare time?'

Devlin nearly said 'Looking after Gabriel Crash,' but remembered they did not know Gabriel or even his name. So he veered to the subject which magnetised his mind, and said: 'Tomorrow I'm going to tea at Sir Randal Belcher's house.'

'Ah,' said Mella, 'how is it we never cease hearing of those Belchers? A year ago I first saw the name in the paper. A month later Paul goes and meets two young girls called Belcher and brings them to a meal——'

'And you know,' said Herzheimer, 'that you liked them very well. The dark one is an exceptional girl. You remember how she danced, Urquhart?'

'I like people who dance,' said Mella simply, and as if she had that moment quite laid aside her more hostile and suspicious self.

'Janet Belcher,' said Herzheimer, 'dances like perfection. We must have her here for exhibition. But I do not suppose she will dance for you tomorrow. I suppose her father will be examining you.' He laughed.

'This poor young man,' he added to Mella, 'was nearly certified as mad. By Sir Randal Belcher himself.' He laughed again.

'Then why are you laughing?' asked Mella; 'there is nothing funny in that.' She rose and walked away. Herzheimer said nothing.

Devlin went home and had a restless night. In the morning he woke up from a nightmare to hear Gabriel playing the piano. The notes fell in a cataract. Devlin huddled under the clothes and managed to sleep again.

When he came down to breakfast at nine o'clock Gabriel was tipsy. 'What on earth are you doing, Gabriel?'

Gabriel wagged his peony head. 'Don't be unkind,' he said, 'it's my birthday again.'

'Oh, Lord, I'd forgotten that. Well, many happy returns, but please stop drinking for a little. You don't want to make yourself ill before lunch.'

'No, I know. But I won't be able to drink in the afternoon, seeing we're going to tea——'

'To tea?'

'To your old Sir Belcher man.'

'But, my dear Gabriel, *you're* not going.'

'I thought you said they said 'bring your friend'.'

'No they didn't. Where did you get that idea?'

'I thought you said it.'

'I'm sorry, but I didn't.'

'So that means I can't come?'

'Yes. You surely don't want to come?'

'No. Unless I can be of some use.'

Devlin laughed: 'You're rather a pet, but I'm afraid far from being any use you'd ruin the whole show.'

Gabriel opened his eyes. Then he said: 'I suppose I'm not really much of a social asset.'

Devlin explained that it wasn't that, but that if he, Devlin, was invited to a strange house he couldn't very well . . .

'But, you see,' Gabriel said, 'Sir Belcher might clap you in a bin.'

Devlin, with apprehension, realised that Gabriel, what with his drink and his nerves, was really worried about this afternoon's tea party. 'Look here, Gabriel,' he said, 'you've got to promise not to bother me. You can't come to Sir Randal's with me, and that's the end of it.'

'All right,' said Gabriel, 'I promise to keep out of it.'

When Devlin left after lunch, Gabriel was settled in the sofa with a big 'Paradise Lost' and half a bottle of gin.

Devlin arrived very early at Waterloo Station. He went up to a penny-in-the-slot machine which contained American peanuts. As he put in his penny he noticed Hogley on his right extracting a box of matches.

'Good gracious me,' said Hogley, covering his astonishment with exaggeration, 'I quite thought you were dead. What *have* you been doing? Why haven't you written to me?'

'Oh, I don't know.'

'How does the job go?'

'It doesn't. I've got another.'

'Such is gratitude. I thought you wouldn't last out. I hope your new vocation is better.'

'Perfect. It's writing advertisements for aluminium.'

'Nonsense. There isn't such a job.'

'Yes, aluminium kettles, aluminium kettlestands, aluminium frying pans, aluminium fish-slices——'

'Please stop, Devlin. You make me quite dizzy. What I should like to know is why you've been hiding your head in the sand so?'

Hogley was trying to reassert himself, to regain his power. They discovered they were taking the same train. Devlin felt Hogley collecting himself to diffuse atmosphere, to repair the recent damages to Devlin's attitude. . . .

'So you're going to tea with those funny Belchers again?'

'Not again.'

'No, it was that day at your school, of course. You were getting off with one of the daughters. That was very quaint.'

Devlin had forgotten how patronisingly rude Hogley could be. 'You know,' he said, 'when you talk about women you're usually a bit off.'

'I think not. Women are all right, but they've got no initiative. I've never met an original woman——'

'I've met several.'

'That's your kind nature, my dear. You create nine-tenths of the picture, I on the other hand am a sober realist——'

'You ought to meet Mella.'

'Mella Belcher?'

'No, Mella Herzheimer. At least, I don't know if she is Herzheimer but she's certainly original.'

'Oh, if she's a Jewess, it's rather different. Even so——'

'She's not a Jewess.'

'My dear Devlin, don't interrupt me. You've quite lost your manners since I saw you last.'

'I've always interrupted,' said Devlin, with a grin, 'and I always shall. It's the only way to make decent conversation.'

'You certainly were always perverse,' said Hogley. He took out his cigarette case. Then he chuckled delicately to himself. 'You *are* a joke, Devlin,' he said, and was silent for a little.

Then he tried again: 'Have you been writing anything?'

'Yes, my aluminium——'

'Be serious. *Writing,* I said.'

'No.'

'You ought to, you know. Don't let yourself go to rot, Devlin. After all, you're not Tom, Dick or Harry; you're . . .'

It was no good. Hogley worked his eyes for a little and surrendered. As Devlin got out at Janet's station, Hogley gave him a last smile through the glass. An insidious and snaky smile, as if to say: 'I know you've cut off from me, me your old patron, who have done so much for your development; well, go off with your girls, give up your writing, *I* don't: mind, *I* don't mind at all – not the least little bit.'

'The Rose Fortress' was a large house covered with dirty ivy and entered through a white marble portico of bastard Ionic pillars. Till passing its threshold Devlin had been self-possessed but, once he had given his name, his mind began to flutter and the objects in the hall to stare back at him as if he were drunk. The floor slid back and he slid forward, he passed through a heavily curtained door and saw a long room full of Janet.

Janet smiled at him very favourably and he was again self-possessed. He could not see Sir Randal. Unless that man – but that was impossible. . . .

'This is Mr. Backshott,' said Janet.

A laboriously begotten, born and reared nobody (or anybody) rose from his chair and shook Devlin's hand. 'Just come up from Town?' it asked.

'Yes.'

'Nice to see a bit of country again, isn't it?'

'Very nice indeed.'

'Ever been here before?'

'No.'

'Haven't you really? Why, I was born here.'

'It must be rather fun being born here.'

'Fun?' Mr. Backshott looked blank.

'I was born in India, you see.'

'Oh, in India? By Jove, that's interesting. I was talking to an Anglo-Indian one day last week, and he'd had a very odd experience, the deuce of an experience, just before coming over. Too long to tell you now. I suppose you don't remember much though?'

'Nothing at all. I left when I was two months old.'

'When you were two? You wouldn't remember much then. Still, I can remember things which happened when I was two. Let me see now. I can remember a whopping great rocking-horse in the nursery——'

'No, no. I meant two *months*, not two years.'

'Oh, *months?* My mistake. Of course that's quite a different thing. Two months – one doesn't remember much from that age, eh? Funny how long one is getting into the run of things.'

'Yes.' Devlin looked round to see where Janet had gone. Janet and Elaine were both standing at the French window.

'Gross unpunctuality I call it,' said Elaine.

'There he is now,' said Janet, who had quick eyes. 'Dads is just coming,' she said, turning round to the room. Devlin was aghast and looked round the room for some last clues to Sir Randal's character. The books, he noticed, were behind diamonded brass caging. A silly little table with fretwork legs stood ready to receive the tea tray. On the floor beside it was a rug of yak's hair – at least Devlin thought of it as yak's. From the ceiling hung a vast glass chandelier with a few pieces missing. Janet interrupted him; she was standing in front of him smiling. 'You needn't be frightened,' she said, 'his rage has disappeared during the last year. He thinks of you now as an unfortunate young man who was led astray by circumstances but has now, apparently, reformed. Elaine and I told him about the reform.'

'You have saved my life,' said Devlin. 'I shall try not to disgrace you.'

'Yes,' said Janet; 'no lunacy please.'

The air in the room went taut. Sir Randal and Maude had entered. Devlin looked up and saw a tall, severe man quite like what one would expect; the sort of man one sees in posters representing the doctor. Beside him was Maude, the eldest and by far the plainest of his daughters: what Hogley would call 'a tweed skirt and sketch-book girl.' (Maude had never *studied* art, as Elaine was doing, but she had, according to Sit Randal, a very fair gift. If Devlin had looked behind him he would have seen two of her water-colours, one of yachts at Torquay and the other of the sky, with two clouds in it.)

Devlin was introduced to Sir Randal. Sir Randal talked to him in the way a dignified professional man talks to any normal young man whom he does not know but still does not dislike. Devlin was thus reassured that Sir Randal was no longer volcanic.

It was when Sir Randal went out of the room to answer the 'phone, that Janet murmured to Devlin: 'All's well, you see. He still remembers that paper of yours though. Elaine stole it one day, you know, and we read it through. I'm afraid it was beyond me. Except that there was a funny joke about parsons.'

'Yes,' said Elaine, 'I liked it on the whole. I saw your point exactly, but what seemed to me to be a weakness was that you seemed to have a certain *complex*——' She broke off on the crucial word because Sir Randal entered. Mr. Backshott seized the opportunity to say to Devlin:

'I say, did I hear them say you wrote?'

'No. At least they were only talking about something I wrote once.'

'Well, that's good enough, you know. If you've written something once, you can write something again. I heard a man just before Christmas – forgotten who he was but someone pretty big – he was giving a lecture and *he* said no one feels they can write to start with, it's all a matter of sticking to it——'

'You're talking about writing?' interrupted Sir Randal.

'Yes,' said Mr. Backshott cheerfully, 'it's always a good subject, isn't it?'

'It is also a serious subject,' said Sir Randal. And, though not deliberately, he opened fire. Elaine, who was now emancipated, put on her sage and tolerant grin. Maude tried to make a diversion by handing Sir Randal cakes. It was no good.

Sir Randal talked at Devlin about Decadence and Disease and what Dean Inge had said. Then he added Bilbatrox.

Bilbatrox was more than Devlin could stand. He did not notice Janet's pursed mouth and infinitesimal shake of the head, but took up the argument as he was accustomed to take up other people's arguments. Crisply, vehemently, outspokenly.

Sir Randal grew flushed. He did not become personal, he made no reference to Devlin's own past, but he ceased to be the generalising theorist and became obviously absorbed in his flowing indignation, in a lava stream of commination and prophecy. 'All very well,' he kept saying; 'All very well.' It was his way of saying 'Damn, damn!'

Mr. Backshott retired, with an excuse; he did not say he disliked heated arguments. Maude retired to blow up the cook for sending in clammy crumpets. Janet and Elaine waited to be in at the death. What sort of death they did not know.

Janet vainly cried out that it was hot and let them all go into the conservatory. Elaine made Sir Randal angrier by throwing some flippancies on his blaze. Even the chandelier suddenly tinkled.

Devlin knew he was making a fool of himself. He had to go on. He was defending his generation.

'Your generation——' said Sir Randal.

There was a violent noise in the passage. The butler came in looking flushed and without a vestige of pomp began: 'There's a gentleman wants——'

'Get out of the bloody way,' said a voice, and Gabriel tumbled into the room in a flash of red hair. The dingy Indian screen reeled against the wall. It was like the Coming of Bolshevism. A roaring drunk colossus he stood filling the room, swaying like a tree in a storm and grinning like a heathen idol. Sir Randal took it in a surprising way. He did not rise from his chair but, sitting like a judge or a Rameses, shot at Gabriel in the soberest metallic voice: 'Who the devil are you?'

Devlin jumped up, hoping to push Gabriel out. 'A friend of yours?' said Sir Randal, by some fatal divination. 'A friend of *yours,* eh?' Devlin stood where he was, petrified.

Gabriel was too drunk to be impressed by personality. 'Hullo, hullo, hullo,' he shouted, in his best telephone voice; 'hullo there, Sir Randal. That you over there? That you Devlin? Hullo, all. 'What's that thing on the mantelpiece?'

Sir Randal turned his head towards Devlin, his body remaining rigid. 'Take out your *friend,*' he said. Elaine burst into semi-hysterical laughter.

Through Devlin's head flashed anger, a bitter amusement, and admiration for Sir Randal. He went up to Gabriel and took his elbow. 'Keep yourself steady,' he said, 'or you'll hurt the furniture.' He made his voice bite. Gabriel, though very drunk, felt the bite and turned at once sentimental.

'All right, Devlin,' he said, 'all right. I didn't mean to put my bleeding foot in it. No, really I didn't. I just thought I might come in helpful. Sir Belcher over there, he'll bear me out. He knows what it's like to be in love. I only wish *I* could be. Say, Sir Belcher, *you've* read Havelock Ellis; well, isn't there any cure——'

'Come on,' said Devlin.

Dragged away, Gabriel looked back at his audience. 'It's bloody hard to be me,' he said to them, with a sad little grin.

Elaine followed them into the passage. 'Take care of the step,' she said; 'I'd take you in the car, only——' She left it at that. The butler held the door open, gaping like a fish. They waltzed down the drive. Gabriel towed Devlin from one side to the other, babbling all the time and spitting:

'Not so fast, Devlin, where you going, anyhow? Bleeding hell and stinks, I didn't mean to annoy you, really I didn't, Devlin. I know you like those girls, I know you do, I know you like Sir Belcher, Sir Randal too, I like him too, I like every one, but don't go so fast – you make me out of breath.'

'Lordy,' said the wife of the lodgekeeper.

Devlin pushed Gabriel into a sitting position on the bank outside the gates. Regardless of five small boys who stood watching, he scooped up a puddle with both hands and slopped it in Gabriel's face.

'Ow!' said Gabriel, 'what you doing, Devlin? I don't like water and my hair's caught in the hedge. What you doing, Devlin? I didn't mean any harm, I didn't really. It's my birthday, you see. And I only thought I'd come and offer you best man; you know what I mean——'

Devlin continued sloshing him with water. 'Get sober, you fool,' he said, in a flat voice; no voice could convey his fury. He guided Gabriel to the station and they waited ten minutes in an empty waiting room. When the train came, he managed to get an empty carriage. Gabriel at once sank into his corner like a sack with his face pressed to the pane. A discriminating small boy cried out: 'I say, mister, you've been drinking.' At this Gabriel burst into tears. But Devlin did not speak to him again that day. When they reached Mrs. Frigate's Gabriel went straight to bed, but Devlin sat up half the night playing patience.

He got up at seven and lit the geyser for his bath. He had his breakfast early. From breakfast to lunch he played patience. By the two-thirty post he got the sort of letter he instinctively expected——

'Dear Mr. Urquhart, – I hope you took your drunk friend home successfully, but I expect you are used to it. I am not at all used to it and I hope to have no more to do with you or your jokes in future. Yours sincerely, Janet Belcher.'

He read it several times. He did not criticise it as crude or unfair; he did not try to consider it as a momentary outburst. Yesterday was for him irreparable. He heard Gabriel getting out of bed, and, grabbing his hat, went out for the rest of the day.

CHAPTER FOURTEEN

The Rose Fortress was outraged. Until yesterday no drunk person had ever passed its gates. Sir Randal took it as a judgment. He had been right all along about this Devlin Urquhart; it was these misguided girls who had deceived him. The young man had probably put his drunken friend up to it. It was a crazy plot to contaminate the Belcher household. Elaine only aggravated his disgust by saying: 'Young men are always getting tight. It's nothing so out of the ordinary.'

Janet had had a shock. She had a physical aversion to drunkenness or to anything such as drugs or hypnotism, which annulled a person's self-control. None of the young men she knew ever got drunk; she wouldn't have known them long if they had. She didn't know boors. The funny thing was this Devlin, this Urquhart rather, was not on the face of it a boor; he had quite nice manners and was quick in the uptake. It must be that he was 'intellectual'; one could not trust intellectuals; they usually were inverted, anyhow. The red-haired man was clearly an invert; Janet usually sensed such things. But Devlin, 'this Urquhart I mean,' it was surprising he should turn out to be a swine.

'That paper seemed pretty silly, of course. Still, I can't really know about that.'

For she was modest. Sometimes she used to moan to herself for an hour on end that there was nothing she could *do*;

there could not be anyone else in the world quite so ungifted. Why, half the wretched girls at school could play the piano. Or, if they didn't do that, they could at least—— Though I admit I wouldn't like to play like some of them. Still, that isn't the point.

'Of course, there are a few minor things I can do. I know what to put on my body, for example. You'd think anyone would be able to do that, but you see how funny people are. Look at Maude. And as for Elaine, what *is* the idea of just hanging things on one like labels, as socialists wear red ties? I mean peasant blouses are all very well, but that's not enough in itself.

'I wish to hell I could afford that hat in the window. But one can't go paying three guineas for a hat. That would be shirking the question. Anyone could dress well if they went on like that. I wonder if it'll be gone next time I'm in London. Sure to be, in fact.

'Though I must go up to London again soon. Hell! Sure to meet Devlin there. Then one would have to cut him and though it's quite fun cutting nasty people——

'Well, it ought to be fun cutting him, too. *I* haven't any use for him. Can do very well without his ugly face. Why have all the nice young men disappeared? Robert Garfield gone off to India; as if there wasn't anything bloody nearer home. All bunk, wanting to make oneself uncomfortable and then call it duty. And he did dance so well – made one feel in heaven.

'And Alan getting engaged, that was a bit silly. All have to go to his wedding, I suppose. Why do people make such a furore of weddings? Wouldn't it be much more decent if two people just went off . . .? Seems outrageous to have all those bells and rice and stuff when everyone knows what the whole fuss is about. When *I* get married, I won't have any of that flap. Not even for Dads. Maude can go and fill the church, but as for me – it isn't as if that was the end of everything, like in novels. Why the whole show *starts* there.

'Talking of dancing, I wonder how Devlin dances? Funny me saying I'd met him at a dance. Don't suppose he dances at all, lots of nice people don't.

'Lots of filthy fellows don't, either. Can only drink cocktails and talk about art. What's the point? To be able to paint is one thing – God! I wish I could – but just to sit gassing and gassing and waving one's hands about——

'The only nice thing about drinks is their colour. Lovely lights port makes on the table. That new ignition-signal on the dashboard is just like it. Must be something barbarous in me this wild craze for anything sparkling' or gleaming. Wasn't Alan amused when we went to Woolworth's and I wanted to buy up all the sparkler counter.

'And it's so wicked that old hags like Lady Spinder can make themselves stiff with diamonds and look like death on top, while——

'The odd thing about Lady Spinder is she looks like an old maid. You don't often find that. Spinsters nearly always look like spinsters – except Mary Graywater, and I expect there's something fishy about that – and widows nearly always look widows. I should go mad if I was an old maid.

'Though marriage is a pretty grim look-out. Always having to live with the same man. Not to speak of babies and miscarriages and——. But think of marrying Robert; it would drive one quite off one's head, Talking away about his socialism; no better than Bilby. Merely to show off, too!

'Alan would be rather a joke. That girl whatever her name is probably hasn't the least slightest idea what an absolute joke he is.

'They're all balmy, after all! Either they're intense and political and ever so conceited, or they're just light in the head. What I can't make out is why they ever like one.

'I suppose it's because I'm not so doughy as most English girls. On the Continent no one would notice it. There's something in having a half-French mother. Though Maude hasn't got much out of it.

'Funny it would have been if I'd inherited all Dads' public spirit. Getting up on platforms——

'Didn't he just get wild with Devlin about literature? I was feeling quite sorry for him before that drunkard came in. I wonder what *was* the reason of that. He *can't* have told him to come. But I don't know – young men are ghastly! He'll get my note today, anyhow.

'Good piece of hush-up of Dads trying to keep it away from the cook. As if everyone hadn't heard the row. Hush-up, always hush-up.

'You wouldn't expect it from a scientist, seeing they're supposed to be such ones for Truth. Yet I never was told anything when I was little. If it hadn't been for Aunt Nora's farm——

'The little girls at school had some pretty odd notions. What a comic show girls' schools are. . . . All the little girls running after the big girls and all the big girls fawning on the mistresses and all the mistresses telling one to be forth-putting and talking about knowledge of Life! And the intrigues and the letters and 'I've done with you, Stella; you have no soul!'

'Who's that friend Davy's staying with now? Nasty little tykes he does pick up. Hillbury doesn't seem really much of a place. That forest is quite nice, but oh! the smells – absolute stables. It was funny meeting Devlin there that time. What a time I had vamping his guardian. I've really taken a lot of trouble over that man.

'It was rather sweet that letter he wrote to me. Ever so polite and carefully written. And then he crops up at Elaine's party. He and Hertzy were the only bright spots on that party. Funny Hertsy becoming another of Dads' red rags. Says he uses his influence wrongly and won't subscribe to things. Lucky he doesn't know Hertsy lives with a mistress. Try and stop me going to tea there next Tuesday. [She had received the invitation this morning at breakfast.]

'Hell!

'Devlin has a job under Hertsy. That doesn't mean he'll be there though. Does it mean he'll be there? No, of course it doesn't!

'I'll just ring up Hertsy and make sure.'

Herzheimer was just going out to a dog show; he offered to take Janet along. His voice sang pleasantly in the mellow distance. He said she really should come and see the Great Danes; two of the Great Danes at the show were practically relations of his. The story was this . . .

'That will be another shilling, please,' said the operator. Meanwhile Janet got the panics; she decided she would cry off tea on Tuesday altogether.

'What I rang up about,' she said at last, 'was that I'm dreadfully sorry, and I'm afraid it's awfully rude of me, but I find I can't possibly come to tea on Tuesday. Please *do* forgive me, but you see——'

'Never mind. Come to tea on Wednesday. The only difference is that there will be no one else on Wednesday——'

'No one at all?'

'No. Are you very sad? I can ask——'

'No, please don't. You know my phobias, don't you? I know it's awful, but I adore coming to tea when there's no one there.'

'I will go out too if you like.'

'Don't be so wicked! Now you say there's going to be no one there, you've no idea how happy I am. You swear I won't meet the King of Poland, like I did last time——'

'Who was he?'

'The man who kept saying 'social regeneration.' He was some sort of royalty, wasn't he?'

'Only a Russian prince. That is not exactly royalty. He is a poor chap, but he will not be there. In fact he is in America. Making a fortune by lectures.'

So Janet was to go to tea on Wednesday. She looked forward to it very much; she felt at home with Herzheimer. Whereas she felt not at all at home through the torpid weekend at the Rose Fortress – Dads in his bad temper and those damned church-bells ruining one's nerves!

On Wednesday she took the car out of the mouths of Sir Randal, Maude and Elaine, and drove off to London.

'Damn!' said Elaine, 'here we are – stranded! And I suppose Maude forgot to get those Turks.'

'Turks?' said Sir Randal, frowning.

'Cigarettes.'

'Oh; cigarettes. Do you ever think of anything else? And I wish you wouldn't swear, Elaine.' He went back to the glass-topped table in his study, feeling sadly disappointed in his daughters. And it was not so much the principle of the thing as those yellow stains on Elaine's nails. (Unconsciously he reversed his public order of values.)

Maude was a good girl, though, and Aileen seemed to be getting on well with that French family (make a very fair linguist, Aileen) but Janet and Elaine. What did Janet mean by sweeping off with the car like that? 'I hope to heaven she doesn't hurt herself! She drives too fast.'

Janet, however, was not driving fast. 'Hell!' she said to herself, 'I feel a bit feeble today, and we all know what that means. Hope I shan't feel awfully stupid having to talk to the Hertsies. It always makes one shut up like an oyster; even before they come. It won't be so bad with Hertsy, though; one doesn't have to *make* conversation with him.'

She was a little late when she entered Herzheimer's big drawing room. The first thing she saw was Mella's flash of teeth. The next thing she saw was Devlin. 'What the devil!' she thought, and felt pleasantly braced. She looked round for Herzheimer and gave him a searching glance.

Mella said: 'You have met each other, I think?'

'I think so,' said Janet, giving Devlin a little formal smile of pointed indifference. Actually, she began to enjoy herself;

she even ceased to feel feeble. And there were some delightful little cakes for tea. One thing about Mella, she was a marvellous housewife.

Herzheimer was soon talking. He had a remarkable way of mixing up the original and the commonplace. He would bring forth the most obvious truths as if they were his own discovery. 'People are too stale now,' he was saying; 'they all play for safety. Look how they decorate their homes. Even these new bright colour schemes the suburban villas have, they too are just playing for safety – stock combinations. Orange and black, bright blue and yellow. House after house has the same blank blue curtains. You may say, 'After all, if those combinations are good, why should only A use them; why should not B and C and D and all of them up to Z – all those in the same street or the same garden city, make use of them also?' But I think you are wrong. A thing is not always good just because it is good. A thing which is good for you may be damned bad for me! And a thing which was good last year is not good this year. They talk about the eternity of art, but that is just sentimentalising——'

'Still,' put in Mella, 'art is something more than a succession of fashions. You can't compare this generation of painters to this season's hats.'

'Yes, but I can. I can and I must! The artistic instinct is the instinct to meddle and tinker. Perpetual change and novelty. It is essentially childish. If you would be a good business man, put the artistic instinct away. That is a thing very difficult to do. I myself, I always want to meddle – to stir up the waters. That may be because I am a Jew – a wandering Jew as you would say. You know the story in Herodotus about the Greek and the Egyptian, and how the Egyptian said to the Greek: 'You Greeks are always children.' Their passionate curiosity, their restlessness, it surprised that Egyptian. The Jews today are like what the Greeks were then. We may be afflicted by many other evils, but we are not afflicted by inertia. Is not that so?'

'On the whole it is,' said Mella; 'not always though. Max now was the laziest man I ever had to put up with. He slept absolutely all day.'

'Ah, but he was too young,' said Herzheimer, 'and, besides, my dear, you demoralised him. We are not so active when we are young. In that Mr. Urquhart has the advantage of us – he always feels strong.'

'Not always,' said Devlin; 'in fact, when I was at school I was ill nearly every term. They thought it was because I was born in India.'

Janet, who had been up to now looking through him, looked at him out of sheer interest. She thought that to be born in India must be really a great handicap. India was to her a nightmare.

'I expect it is the curse of the East,' said Herzheimer jovially.

Mella, as so often, turned at right angles into the serious – even into the sinister. 'You are right,' she said; 'the East is horrible. I went to India with my second husband. He must have been mad to want to go there.' She told them how George, her second husband, was a wealthy American who believed in what he called 'The Orient.' 'And he was so confident,' she added; 'he was so good humoured he believed in everyone else. That was how he trapped himself. He *would* make friends with people.' The story came out, vivid like burning coals against a black background: George had gone off with two natives who said they would show him a temple, show him over a temple. Europeans rarely saw it; it was a very special temple. Anyhow, they killed him and returned the corpse to her house in a great basket used for packing fruit. And the motive was merely robbery; they had taken his wallet of notes. He always used to carry an excessive amount of money.

Devlin felt his face go stiff of itself, as he listened. When she stopped, he looked into the fire and saw there the pillars of a temple suddenly crumple and fall. Then his mind filled with his father.

Whereas Janet had no connection with India, but its horror had always haunted her. And now this horror had become palpable; here it was in the room, close to her, breathing on her neck. Instinctively she turned towards Devlin and smiled like a person rescued. Devlin smiled back.

It was reconciliation, but it was much more. What the much more was was not defined, but it was startingly much. And each of them felt it was only natural that they two should fall together as against the other two, against Herzheimer with his eyes like black stones and the vast depths of his mind; against Mella with her terrible story, against the union of Herzheimer and Mella in their barbarously intimate, rigidly exclusive affection. For even Herzheimer, though both so brilliant socially and so sympathetic to individuals, was yet cut off from one in a circle of stone and iron, a circle which contained Mella and no one else at all.

Conversation flashed back to frivolity. Mella, having told her evil story, became unusually and astonishingly merry, like a pilgrim who has done his penance. She made Janet dance for them. Herzheimer again cried, 'Perfection, perfection,' and Devlin was once more enchanted.

But it made Janet very tired. She felt when she had finished, that she had lost her grip; she felt like laughing and talking nonsense; she knew why that was of course. She sank back in a deep armchair and said: 'I feel absolutely balmy!'

'Never mind,' said Herzheimer, 'I will tell you a story. It is about a rose fancier I knew in Constantinople.'

Herzheimer told his story. Listening to it was like living in an idyl. He had put some sort of spell upon Devlin and Janet so that they had forgotten all about their catastrophe and Janet's note, so that, while they listened to him, they kept smiling at each other.

At last Janet looked at the clock and said: 'Oh dear; I must go.'

'Disaster!' said Herzheimer, 'don't go yet, my dear.'

'But I must. I must be back by dinner-time.'

'You will be late, I fear. That clock is twenty minutes slow. But never mind. Stay here to dinner.'

'But——'

'Yes, that is the solution, of course. What luck we are in today.'

'But, Hertsy, thank you ever so much, you're sure——'

'Good! Then if you're staying to dinner, we may as well go to the theatre afterwards. Have you been to *Merrythought?*'

'No, but I can't——'

'You've not been? Excellent! I have got some tickets for tonight by a mistake, and I had thought they must be wasted. Now we can enjoy them. Let me see. Urquhart, there is one for you! Will you come?'

'I should adore to,' said Devlin; 'thank you very——'

'But, I say,' said Janet, 'I should never get home, and besides I've got no clothes——'

'Clothes? Why?'

'But I mean, won't I need them? The tickets?'

'Oh, the tickets are for the stalls.'

'But then, of course I need clothes. You *are* wicked, Hertsy. First you produce these wonders and then——'

'Never mind about clothes,' said Mella, who was still extraordinarily merry, 'I'll lend you some clothes, my dear. I'm a little taller, of course, but with these sweeping dresses——'

'So much for the dress question,' interrupted Herzheimer; 'as for the getting home, of course it would be too late for you to go driving alone through the country. You must, therefore, stay here.'

Janet accepted. She knew when people meant their invitations.

'Now, my dear young man,' said Herzheimer, turning to Devlin, 'you will not try to shirk, I hope? The man will run you home in the car and wait for you while you dress. Then you will not miss dinner.'

Devlin was dazed. Herzheimer was a conjuror; that was all there was to it. Not the sort of man you meet in real life.

People in real life are often exceedingly kind but they never do you any good. They're all much too shiftless.

Mella, who seemed transformed, led Janet from the room, rattling out at a great pace the possibilities of her wardrobe. Janet smiled back at Devlin for they were now good friends without a word having been exchanged.

Devlin got out of Herzheimer's car and ran upstairs with his hat and coat on. He had not spoken to Gabriel since the day of the tea party, but he would speak to him now. Gabriel, after all, had been looking terribly ashamed. He swung open Gabriel's door and bumped into something large and soft. Gabriel was always moving the furniture about, but this time it was a dog. A vast, shapeless, shaggy dog without a tail.

'Good God!' said Devlin.

'Hullo!' said Gabriel, beaming with delighted astonishment, 'what's happened?'

'What's happened in *here?* What's this?'

'Isn't he a wonder?'

'What *is* it?'

'It's a love. I bought him this afternoon. They told me he was a trained watchdog.'

'Good Lord! What do you want a watchdog for?'

'To look after me when I'm blind, of course. Haven't you heard of the blind man's hairy friend?'

'But a watchdog doesn't do that. Besides, his *size!*'

'But that's the point of him, Devlin. And today I felt so lonely I felt I must really have something, I'm going to take him early runs to Covent Gardens and rural places like that.'

'Well, God be with you! I've got to go and dress. Herzheimer's taking me to *Merrythought.* He's taking Janet, too!'

'Janet?'

'Yes.'

'Oh, grand! I *am,* glad. I say Devlin, wait a moment——'

'I've got to dress.'

'Well, *you are* lucky. May I come up and talk to you? Is he the Almighty, your old Herzheimer? But I say I'm not half glad it's all come all right. . . .'

Gabriel sat on the bed admiring Devlin's neat methods of dressing. He had shut the dog in his sitting-room, where it could be heard knocking things over.

'I say,' said Gabriel, 'I've thought of a new name for the two-backed beast.'

'You filthy old swine! What is it?'

'Well, first I'll tell you how it evolved——'

'You needn't do that.'

'I was reading the paper today, which I've not done for three months – it all comes of having nothing to do – and do you know, there's the hell of a thrilling divorce case on, all about a Welshman and a Dutch lady——'

'God help us all!'

'No, it's really very amusing. Well, these two people they went off to a place called Pontypridd and there they lived nominally as man and wife until eventually the real wife of the man, she was Scotch, I think——'

'Gabriel, *do* come to the point. I'm almost dressed.'

'Oh, no, you're not. Well this Scotch lady. . . .' Gabriel told Devlin the whole immoral story up to date.

'Well, what about the word?'

'Oh! I'd nearly forgotten. Can't you guess?'

'No.'

'The word's Pontypridd, of course.'

'Oh.'

'Don't you think it rather a nice name?'

A loud crash shook the house. 'That must be that revolving bookcase,' said Gabriel.

'Hadn't you better go and stop him?'

'I suppose so. He *is* a sweet, isn't he?' Gabriel went downstairs to wheedle his dear dog. As Devlin went down fully dressed five minutes later, he heard Gabriel say to the dog, 'Now do be good and I'll sing you a little song.' Devlin stood on the landing and listened. After a little scuffling, Gabriel began – to the tune of 'My Tarpaulin Jacket':

'Wenn der heilige Hogley macht Wasser . . .'

Crash! Gabriel stopped singing. There was more scuffling. Devlin hurried down to enter the waiting car.

CHAPTER FIFTEEN

Devlin was always so cool, Devlin thought to himself; knew himself perfectly well; was in a minority there; among the few people whose reason always dominates. Like Hogley perhaps. Not like Gabriel. Devlin's reason always dominates. Always except in unfair circumstances. For example, intoxication; but he had given that up since Oxford; it made one look such a fool. But there were other subtler and undermining dangers. The theatre had always been dangerous; ever since he first went to a play at the age of nine or ten. A single scene could demoralise him, upset his regular values.

And now, in this whirl of legs and fluff and blond, bland comedians, the world of daily bread, the world of logical argument sunk away beneath him; he felt in his seat as if buoyed on a cloud. Beside him was Janet in a red dress of Mella's which was now completely Janetised. What Janet was thinking he did not know, but she seemed to give herself up to the scene on the stage, to participate in it through sheer sympathy and thrill. Devlin in his turn thrilled to her laughter as it rippled over his cloud like June sunshine.

That was a very good dinner. This, too, was a very good show. But those were just accidents. Though, like many accidents, they had a purpose. With each course of the dinner, each falling and rising of the curtain, he felt himself advance. As he advanced, his ordinary values receded. With all that dinner and brandy and show inside him, he felt re-born, diabolical. Satan-like he clambered and plunged among clouds, bathed in their ripe foam, their bubbling ebullient possibilities, their whipping specks of salt and white excitement.

'I have been a puppet,' he thought, 'pulled by wires; always masked. People like Gunter approve of masks; so does Hogley; masks are always successful. Reposeful things, masks. Angels' faces are masks, clean, white and starched; that's why they get on. But a devil, a Satan, has features. He has a fiery mobile face; he could sit to Michelangelo. I shouldn't half like to be a Satan.

'The Satans are the people who make havoc. Who make scandals and wars and eat up the weaker. But they make other things too, all the things which are good.'

He began to feel strong and alive in the thought that perhaps he too was Satanic. The insistent music helped this self-flattery, these doped and dangerous thoughts. All the time he glimpsed Janet beside him.

Therefore and therefore this show must never end. For then she would get up and put on Mella's cloak and go away into space. While he would take a taxi back to Mrs. Frigate's and all this would never happen again.

It must go on and on, this show. They were only at No. 6 and No. 15 was the last. If it would only crystallise, hold as it was like a bubble, sun and moon stand still.

A real Satan perhaps would force the issue. How does one force issues? His heart beat like a piston. Logic had deserted him at last. Something came over him from the seat beside him, came like the arm of a dream with the sweeping sleeve of an irrepressible dream, removed like a cobweb what had seemed a hard shell. He was quite exposed now, like a grub broken from its chrysalis with its wings still furled. He was all open to the air. But not the common air of day; the gentle-scented thought-assuaging air which was, in its essence, Janet.

From his cloud he saw them all come out before the curtain, hold hands, and bow, and realised with dismay that the show was now ended. Everyone was babbling and shuffling. They began to move out in file, himself behind Janet. Her hair was clumped tightly rather low on her neck, and Mella had made her wear pearls. They showed up the softness of her skin, the noiseless ambush of the outer border, the skin of the flesh of the body of her being.

Herzheimer and he were waiting by a marble pillar with a capital of gilt foliage; among the swish of evening dresses and the parched faces of ladies past their prime; hands held bags, voices made remarks. Herzheimer for a change said nothing, but looked at his programme. Devlin felt he was looking at him.

Then Janet was again, and the air was revived. They were all in the car; in silence. Herzheimer and he sat on the two little seats with their backs to the driver. Janet was opposite, Herzheimer. Devlin's knees were touching Mella's. Mella looked at him out of her dark corner, rather ironically, he thought, as if she was saying: 'You are very young; you have had no experience of the future.' But except when it concerned Herzheimer, you were never sure what Mella meant.

Light kept flashing on and oft Janet's face. She still smiled with pleasure at the show. Her smile gradually brought an echo on Herzheimer's face; his white teeth shone.

They went up the steps of Herzheimer's house. There had been a shower and the pavements looked like water with mild lights reflected. There was a fresh smell after the rain. The next moment they were sunk in the comforts of the drawing-room, in cushions soft as oblivion.

Mella and Janet and Devlin were all on the big sofa in front of the fire. Janet was between them, only a foot from Devlin. The huge fire flicked its tongue like a tame dragon. A man-servant, came in because Herzheimer had rung.

'What would you like, ladies?' said Herzheimer.

'What would you like, my dear?' Mella said to Janet. 'Have something to drink and some fruit and cake. What would you like to drink?'

'Nothing please. Alcohol's wasted on me. I've tried and tried, but it's no good.'

'Try some cherry brandy.'

'No, really, thank you ever so much, but I've tried that too. They all taste alike to me. So it wouldn't be any good, would it? I mean, it would really be sacrilege.'

'Ah, you will learn,' said Herzheimer, 'but you like lemonade, I trust? George, bring some lemonade at once. And also you must bring some fruit and the benedictine and brandy and any sorts of cake you can find.'

'Yes, sir.' George disappeared like an automaton.

'Where are those sweets?' said Mella. 'They must be somewhere in here.'

'There they are, my dear, on your little chair.' Herzheimer brought over to them a great box of chocolates and a round box of marrons glacés

'Ah!' said Janet.

'You like them?' said Mella. 'Good girl!'

'Of course she likes them,' said Herzheimer, 'What would life be if one did not like what is good?' He stood in front of the fire with his hands on his hips and looked from Mella to Janet to Devlin and back again.

George brought in a great silver dish of fruit and put it on a table by Mella. By it he placed a pineapple on a plate. Then he placed on another table by Herzheimer a tray with bottles and glasses. Devlin carefully watched all this; he could not quite make out why he was here and not at Mrs. Frigate's. He wanted to laugh. The gods, or rather Herzheimer, were favouring him absurdly. And no one knew how he felt!

'I'll only have a tangerine,' said Janet.

'Oh; but you must have something more. You start with a tangerine,' said Mella, touching Janet's wrist with her fingers.

What was wrong with Mella? Why had she gone so motherly? And how could they be having tangerines at this time of year? Surely they were only things one had at Christmas?

'When I was little,' said Janet, 'I always thought tangerines were like elephants. Because their skin is so loose.'

Mella laughed heartily like a child. 'Did you hear that, Paul?' she said, when she had stopped laughing. 'Did you hear what Janet thought about tangerines when she was a little girl?'

'Yes,' said Herzheimer, 'I always hear anything clever.'

'Don't make fun of me,' said Janet. She was pink and laughing. The light glowed on the silver and the fruits. Devlin was reminded of innumerable paintings and of mansion scenes on the movies. But they were the burlesque; this was the reality. He was afraid that in a moment he would forget and touch Janet's wrist just as Mella had been doing.

'The people in this country do not understand good things,' said Herzheimer suddenly. 'Neither music nor the theatre nor humour nor anything good. All they can understand is Gilbert and Sullivan. And hymn tunes. Hymn tunes and Gilbert and Sullivan; that is what they are born to. And why do those things take so well? not because they have go. They have no go at all. Listen to an English band; they are all tired; moribund. Gilbert and Sullivan, what go is there in that?'

'A sort of spurious go,' suggested Devlin.

'Yes, you are right. A spurious go and that is no go at all. Just like their public speakers. I tell you, it is abysmal. I have just been reading in the paper about the Mission to the Midlands. What is the idea of that?'

'That's Bilby's idea,' said Janet, quietly.

'Don't you think,' said Devlin, 'it's because we're retarded in this country? Everyone wanting to be some sort of a missionary.

Surely, that sort of spirit is what everyone has in their adolescence and it's only afterwards that it's so tiresome?'

'You are right,' said Herzheimer. 'You are quite right, my dear young man. But sometimes that spirit is very good, eh? It all depends on the adolescent. Or, if you like, on the overgrown adolescent. It is very good that there should be some people narrow-minded. An artist must be narrow-minded. Narrow in one sense and wide in another. But you all know what I want to say.'

'You are forgetting the drinks,' said Mella.

'Yes, I am a bad man. What would you like my dear? Your little glass of what you like? Ah; you are a good girl.' He gave Mella a glass of benedictine.

'I do love the colour of that stuff,' said Janet. 'I wish I liked the taste. It makes me angry to think of all you people enjoying something which I can't.'

'You should try something sweet,' said Devlin.

'No; I've tried all sorts of things and they all taste like poison to me. I can't even distinguish one of the poisons from another. It's very odd, because in anything else I can tell the minutest differences. Even with my eyes shut.'

'I wish I could,' said Devlin. 'I haven't much of a sense of taste.'

'Ah, well,' said Janet, slyly, 'you can't have everything. Now I have a sense of taste all right, but I can't talk about lofty things like spirits and being retarded. It's very foolish, really, not to be able to talk like that.'

'Please don't accuse me of being lofty,' said Devlin.

'I wasn't *accusing* you. I don't mean that you're unique All I mean is that I'm uniquely *not* lofty. Everyone one meets seems able to talk for an hour on end about reactions and tendencies as if it was a matter of course. I expect the Lord must have left something out of my makeup.'

'He was a wise Lord.'

'Nonsense. If I met whoever made me up, I'd tell him what I thought of him.'

'Janet,' said Herzheimer, 'have some more lemonade.'

'Yes I will, please. *We* can never make lemonade like this.'

'I'll give you the recipe,' said Mella.

No one spoke. For some reason they all looked at Janet as she sipped her lemonade. She had a pretty way of drinking. Slightly suggested a kitten.

The silence was broken by a bark.

'Oh, poor Karl!' said Mella. 'We never said good-night to him.'

There were more barks.

'I'll go and pacify him,' said Herzheimer.

'No, no. I must go. He doesn't want you.'

'Nonsense, darling.'

'Well, we will both go then.' Mella stood on her toes, kissed Herzheimer behind his ear, then led him out of the room. Devlin realised with alarm that he was alone with Janet.

Janet finished her lemonade and put the glass on the little table. 'That *is* good lemonade,' she said.

Something fluttered inside Devlin. It was the little Satan, who had been for some time shrinking. He was saying: 'Now, is your last chance. Probably it is. They won't be away long.'

Devlin stared at the fire.

'I shall soon disappear altogether,' said the little shrinking Satan.

'Oh, damn!' said Devlin aloud, unconsciously.

'What's the matter?' Janet looked at him with astonished eyes.

'What? Did I say something?'

'Yes, you said 'damn'.'

'Nonsense; I didn't. I'm so sorry.'

'I don't mind. I thought you'd hurt yourself.'

'No. It's only I suppose one sometimes thinks one's thinking something and one's really saying it.'

'But why were you thinking damn?'

'Oh, I don't know.'

Devlin looked at her. She looked into his eyes and then away.

'I liked what you said about tangerines,' said Devlin.

'How funny you all are. Why, didn't you think things like that when you were little?'

'No. I was very dull. I wish I'd known you when I was little.'

'Oh! you wouldn't have liked me.'

Devlin realised this was an opportunity to say something pretty. It was the last flicker of his conventional self. For at the same time his Satan rose, bulged over his mind, and, instead of saying anything he slid close to Janet and kissed her. She turned away her face so that he kissed the hair over her ear.

'Let me go,' said Janet, pulling away.

'Why?'

'Why? No; let me go. They will come.'

'Do you hate me a lot then?'

'No, no. I think you're dotty.'

Devlin drew her towards him, trying to kiss her mouth, but she kept her face away. In her mind all sorts of Japanese flowers were unfurling their flags and petals.

'Let me go!'

'But Janet, Janet darling, I can't let you go; you'll only go away and then I shan't see you again.'

'No, I shan't go away. I mean I shall be about – but you, you're only being silly. I've a good mind to slap you.' Janet suddenly laughed. A full corolla rocked on her mind's waves. The other young men all went down, drowned. She realised fully that this Devlin behaving in this odd way was all that she now wanted.

'Be good now,' she said, 'or I shall begin to think I'm a slut.' Devlin, sensing her surrender, drew her back to him. At that moment Herzheimer and Mella came in with their arms round each other's waists.

'Don't move,' said Herzheimer, in his deep voice.

'Don't move,' said Mella in her silver voice, which splashed through and crested Herzheimer's deep voice.

So, as if petrified, they sat where they were.

'After the theatre,' said Herzheimer, 'one always behaves more naturally. Look at Mella and me now.' He and Mella kissed each other. Then Mella waved her hand and cried: 'Back in a minute,' and like one creature they moved out of the room.

'Come,' Devlin whispered.

'No. Let me go.'

'But do come. I love you so much.'

Janet looked at him with vast eyes. 'Nonsense,' she said.

'But I do.'

'You only think you do. You're excited.'

'But I do, Janet. I have ever since I saw you at Wytt.'

'Oh! that's longer than me.'

'What?'

'Oh, nothing.'

'Come, darling.'

'Oh, damn it,' said Janet, and with a sigh of contentment, slipped on to his lap.

'Have you really?' she asked.

'Yes.'

'How funny. I can't say you showed any sign of it. In that letter for example?'

'No, of course I didn't.'

Janet kissed him on the mouth.

'I didn't realise it was all up with me – not till just now,' she said. 'It's because I like you too that I haven't gone away.'

'I love you,' said Devlin, and they said nothing more.

In a few minutes Herzheimer and Mella crystallised out of the opulent haze. Janet still sat on Devlin's lap. Mella came up and stroked her head. 'Have something more,' she said, 'to eat or drink for a change?'

'Another tangerine please,' said Janet.

'And what about you?'

'No,' said Janet. 'He'll share mine.'

'It is a symbol you know, sharing fruit,' said Herzheimer.

'Well, that's all right,' said Janet.

'We want a symbol,' said Devlin.

'Move up a little,' said Herzheimer. 'Two couples can get on a sofa easier than four people.'

Janet and Devlin tumbled into one corner of the sofa. Herzheimer sat in the other and Mella sat easily on his knee.

'What shall I do with the pips?' asked Janet.

'Spit them into the fire,' said Herzheimer.

'It's too far.'

'Well, use that ash-tray,' said Mella, 'or, no, use the lemonade glass. When you are comfortable I will give you a few tips. You approve don't you, Paul?'

'Yes, darling; but don't depress them too much.'

'Listen now, both of you,' said Mella, 'while I preach to you with the voice of experience. I expect you think I am fooling?'

'No, no.'

'Good. Well, the first thing to remember is not to have doubts, or, at any rate, not to pay attention to them. For, if you pay attention to your doubts, you will never get anywhere. I don't know if you are going to get married – perhaps you will just live together. Of course, you are going to do one or the other. On the whole, you may as well go the whole hog and get married. Don't interrupt, Paul. Now, I have been married twice, and I have also lived with several men and none of those men was the right one until I found my own dear Paul. My first husband was a genius and very lovable, but he was not tight for me. And I must say that the odds are very much against finding the right man. But when one does find him it is so good that it is always worth trying the odds. So now as to you two, I have no doubt that you are all wrong for each other——'

'Come,' said Herzheimer, 'that is rather strong——'

'I mean that you are very likely to be wrong; you cannot help it. But there is just a possibility, perhaps more of one in your case, that you may be right. So go ahead. For God's sake go ahead.'

'Yes, go ahead,' said Herzheimer. 'Mella is very wise; the only thing is she is too gloomy. You will very probably get on well. And if you don't, well, you can get divorced. And now let us all drink to everyone's health.'

'And yet it is funny,' said Mella, beginning to laugh. 'Here are you two, only just met – well, only a short time – and now you must needs go off and pretend to be grown up. After all it is not too bad being unmarried.'

'It is cowardly, though,' said Herzheimer.

'I suppose so.' Mella thought for a little and then said dreamily: 'And I don't suppose if I *had* met you first, I'd have married you. Gabriel took me by storm; it was mainly his playing I think.' She got off Herzheimer's lap and walked over to the tray of bottles.

'Isn't this funny?' said Janet. 'Let's ring up Dads.'

'Nothing too hasty,' said Herzheimer, 'though I admit it would be fun. You must do everything carefully. When should they be married, Mella?'

'Hi!' said Janet.

'We'll arrange that,' said Devlin.

'Quite right,' said Herzheimer. 'Don't be bothered by us.'

'Well, when shall we?' said Devlin.

'I don't know. What about money and things?'

'I don't know. We must work all that out.'

'Well, let's see. When I go home tomorrow I'll tell Dads about it. I doubt under the circumstances that he'll take it well. Meanwhile you tot up your income. Mine's pretty simple; it's five pounds a year. I can always char of course.'

'Mine's pretty simple too. It's just under three-fifty a year.'

'Oh! that sounds a lot, but I suppose it's not much really. Hertsy will know. Hertsy, can two chaps live on three-fifty a year in London?'

'Not in London. At least not you two chaps. And remember, my children, it is not very tactful what you do, discussing the poorness of your income, seeing that half of that income comes from me.'

'I know, Hertsy, I know; it's only——'

'Now, look here. I don't believe in spoiling people when they're young. You think, no doubt, that it is a very mangy salary I give your young man. But remember, my dear, that the work which he does for me must take up very little of his time. If he wants more money he must either work more for me, or work, in addition, for someone else. I myself could make a suggestion, but I know he would not follow it, so I leave it unsuggested. Now, as I said before, people when they are young should above all not be spoiled. If they have any character, it is better for them to be poor; if they have not, it is better for them to be bachelors. So you need not think that I am going to do myself in order to line your purses. So what you must do is see to your own lives and avoid doctor's bills.'

'That's very true,' said Devlin. 'I know well my luck in having this job at all. We shall get on all right. We've characters; haven't we, Janet dearest?'

'It sounds like cooks,' said Janet.

'But listen again,' said Herzheimer. 'If you have only this job with me, you need not live in London.'

'Nor we need.'

'Somewhere in the country not too far away would do you and living would be cheaper there.'

'Of course it would,' said Janet, clapping her hands. 'Let's do that.'

'In that case, if you like the locality, I can let you have a cottage at Furberley. It is not a bad cottage and the rent is twenty pounds.'

'But Hertsy, twenty pounds did you say?'

'Yes, it was twenty pounds when it was a young cottage, before I bought it. It may as well be twenty pounds now it is old. It is not furnished, of course.'

'But Hertsy, how magnificent. You really are a good man. Look here, Devlin, what——'

'It has quite a nice bed in it, and a good kitchen table. It has a little strip of ground in front with wallflowers, but otherwise no garden. However, there is a neighbour's lilac bush which leans over and looks in at one of the back windows. It is also, for a cottage, reasonably spacious.'

'But you're an angel. Tell us all that again slowly—— It's——'

'It's merely a business proposition.'

'Business? What an old joke you are. Why, we'll be able to get married at once.'

'As you will,' said Herzheimer, 'but that's all I do for you. You'll have to get your own licence and *I* shan't pay for the divorce.'

Then they ate more tangerines, it was all like a dream and at last, when the clock was at two, Mella and Herzheimer patted and pushed Devlin downstairs, and Janet kissed him on the steps under the porch, and there was a taxi ready, and, before he knew where he was, past all those spinning lights, reflections in the road, took out his latchkey, made a great noise in entering and roused Mrs. Frigate, whom he met on the stairs in her dressing-gown with her hair on top of her head.

'Sorry to wake you up, Mrs. Frigate. I'm engaged to be married.'

'You're *not*, sir? So late at night, too.'

'Yes, I am. On my word.'

'Well, I never, I knew there was something in the wind.'

Next he opened Gabriel's bedroom door and turned on the switch. From under the dressing table a shaggy head raised itself, followed by a vast body. But it seemed to know Devlin was not a thief. It stood looking at him guilelessly.

'Gabriel, wake up.'

'What is it, damn you.'

'Wake up, I've got news for you.'

'Hell take your news.'

'I'm going to be married.'

'What?' Gabriel sat up, with staring eyes like a gargoyle, and his hair shagged like the dog's.

'I'm going to be married. To Janet.'

'Hurrah.' Gabriel threw his pillow to the ceiling. It dropped on the floor and was promptly murdered by the dog. 'I knew you'd do it. I'll come and play the organ.'

'Oh, I fear it won't be like that.'

'Well, never mind. I say, I *am* glad. Tell me more.'

'I'll tell you the details tomorrow; I'm much too dotty tonight. I feel all up in the air. But I'll tell you it all tomorrow. I say though, you don't look very well.'

'Oh, I'm all right. I say, I am glad.'

'Well, good-night, Gabriel.'

'Good-night, Devlin. Say good-night to the dog.'

'Good-night, dog.'

Devlin floated upstairs on his brand-new wings, vividly remembering and vividly expecting Janet. While Gabriel lay on his back quite exhausted, thinking how now he had got no job, no ideal to follow, and soon Devlin would go; and then, except for this poor mutt of a dog, there would be no one to keep off the loneliness of the silence, the terrible, noisy silence.

CHAPTER SIXTEEN

Sir randal and Colonel Hardle sat in evening dress in the Colonel's study. The friendly odour of leather books and cigars cajoled their worried spirits.

'You see,' Sir Randal said, 'I know Janet like a book. It isn't the first time that she's had these sudden crazes. Why, about a year ago she fell in love with a boy called Garfield – a conceited young charlatan. I suppose it's part of a young girl's make-up, suddenly to fall blindly in love and then fall out of it again. For, thank Heaven, they always recover from it.'

'So you think she will recover?'

'Think she will? Of course she will. Why, I've studied her since she was a baby and I know every one of her reactions. I've done the same with all my daughters. She's only once really lost her temper with me. That did surprise me, but I knew it was only nerves – all girls have nerves about that age. Especially nowadays, with all this – this atmosphere and tension, it needs gentle treatment. I smoothed it over as well as I could and ever since things have run quite smoothly. And now what happens? She comes along and tells me she's going to marry, actually going to marry, the most typical young – typical young wastrel and decadent I have as yet had the bad luck to strike. You know him yourself as a mean and cheeky rogue. I told you about that essay he wrote – filthy profane rubbish; and I think I told you too how Janet insisted on bringing him to the house. I knew it was a mistake – I have always tried to close the door to undesirables –

I knew all along it was a mistake, but I tell you I was trying to be kind to Janet. Well, what happens? He not only comes himself and insults me to my face, but he brings in after him a contemptible young man dead drunk, a half crazy creature – brings him into *my* house where the whole of my family can see him. And that is the sort of man my daughter wants to marry.'

'He's got a job, yon say?'

'Job! He somehow or other gets money from Mr. Herzheimer; I don't know if you can call it a job——'

'Herzheimer? He might get quite a lot out of him.'

'What difference does that make? I tell you I don't mind about money. I shouldn't mind if my daughter married a crossing-sweeper provided he was a decent, healthy fellow who washed himself and had a sense of honour. As for this Urquhart, I shouldn't care if he was getting twenty thousand a year. I'd never give my consent to any daughter of mine marrying a man like that. A man who's mentally and morally unstable. You know all about that yourself; didn't he come sneaking into your garden, masquerading, pretending——'

'He did. He did, indeed.' The Colonel's cigar ash fell off on his trousers; he brushed it off leisurely.

'Well. What did you think of it? Did you think he behaved like a gentleman? Did you——'

'To tell you the truth I was very angry at the time, but afterwards I was somewhat – somewhat amused. To think of my wanting to show him off to Wilkins. I haven't told Wilkins yet; afraid he would rag me. But, you know, he must be a clever chap, anyhow. And got nerve too!'

'Nerve? I should think he has. That type often has nerve or something that looks like it. But what is the reason? Simply that they are totally lacking in conscience and sense of honour.'

'You may be right. You may be right. I defer entirely to you. You are an active man and it is your business to look into these things. You know, Randal, I've become such a recluse I'm quite out of my depth in questions like this. Half the time I'm a bookworm and half the time a potterer in my garden. I just can't judge human beings at all.'

'It's easy enough to judge in this case.'

'I suppose so, Randal. I fear my moral anger is not as ready to spout as it used to be. Time——'

'You're not a father.'

'No; I suppose that is the reason. I only wish I were one. You are very lucky, you know, Randal.'

'I sometimes doubt it,' said Sir Randal, throwing his cigar-stump into the fire. 'I suppose people will begin arriving soon.'

'They' should. They should indeed. It's a pity it's such awful weather. No one would believe it was May.'

'You know, George, it's very admirable of you to keep up this annual affair. I don't know how you do it.'

'Oh, I like it. I'm an idle fellow you know, and I like a little fuss once a year. I don't even write letters to the daily papers – as all retired colonels are supposed to. So I must do something. I can't tell you how glad I am all your family were able to come. Last year when you were all abroad, it nearly broke my heart. Aileen's looking very well, by the way.'

'Yes, she enjoyed her stay abroad. But she says she's glad to be back.'

'Of course. We're always glad to get back. Well, shall we go and rescue your daughters before the crowd arrives?'

Sir Randal got up. 'Hullo!' he said, 'I've been sitting on a book. I'm so sorry, George; I trust I've not hurt it?'

The book had been left open on the chair, and now its pages were a little crushed and the corners of two or three turned down. It was the Aeneid. Sir Randal held it out to the Colonel, who said: 'Lord bless you, it doesn't matter at all. That's only an old copy. It doesn't matter at all.' He shut it hurriedly and shoved it into a shelf.

'I told you I was a bookworm,' the Colonel went on. 'Do you know I've spent nearly all last week reading my school classics, and, you know, they give me a pleasure I don't get anywhere else. It may be their seriousness. English literature seems so flighty after them.'

'The latest English literature anyhow,' said Sir Randal; 'if it *is* literature.' They went out of the room together.

Ten minutes later the Colonel slipped back, took the Virgil out of the shelf, opened it, turned back the corners of the pages, smoothed the pages with gentle palm, and, after gazing at it for some time, replaced it in another shelf, the one where it belonged. Then he slipped out again to chat merrily with the four Miss Belchers.

In a quarter of an hour the first guests arrived. More and more cars followed them. The rain crashed and lay round the house in pools. The raindrops danced on the steps round the incoming evening shoes. To everyone who came the Colonel was equally courteous.

Among those who arrived were a number of Smiths. They had brought a young man in place of 'John,' who was ill.

'Good gracious me!' said the Colonel, 'I'm glad you haven't forgotten me.' He laughed very heartily.

Devlin, who had half expected to be thrown out, laughed also. 'I'm not pretending to be anyone particular now,' he said.

'I hope not,' said the Colonel, 'I hope not. Ha! Ha!' And then he was rapt away by the appearance of an average young man and an average young woman, who were wondering which door to go through next. He turned to them with the smile of a guardian angel. Devlin, much relieved, followed the Smiths into the ballroom.

'Good Heavens!' said Maude to her partner, 'There's Janet's young man.'

'Who? Where? That Garfield chap?'

'No, he's in India. That little man over there. I don't know what he's doing here.'

'What? That fellow with the funny face?'

'Standing by the pillar.'

'Yes, that's the one I mean. Odd-looking chap. Pale face he's got. Not enough vitamins or something.'

Maude gave a little absent laugh. It was very upsetting, this. She was definitely upset. Where was Janet? Was this Janet's doing? Didn't the Colonel know he was here? Wouldn't he turn him out? Dads said the Colonel detested him for playing him a dirty trick. Where was Janet? And what would happen if Dads saw him?

Devlin stood in the protection of the pillar while everyone swayed past, enjoying themselves gravely. Most of the women looked at him and asked their partners: 'Who's that man by the pillar?' 'Who's that odd-looking bloke?' or 'Who's that distinguished looking young man?'

No one knew him except one Gotthard, who said: 'Why, that's Urquhart. He was at Hillbury with me. Not much of a chap; rather a slacker. Chap to keep clear of. Not quite the sort of man one wants about.'

Devlin did not notice Gotthard; he was ambushing the door the other side of the pillar. He nearly jumped as he saw Elaine and Aileen come through the door; but no one followed them. They came straight round the pillar and——

'My God!' said Elaine. 'How did *you* get here? What a god-awful joke.' She laughed shrilly and put her hand to her necklace of painted wooden beads, orange and green. She seemed to have done something to her eyebrows since Devlin saw her last. Aileen was perplexed; having little memory she did not remember Devlin's face.

'Oh; you don't know each other,' said Elaine. 'What a bore introductions are. Look here, this is my sister and this young man is Janet's young man you've just been hearing about.'

They shook hands – Aileen gingerly as if Devlin was something venomous. She was a simple-minded girl. 'I think I've met you at Hillbury,' she said.

'Yes, of course,' said Devlin, and looked vaguely through her.

'You want Janet, I suppose?' said Elaine. 'Well, you can't have her – at the moment. She's got such a complicated dress she's had to go back and rearrange it. You'd better come along with me or some of these people will eat you; the Colonel would kick you out, you know. Not to speak of my father, who's lurking about somewhere.'

She took Devlin into a little room where there were two great eighteenth century globes in stands – one of the earth and the other of the heavens. They sat down on an ottoman.

'Grotesque furniture the Colonel goes in for,' said Elaine.

'Yes. Some of it's rather nice.'

'Do you think so? But, look here, don't get me off the track. What I want to ask is: Do you really want to marry Janet?'

'Yes.'

'Well, if you've any sense, you won't actually marry her. Marriage is played out. What's the point of it, anyhow? Why not just live with her?'

'We're old-fashioned fellows,' said Devlin.

'I don't believe it. Why, can't you see? Can't you? You don't want to be like all those people dancing in there? All those dreadful English people, so very very English!'

'But we're English too, after all. And after all, it's only a question of convenience.'

Devlin looked at Elaine, at her short lop-sided dress, her art-student necklace, her face, her hair.

'Convenience?' said Elaine. 'Why, its just weakmindedness! The trouble with Janet is she never goes far enough. I mean she's not like Maude and Aileen but on the other hand. . . .' Elaine talked for some time about herself, ending up: 'I'm terrible thirsty; let's go back into the crowd.'

'Look!' said Gottbard, 'Urquhart's been getting off with that little vamp there.'

Meanwhile Maude had thought of telling Sir Randal that Devlin was here, but she had not the courage. Sir Randal sat in the Colonel's study, resting. He was, as always in the evening, very tired. He had looked over the Colonel's books but they did not much appeal to him. The music came to him from the distance; he found it distasteful. It was a social convention, of course; opportunity of good fellowship, but otherwise rather poor. Poor stuff, this jazz; hypnotic, too. Take the case of that fellow in the sanatorium, who had been found charlestoning in the factory.

All the time the thought of his daughter's folly disturbed him. Of all people. Of all people to choose that derelict, that dirty-minded——

'She'll get over it, though,' he thought; 'and I'll keep my eyes open.'

Meanwhile Devlin was waiting for Janet by the door of the ballroom. But Janet was still upstairs. Presumably she did not expect be would bring it off. And he only just had. Only at the last moment had forced himself on the Smiths. Old Hillburians proving of use again. Bloody bores at that!

Here came Smith now.

'I say——' said Smith excitedly.

'Yes, what's the excitement?'

'I say. I'm in love again!'

'You're what?'

'I really am. It's the real thing this time. I say, old man, it's staggering!' Smith's pig eyes glittered in the vastness of his face.

'You don't understand,' he said, 'what I feel like. Still, you were at school with me and these other chaps . . .'

'God!' thought Devlin, 'how many more people want to gas at me.' In the middle of Smith's talk a spear pierced him. Instinctively he turned and caught Janet's hands.

'Janétski, dear!' he said.

'Darling, I was sulking upstairs and suddenly I knew you were here. You *are* clever.'

'Come, darling. There's a little room here.' But the room with the globes was occupied. They went through it and found a dim passage containing the servant's stairs. There they sat.

'Well, darling?'

'Well, darling?'

'Everything's nearly fixed,' he said, 'what about you, dearest?'

'Oh, me? I've been having the hell of a time! Dads raging and Maude weeping and Elaine talking advanced. Not that she says anything when *he's* there.'

'I know, darling. She's been talking to me. She's all for us living together.'

'As if she'd ever lived with anyone,' said Janet.

'What about your clothes and things?'

'I'm packing them by degrees. And I sent a trunk up to Paddington this morning which contains enough to get on with.'

'Can't we do it before Monday?'

'God! I wish we could. But we'd better wait, I think. I'd like to sail out in the open. Not minge off without telling them.'

'Hell! All right then. How sweet you look.'

Janet was in a sweeping cherry-coloured dress with the skirt supported on paniers. It was cut low at the back, but at the moment she had a flowered silk shawl over her shoulders. The paste on her shoes glittered on the dark stairs and her eyes shone like dark lights. It was even rather frightening.

'And now let's go and dance,' she said.

They danced. All among Elaine's typical English – the Smiths, Smythes, Spaldings and Piddocks; Maude and Aileen and Gotthard. There was the Colonel. He saw them but seemed to smile to himself.

'He's probably told Dads,' said Janet. 'Never mind. The move the merrier.'

'Look how grim everyone looks,' she said, 'and it's such a good tune, this. Pretty dull band, though.'

'Gabriel's the man to dance to.'

'Gabriel? Do you like him really?'

'Yes, darling. I know he nearly mucked us up, but I can't help liking him. He's like a child.'

'I know. It's a pity be gets drunk. That's one thing always puts me off.'

From a little S-shaped sofa with a back like a dromedary (a relic of elaborate Victorian modesty) Miss Hardstaff and Miss Lylie watched the modern generation. Both smiled obscenely like conspiring gargoyles.

'What a fine tall young man Mr. Gotthard is,' said Miss Hardstaff.

Miss Lylie, who was herself six foot, was not impressed by this. 'Look!' she said, 'there's a distinguished-looking couple. That's one of Sir Randal's daughters.'

'Yes, that's Janet. Who's the swain?'

Miss Lylie stretched her scraggy condor's neck. 'I have no idea,' she said, 'but he reminds me of someone.'

'Yes, I certainly seem to have seen him before.'

'Unusual dress, Miss Belcher has,' said Miss Lylie.

'Long dresses are coming in again,' said Miss Hardstaff, runkling her nose.

The music stopped. People subsided out of the room. Colonel Hardle touched Devlin's arm, smiled and said something, led him away.

'That's very curious,' said Miss Hardstaff.

'What is curious?'

'Seeing him with the Colonel reminded me. He's exactly like that gardener the Colonel had some time ago.'

'Oh! that gardener's boy? Yes. Yes, you're right. Came from the North Country, I think. The. Colonel had to dismiss him. I rather inferred that he stole.'

'Or half-witted, perhaps,' said Miss Hardstaff. 'I remember speaking to him about the Men's Club and he answered me most strangely.'

'North country villagers have no manners,' said Miss Lylie.

Meanwhile the Colonel and Devlin had entered the Colonel's study. Sir Randal Belcher had, unknown to the Colonel, just opened the study french windows and stepped out on to the verandah. The fierce rain had stopped for a little. In spite of the cold and damp Sir Randal sat down in a damp wickerwork chair and looked into the gloom where the circle of cut yews made clumps of more definite darkness. There was a ceaseless sound of dripping. A pale streak in the sky wavered for a moment and vanished. It was the moon, bemarshed deep in clouds. Sir Randal's chair creaked under him. Heavy drops fell from a thick creeper on a trellis. The jazz could hardly be heard. Sir Randal wandered far into a deep fog of thought.

'Good Lord!' said the Colonel. 'Someone's left the garden door open.' He went over and shut it.

'Now,' he said, breezily; 'I'd just like to talk to you. I know it's none of my business and in any ordinary case I wouldn't dream of poking in my finger. But the fact is, Urquhart, I have a double connection with this case. Firstly, I'm a man, who when I was young, had a very great respect and even reverence for your father. And I think I see something of your father in you. I have just heard from her father that you wish to marry Miss Janet Belcher. In fact – ha! ha! – I presume you came here tonight to see her. Well, Sir Randal Belcher is one of my greatest friends, and I should be very much against anything. . . .It's not that I don't wish you and Janet every success; I myself should say you had the right stuff in you, Urquhart. But one *must* do things the right way. If a father is definitely against your marrying his daughter, your duty is – well, you see what it is. You must win the father before you win the daughter. It's the only honourable course and it's a perfectly possible one. Just think a moment. Remember——'

'I know——' began Devlin.

'Just a moment. Imagine for a moment what it is to be in Sir Randal's position. What, from the little he has heard or seen of you, you must appear to him to be. Something, no doubt, very different from what you are. Your actions, you see, all the actions in fact which he knows of, have not been such——'

'I know that, but——'

'In fact, my dear Urquhart, you have made a very fair fool of yourself. Of course – ha! ha! – I know that's a way with young men. Still, when you become a suitor for a great man's daughter, you have to drop all that sort of thing. If you can't drop it, drop your suit. You've been too precipitate, Urquhart. Do you know, Sir Randal firmly believes you're mad? And immoral at that. You needn't think *I* think that. But what I do think is that you've been extremely – well – inconsiderate. All these extraordinary tomfooleries of yours. A young man who wants to marry immediately, does not begin by making a bear-garden of his prospective father-in-law's house. Now just a moment. I want to be scrupulously fair. You are your father's son, and I myself, if I had a daughter, could prefer no other man's son to his. Still, I should not accept you as you are. The man and the girl must know each other first. Before they even count themselves engaged. Why, how do you know you ought to marry Janet? And how does she know – why, to cut it short, neither you nor she has really had time to weigh the pros and cons. What you want, Urquhart, is to let a little time elapse. A little time for you and Janet to get to know each other and for you to reconcile Sir Randal. What yon want to do is to work seriously for a year or so. A little time works wonders. There's nothing to be gained . . .'

And so the Colonel went on. With time and what you want to do and wait a little time and don't force the issue and think it over and weigh the pros and cons and but and if and how and when and considering, notwithstanding . . .

At last he let Devlin go. As Devlin shut the door, the noise arrested Sir Randal, propelled forward through fog-bound ways in his invalid wicker chair. But in all the spas of the mind, which he himself recommended, he had found no rest or ease. Very bitterly he longed for his dead wife. And his daughters would all go. And Janet was the best of them. And these young men were spongers, tricksters, played dirty. He would not give up Janet to anyone who played dirty. Or to anyone of warped mentality. When Janet looked at him someone else looked too. And moved Janet's hands in delicate, light movements. He would not give her up. Except to a hero, some eminently ideal, some outstanding, some——

He looked at the heavy pudding yew trees. All round were drippings. Meshes within meshes within nets within nets of the desolate traps of nature. Nature was full of disease, of spite, of false turnings. The world was pockmarked with stale ditches and pools. Caked and clotted with spawn. But as for Janet and the other person in Janet, you did not find them anywhere near such places.

Sir Randal stood up and tapped on the window. The Colonel let him in. Sir Randal walked up to the fireplace and rallied into a laugh.

'So you locked me out, eh, George?'

'Upon my soul, I never knew you were there. That's really very funny. Quite a situation. Didn't you hear us?'

'No. Who've you been talking to?'

'You'd never guess.'

Sir Randal beat his drum and charged into hilarity: 'Let me see now. You've been proposing to Miss Hardstaff?'

'Ha! ha! ha! No, it's even funnier than that.'

'Not Bilbatrox?' said Sir Randal hopefully.

'What heresy. You don't think *him* funny, Randal?'

'No,' said Sir Randal, honestly, 'but of course the idea of him turning up would be rather a coincidence. Like the picture of the parson at the frolic, eh?'

'Yes, but——'

'I ought to write to him,' Sir Randal went on. 'You know George, he's really the best of fellows. He works like an ox and what a brain he's got——'

'Yes? Yes, Randal. I admire Bilbatrox as much as you do. Still, don't you find him on the *human* side a little, a little, er?'

'Oh! the *human* side? Human side? No, George, I don't think you do him justice there. I find him a perfect companion. Quite good company indeed.'

'Well, to return to our guessing game. One more guess for you.'

'Oh! I give it up, George.'

'Well, don't be angry with me. It's your *enfant terrible*.'

'My what?'

'It's Devlin Urquhart.'

'What?'

'Janet's young man you've, been telling me about.'

'It's not? He's not come here? Of all——'

'Wait a moment, Randal.'

'Did you kick him out?'

'No.'

'Then I'll go and do it myself.'

'You can't, old man. He's one of the Smiths' party.'

'The Smiths? Fools.'

'Just a moment, Randal. I've been talking to him. He's not a bad lot, you know. I know he must appear pretty bad to you, but that's more a misfortune than anything else. Well, I took it upon me to appeal to his commonsense. I told him that with time he could redeem himself in your eyes——'

'He could certainly not.'

'I told him not to do anything rash, that one must have time to get things straight. I think he was quite impressed. And I say, Randal, don't be too hard on him. Remember his father. He was a wonderful man.'

'Yes, but that's not the same——'

'Oh! a wonderful man. He saved India, you know. Have a cigar, Randal?'

'Thank you. Well, well; this is a shock to me. The impudence. You can't be right, George. I know he's a rotter. I'll stay here for a little and think it over. And I tell you what, I'll give him one chance. He can come in here and talk it. out with me. If he can defend himself, well and good. But I suppose he'll be afraid to come.'

'Oh, no. Not afraid. He's got a lot of his father in him.'

'Has he?'

The Colonel went out.

'Has he, eh?' repeated Sir Randal, and sitting down, glared into the fire.

Meanwhile Janet had been asking Devlin what he meant by sitting all that time talking to the Colonel. 'And what did he say to you, anyhow?'

'Oh! nothing but time, time, time. Telling me how we must wait——'

'Silly old boob.'

'They don't see the point of course.'

'See the point? What do you take them for? They wouldn't see the point if one argued till all was blue. No, no, Devlin dearest, one's just got to ignore them.'

The jazz contracted on their nerves, clenched like a hand, twanged their nerves and tendons; all the time they danced they felt wired off from the others. As if they were dancing on a table, high and apart.

There was Elaine baiting the local artist, Aileen flirting heavily with a naval man, Gotthard talking fishing to a girl who ran a teashop, Smith in raptures with a girl like a tea-cosy, Miss Lylie dancing grotesquely with the Colonel, Miss Hardstaff sitting on the museum specimen sofa and talking about the country to a clergyman. First she talked about it with a small c, about the greenery and the feeling of May, and the view from the top of that hill; and then she talked about it with a large C, about the economic problem and the Labour Party and the Reform of the Prayer Book, and the King's health and Bilbatrox.

But Devlin and Janet floated high like swans.

Suddenly, Devlin said: '*What about it?*'

'*Yes*,' Janet said.

'Shall we tell your pa first?'

'Hell! no, darling. I don't like slinking off, but we can't spend the whole night talking. Never get anywhere.'

'Let's go then.'

'Yes, let's go. What a good idea of yours, darling. How are we to go though?'

'Car, preferably. I know; Bearley will get us a car.'

'Who's Bearley?'

'He's the gardener. My old friend.'

'But is he about?'

'He's sure to be about. Protecting the house.'

The music stopped. They went through the globe-room into the back quarters and found the kitchen. The cook was surprised and flattered to see them. 'You want the gardener?' she said. 'Why, he's just a-sitting in the scullery.'

Bearley appeared, smoking his thick twist.

'Hullo!' said Devlin. 'Do you remember me?'

'Why, sir, yes. Certainly I do.' Bearley took his pipe out of his mouth and looked at Devlin in a slow contemplative way, gradually opening into a grin. 'Not play-acting any more, sir?' he said.

'No. Except that I'm going to be married.' Devlin explained the situation. 'And now can you get us a car?' It will save our lives.'

'Just a moment, sir,' said Bearley. 'What does the Colonel say about it?'

'The Colonel won't mind,' said Janet, quickly.

'Well, in that case I can get you a sort of a car. I can't say it's a very good one. It belongs to the grocer.'

'Oh, that will be all right. Do you mean it's a van?'

'No; it's a private car. Second-hand, that is. He won't mind it borrowed – not tor a bit of romance. No one can drive it now his son's in London.'

'Well, how are we to get to it?'

'Oh, I'll bring it up for you, sir. Won't take me long. I knows the ways of it. . . .'

Bearley went off into the rain. 'He'll be about a quarter of an hour going to the village,' said Devlin.

'Oh,' said Janet. 'Let's go back and dance then. Listen, it's a waltz.'

They went back and danced, feeling, in spite of the crowd, like two interorbited stars in a velvet and empty night.

As the dance ended the Colonel came up to Devlin and drew him aside. 'Sorry to attack you again,' he said, 'but Sir Randal would like to speak to you for just a moment. He's in the study. Go in, my boy; I believe he'll treat you fairly.'

'Right you are,' said Devlin, and went out into the passage.

Janet nipped after him and caught his elbow.

'Well, what am I to do?'

'You can't go and talk to him now.'

'It would only be decent, darling.'

'Decency be hanged! Do you know what will happen if you go in there? I suppose you think you'll have a beautiful argument and Dads will fall on your neck and send us off with his blessing. Well it won't be like that at all. You'll be talking there all night, and how do I know you won't be joining the Y.P. something or other by the morning? No, look here, darling, seeing we're determined to go, let's go. It's no good tempting fate by dawdling around here.'

'But——'

'He'd *never* understand, darling.'

'All right. Let's run and dress. My coat's in a cloakroom round here.'

'My things are upstairs. You wait in the back passage. By the stairs, there.'

They kissed each other, and feeling amazingly exhilarated, went their different ways.

No one went to the Colonel's study where Sir Randal sat straight in his chair with both hands on his lap. 'Why doesn't he hurry?' he thought. 'Can't he even do that? He doesn't know the man he's dealing with.'

But no one came. The next dance began.

'Damn him,' thought Sir Randal. 'Flirting with my daughter and doesn't condescend——' His face went red and square.

The clock's long hand moved ten minutes on. The Colonel fumbled tactfully at the door and came in. He looked round apprehensively. 'Hullo, Randal' he said. 'Had your say?'

'No, I've not. He hasn't even appeared.'

'What? But I left him on his way to you!'

'Well, he must have funked it.'

'Funked it? No. But that's very odd. Very odd.'

The Colonel walked up and down. 'I'll go and have a look for him,' he said.

In all the flap and muddle it took some time to ascertain they had gone. It was Maude who voiced the astonishing suspicion. She and Aileen went to where Janet had left her cloak, and it was not there now. They asked the servants if they had seen anyone going out. The cook said that a young lady and gentleman had had a long talk with Bearley.

'That settles Bearley,' said the Colonel. 'Where is he now?' But Bearley was not about.

It caused quite – as they say – a sensation. Miss Lylie said it reminded her of one of her uncles and Gotthard said the man must be a cad. But people went on dancing, chattering. Sir Randal and the Colonel talked in the study.

Sir Randal was terribly calm; it was almost the calm of a Rameses, a mask like stone, but more tired than stone. 'An elopement, I suppose?' he said. 'Very romantic. Very romantic. It's funny they never think about their parents. Personally I shall do nothing. They are both of age. I shall not cut my daughter off or anything so old-fashioned, George. She will always be my daughter. I hope I shall be able to help her.'

The Colonel was horrified. That this catastrophe should have happened in his own small world, in his own divine blind alley, to his greatest friend and hero; this was unbelievable. If only he could make Sir Randal think it was not so bad. For after all the boy had his good points. His father had saved India.

But Sir Randal said: 'I know all about his father. The man himself is what I go by. He is a funk, a sneak and a liar. And I am sure he is unsound. I see nothing – nothing at all in him.'

Outside, Elaine was laughing and saying to Smith: 'Look what a viper you brought in your bosom,' and Smith was saying 'Good Lord,' and almost forgetting he was in love.

Farther outside still Devlin and Janet crashed through the rain, the windscreen wiper working like a crazy pulse, while Devlin's left hand lay on Janet's knee, on her soft black velvet cloak. Just about dawn they got out of the grocer's car at Mrs. Frigate's door. They stood on the pavement looking at the car. The rain was now only drizzling and the sky grey. 'Where shall we put it?' asked Devlin; who looked like a movie hero in a tight blue coat over his evening dress and a white silk handkerchief round his neck.

'We can't leave it here can we?' asked Janet, looking wan, but radiant.

'I don't know. We can't do anything else with it. Do you know, I've only got sixpence on me?'

Janet looked in her little black evening bag that glittered coldly with paste, 'I've not got a sou,' she said. They turned spontaneously and Devlin fumbled at the door with his latchkey. 'What about that sheepdog?' she whispered, catching his arm.

'I don't know,' said Devlin. 'We'll trust to luck.' They went in and there were no barks.

Thus they began their new epoch, or epos, and left behind them the dry sands of youth. There were no barks, there were no voices, there was no setting of the stage.

Graft fire on ice, let the flowers and stars go drunk, and the sky tilting take us back to its bosom; close and near now beneath the cold, gold, grandiose quilt of essential being let your heart barge its way, let its red petals pelt, let the world's brim swim with the spilth of the blazing, crazy mount, the fount and font of flowers, let Ygdrasil and all other tall trees tug, and sleep so come down a long approach of trees, the air sweet with bees' trove and the sapphic of doves' calls.

CHAPTER SEVENTEEN

Gabriel got up about half-past eleven. His head ached. What a bore meeting that man last night, and going to see those Germans. Bierabend – silly damn dullery! All those women, and men too, all kissing each other. All so ugly too. Cult of the ugly mug.

He looked at himself in the mirror on his dark varnished dressing table; a mirror hanging awkwardly between two fantastic growths of knobbed and curling woodwork. He didn't look up to much. But he liked, as always, the tawny hair on his chest. 'It's really rather good,' he thought. 'Nearly as nice as the little imperial Devlin has on his chest. Wonder when Devlin got back from that dance. Perhaps he didn't. Perhaps someone knocked him down. Well, I suppose there's not much chance of his not marrying her now.'

He ruffled his hair and made it look musical; shocking bad taste, he knew, but he rather liked it like that. He wondered how Cadwallader had enjoyed his night in the basement. Mrs. Frigate had made him a lovely bed, but it was rather hard on him. Still . . .

He slouched into his sitting-room and pulled the bell-rope which looked like a dressing-gown cord. Mrs. Frigate's kind but inscrutable face appeared almost at once.

'Good morning, Mrs. Frigate. How's Cadwallader?'

'Oh! he's very well indeed, sir. What would you like for breakfast? Try and make up your mind to something nice and substantial. Seeing as——'

'Is Mr. Urquhart back?'

'Yes, sir. Must have come back very late. He's having a lay so I've not disturbed him as yet. This dancing you know, sir, it takes it out of one.'

'I'll disturb him soon enough.'

'Oh; you wouldn't be so unkind, sir? Poor Mr. Urquhart come all that way back in the rain; can't have been asleep more than——'

'His own fault,' said Gabriel. 'The only sort of dancing that's any good is when the people kick their own heads. Ever been to the Russian Ballet, Mrs. Frigate?'

'No, sir. Highbrow isn't it?'

'Well, you listen to this,' Gabriel sat down at the piano. Mrs. Frigate's compactly ample body slid rapidly through the door. 'I'll bring you up two eggs and bacon,' she shouted.

'. . . Petrouchka . . .' murmured Janet, rolling over in a half sleep on to Devlin's crooked-up knees, just as if she was sitting on his lap in a horizontal plane. Devlin woke up. 'What?' he said. 'What's that?'

'Eh?' said Janet, rolling over again and looking up at him out of one eye, while the other was still screwed up.

'Darling,' said Devlin, gathering her to him. They kissed each other and both began to laugh. 'When *did* we get here?' said Janet.

'Some time or other. Here we are, anyhow.'

'So this is your room? How funny. Lord, I feel stiff. Do J look all goggly-eyed?'

'Piggy, piggy piggy,' said Devlin.

They subsided into a semi-conscious doze, occasionally stroking each other and hearing all the time, as if through water, Gabriel playing Petrouchka. Suddenly, the music stopped; its cessation woke them like a shock. Steps came up the stairs. 'Good Lord,' said Devlin. 'Old Gabriel will be in on us.'

Gabriel flung upon the door so that it bounced back on him from its little rubber buffer. 'Hello, you bloody old swine,' he said. 'Good God!' There was a red dress on the foot of the bed, and there was a woman in the bed too.

'Don't go away,' said Devlin. 'This is my wife.'

Gabriel stood gaping like a tousled yokel. 'I *am* sorry,' he said. 'I didn't mean to come in——'

'Don't be silly, Gabriel. What you ought to say is something congratulatory.'

'Yes, yes. That's what I want to say. I——'

'You don't mind us coming into your house then?' said Janet.

Gabriel smiled. He did not think of women as lovable or admirable, but some of them could say ordinary things very nicely.

'I say, husband,' said Janet. 'Do you think he could order us some breakfast?'

Gabriel liked being talked about in the third person; it made him feel happily like Cadwallader. 'Breakfast?' he said. 'Of course. Mrs. Frigate's got a passion for cooking breakfast this morning. I'll go and tell her at once.'

'She'll have a fit,' said Devlin.

'Oh, no, she won't. I know my Frigate. If she stood Cadwallader, she won't mind you.'

And Mrs. Frigate was, in fact, much pleased. 'The only-thing is,' she said, 'it's getting a bit latish for breakfast. Why not make it lunch? Well, THIS IS a tribute to the house. Must be the first honeymoon couple it's seen for many a year.' Gabriel grinned at her foolishly. She looked at him out of her clean, inscrutable face and then said sharply: 'Well, there's your dog. It's about time he had some exercise.'

'I'll take him upstairs to see the bride,' said Gabriel. He patted Cadwallader and led him out of the kitchen and up the basement stairs. Mrs. Frigate sat down, smoothed her neat, almost quakerish grey hair, and smiled very wisely. 'It's difficult for people to get married in the night, but never mind. Forms is forms and love is love. There ain't much of the one and there's a terrible clutter of the other. Mr. Urquhart may be or be mayn't be. Or again he may be going to be. None of my business, and I wish him all good fortune. And I'll cook them a real nice lunch.

After all she herself had been born four months after her parents' marriage – 'I know it counts respectable, but I don't give much for that' – and her sister Irene had got into trouble twice; and her own husband had gone off to Australia with who do you think, a *nippy* from *Lyons*. Just like him, just because she was always having her hair waved and never noticed her squint.

She beat the table sharply like a magistrate, rose and went out to the bottom step of the stairs. 'Mr. Crash,' she shouted. 'Yes?' came Gabriel's voice, rising to a feminine pitch from excitement.

'I gave you a large coffee pot. There'll be enough for three there. Lunch will be ready in half an hour.'

Gabriel shouted this up to Devlin. Then he went into his sitting-room and sat talking to Cadwallader. 'Well, Wallader, my dear, I hope you feel honoured. It's not every dog has a bride honouring his house. No, it's not. No, it's not, you balmy old shagster. You silly old tailless gosling. You've got to behave well now. Thank God, you've not got a tail to lam into the coffee pot. You poor old moozled funny-face. . . .'

While Devlin sitting on his bed looked at Janet.

Janet laughed. 'What's really odd,' she said, 'is how natural one feels. Why this time yesterday I was fugging away at home helping Maude with the flowers, and now here I am in a room with a strange man, running about in my undies and feeling as if I'd done it ever since I was born.'

'That proves we're all right,' said Devlin.

'Mella ought to be pleased,' said Janet. 'She says chaps who're going to hate each other as often as not hate each other at once. Can you lend me a dressing gown, darling? I can't put on my evening dress. After lunch I'll send round to Paddington for that trunk.'

'This dressing gown's really Gabriel's, but I've left my own at home, and he's given up wearing them. It's rather too long for me so I don't know what——'

Janet slipped it on with her usual amazing quickness. 'But it's perfect,' she said. 'Now, I look like Queen Victoria being coronated. I've always longed for a dressing gown like this.'

Five years ago Gabriel had had it specially made by a tailor to whom he had brought the stuff. The stuff he had found in an old trunk of his father's, five yards of it buried beneath books of music. It was all over parrots and squirrels and rabbits, chirping and cheeping and holding up their paws. 'Won't he be very angry?'

'Not he,' said' Devlin.

When they walked into Gabriel's sitting-room, Gabriel cried out: 'Hurrah, now at last it suits someone.' He gave Janet a chair, having put a cushion on the seat and another balanced up the back. Janet in return, admired enthusiastically his room and his dog. She felt light headed and very well.

Mrs. Frigate's face appeared, looking at her in interested composure. 'Good morning, ma'am,' she said. 'Everything quite comfortable I hope. I wanted to ask you about your lunch. There's no time for any roasting so I'm making you some steak and chips. But if you don't like steak——'

'I love it,' said Janet.

'She cooks it red,' whispered Devlin.

'I like it underdone,' added Janet, sincerely, as Devlin knew.

'Ah,' said Mrs. Frigate. Her smile became for a moment vehement.

'It makes me most unhappy,' said Janet, 'when people dry away all the juice.'

'You're quite right,' said Mrs. Frigate, 'but of course they often don't grill it. It's a great mistake not to grill your steak.' She suddenly looked Janet in the eyes, perhaps to see if she was pretending. Then she went out. In spite of being eleven stone she made no noise on the stairs.

'It's quite true,' said Janet to Gabriel. 'I simply adore it red.'

Gabriel simply smiled; it was his way of talking to Janet.

Devlin said: 'You have sweet taste, darling,' and kissed the side of her head. Her hair was warm and alive.

'Where are you going for your honeymoon?' said Gabriel.

'Good Lord!' said Janet, 'I'd forgotten that was its name. We haven't really thought about that, have we, darling?' She and Devlin began a long discussion. Gabriel sat smiling till, without knowing it, the smile faded and he was looking vacantly at the wall. He had made a discovery that this girl was very nice (made one feel like one felt sometimes in the nursery, that the world was a warm place and full of painted bricks and bears that you made grunt – rather like Cadwallader). But this discovery was small beside the vast certainty, cold, overhanging like a cliff, that Devlin was now gone. He would soon leave these digs, and anyway he was gone.

But he tried to not show his depression and anyhow he was excited too; and finding he'd gone and let his smile go he retrieved it quickly and wagging his tail showed his face to all. And Cadwallader followed suit. And Janet patted Cadwallader and smiled at Gabriel.

While Devlin too kept himself in, showed a respectable front. For whenever he looked at Janet he wanted to scream with delight. But he talked quite calmly and listened to the others' talk. 'What shall we do about Herzheimer?' he said.

'Hertsy? Yes, we ought to let him know of course. He'll be amused to hear how it happened. By the way, darling, did I tell you about Mella?'

'What about her?'

'Why, I found out her real name.'

'When?'

'The night I stayed there – the beginning of our show. I don't know how I forgot to tell you. At breakfast Hertsy made me sit next to him, where Mella sits usually, and I found a letter on my plate addressed to Mrs. C. V. Edwards, and it turned out to be Mella.'

'Did she mind?'

'Not she. But would you ever expect her to be Edwards?'

'He was the man in India, I suppose?'

'I suppose so. Do you think C. V. are his initials or her's? Because where does 'Mella' come in?'

'Oh, I expect they're his. Though it's quite possible. 'Mella' *isn't* a real Christian name. Hertsy probably invented it.'

'Yes. Well, I *was* pleased with myself. I thought she'd be Mella and nothing else till the end of time. Hertsy never introduces her. Mrs. C. V. Edwards!'

'C. V.?' said Gabriel.

'Yes.'

'C. V.,' said Gabriel to himself, 'how very funny. I've hardly ever found anyone else C. V. Except that boy in the Maths Sixth – C. V. Wilkes wasn't he?' Gabriel turned moody. To rouse himself he ran about poking the fire, fetching things.

During lunch conversation flagged; Gabriel felt out of it; he felt they wanted to be away, like birds flying from the land. After lunch he insisted on going to Paddington to fetch Janet's trunk. He made the taxi go round by a confectioner's and bought a box of liqueur chocolates. But when the taxi was nearly at Mrs. Frigate's, he remembered Devlin had said at lunch Janet couldn't bear alcohol. So he drove back and changed it for a box of ordinary chocolates, which he gave to Janet and she was very and charmingly grateful.

The next moment Janet, very elegant and fresh in a coat and skirt, was going away and Devlin going too. With many smiles and thanks and Cadwallader wanting to jump up, Janet said good-bye and Devlin said good-bye. The taxi went, taking away Janet and Devlin – taking away Devlin.

Gabriel was back in his room trying to talk to Cadwallader. 'Well, my poor old creature, what are you looking so glum about?

What about a walk somewhere? You're getting quite seedy with never having a walk? What would you say to going – oh! damn it, Wallader; I think we'll cut the walk. I'll take you a walk tomorrow.'

He could not talk to the dog or play the piano or even pour himself a drink. If only he were in the country and could sit in a field. But no people. No people, for God's sake.

A knock startled him. Mrs. Frigate's face appeared, saying: 'A gentleman to see you, sir?' and Hogley's face appeared, saying: 'Hullo Gabriel!'

Gabriel stared at him. Hogley stood miles away at the end of a desert of carpet. Tall, spruce, cynical, fatuous, there he stood, the other side of a Sahara. There he stood, as small as life.

'What's the matter, Gabriel? In the doldrums?'

Gabriel stared at him. Hogley was cartooned on the air and the air round him was all pepper and salty. Or perhaps more like emery paper. Everything had gone dull and grating. It was like before Devlin came. 'Nothing,' said Gabriel. 'Let's go to a movie.'

'Now, don't be so abrupt,' Hogley laid his gloves on the sofa end. His voice too was gloved – no finger-prints, no index to the soul. 'It's quite a long time since I've seen you,' said his soft kid-skin voice.

'Yes,' said Gabriel's own voice, dully.

'I saw Devlin though the other day' – with a meaningful inflexion on the 'Devlin' – 'all got up regardless. I suppose he's out?'

'Yes.'

'Well, Gabriel dear, stop being patience sitting on a pouffe. What are the news in these parts?'

Gabriel winced. He must not tell Hogley about Devlin and Janet. Because Hogley would make some remark, and that would smash that too. 'News?' said Gabriel's voice.

'Yes. News. Events. Small-talk. Have you a job for instance? And how is Devlin's benevolent old Jew? And how——'

'Let's go to a movie.'

'My dear, what *is* this passion? Everywhere will be in the middle of their programmes. Wait a little and——'

Gabriel had a brilliant thought. He pointed at the shaggy breathing heap on the floor, and said: 'You've not seen him?'

'Your dog? No. He's what's called a *bobtail* isn't he? Very sweet. What's his name?'

Caught again. If he said Cadwallader, Hogley would mock him. He did not want to look a fool. So instead of telling him his name he told Hogley exactly how he got him, how he was a guaranteed watchdog, how Mrs. Frigate worshipped him, how——

Hogley was soon bored. He broached his scheme. 'By the way, you wouldn't like to come round to Eddie Hynes' for tea?'

'Who's Eddie Hynes?'

Hogley was surprised at even Gabriel; for Eddie Hynes was one of the few people Hogley called geniuses. He was small and finicky with red cheeks like a yokel, huge owl-like spectacles, a big pipe, and mousy hair coming down over his collar. Hogley could be quite funny about his appearance, but his respect for him was great.

'You don't know Eddie? Then you certainly ought to. You must play for him.'

Hogley thought this was not a bad idea. Eddie would then say that he (Hogley) was great at discovering people.

Gabriel did not want to but he acquiesced. He always acquiesced with Hogley.

As they ran for the bus, Hogley absorbed in not splashing himself, Gabriel saw his chance. He followed up to the bus, and then, when Hogley was struggling in its interior, stopped on the pavement and turned away. The bus started and Hogley, peering through the sweaty window, saw Gabriel's back walking rapidly away.

Walking away at random. He wanted to find sordor, back streets, scribbles on walls. But he could not get away from the respectable. Some dull little antique shops and a sort of taxidermist's – old musty fur and armadillo's mail. Then a flowershop. Very narrow, going back from the street like a wet green cave. He went in and bought a dozen yellow tulips.

Small unopened spears they were all one could want for shape. He would put them in that earthen bowl and at first they would be straight and then they would snake outwards, opening their——

A sort of nostalgia hit him, knocked him giddy. He wished he were in a field, a flat field with hedges. It was no good playing with these toys. He dropped the tulips on the pavement, with a clangour like painted brass.

Having walked on ten yards, he stopped with his lip quivering. He wanted to cry. He wanted to go back and pick up the tulips. But he would not.

He had tea in an A.B.C., little marble tables, washed-out efficiency. Then he went back to his digs.

There had been no fire for several weeks; the grate had the forlornness of early summer. He opened the cupboard to see what there was to drink. Only whisky; he did not want whisky. He went to the piano and played.

As he played the ceiling grew coffered with massed gold, heavy pillars writhed under the weight; Maya or Aztec idols frowned over his shoulder. John the Baptist's head was brought in on a cymbal.

On a time your John the Baptist was a fine man; though subject *to* ups and downs (psychosis they called it). Won the half-mile; magnificent physique. But he must have had some kink which came out in him at last.

'My father and my mother were not like most people's. They were both adorable and they were both impossible. My mother ran away and became many men's mistress; my father stayed at home, became a suicide. 'While of unsound mind.' As if one couldn't do it from sheer force of logic!'

What else was there in the papers? The 'Turvey Treatment,' 'Mend your Shattered Nerves,' 'The Headmaster of Harrow speaks on Education.' Tasteless all, like over-masticated meat.

'No one has ever told a lie, and no one has ever said a truth. There's something in everything, but it's not much. And they call this May with this cold dull breeze. If I'd brought those tulips now——

'Christine Vivian her names were. Silly names for her to have. Funny that Jew's mistress being C. V. too. My father called her Vivvy. What did I call her? I really can't remember.

'C. V. – Christine Vivian.'

He went from the piano stool to the cupboard and looked in. There was only whisky there; he slammed the cupboard to. Drink was a false escape anyhow. Soothed the nerves but just running away. Self-flattery too. Liked to sit at a table with one's chin in one's hand like a Tchehov hero or a Picasso blue period, doped by a sense of magnificent failure, a glorious aura of futility.

'Though I've had some splendid moments drunk. Never mind; that's all played out now.'

He took up his shapeless hat and went for another walk. Without Cadwallader; he did not feel sociable. This time nothing but Nonconformist chapels. Pretentious plaster pinnacles and posters in red and blue letters: 'Are You Saved?' 'Has Christianity a Future?' 'Is there a Hell?' 'Christ and the Unemployed.' 'Daniel an Old-Time Saint.' Gabriel began to laugh.

'There were two sorts of religious people who were all right – the simple-minded and the mystics. I suppose each had a touch of the other. St. Francis for example and George Fox. And the rosy-cheeked sit-up-with-you-by-night, give-you-magazines, lift-you-over-stiles, make-you-a-packet-of-sand-wiches, fond-of-birds-and-dogs, always-ready-for – well, they were all right. Comfortable sort of people.

'But Bilbatrox and the plaster and hell. How funny Devlin could be about Bilbatrox. It's funny people stand it.'

With a flush of annoyance Gabriel saw two small boys staring at him. He put his hand to his hat and settled it. Then he put both his hands in his pockets and hustled forward. Small boys were ghastly; they were so sharp, sophisticated, inimical. He could not bear inimical people. He hated being disliked. Like at Cambridge where, as he passed in the streets, he always heard men saying: 'My God! that man Crash,' 'Look at that man Crash.' Devlin, now, could get away with it; he would feel a match for the small boys and the sneering loutish undergraduates. How does one feel a match for people like that?

He went home, greeted Cadwallader, and, sitting down, began to play. After an hour he stopped and went to the cupboard. He poured himself a whisky and gave Cadwallader his hand to lick. 'So you like whisky, my dear?' he said, imitating Hogley.

The thought of Hogley annoyed him. He would like to go off somewhere and see none of them again. Not even Devlin. 'A chap like me, who's all perverse, doesn't want to see people. He ought to be a coal miner or a timber king or something.

'And Devlin was not entirely sympathetic; too metallic or something. Not like my father.'

He went and rummaged in a drawer in the desk. He could not find his father, but here was his mother. Magnificent, in spite of her long bunched skirt and straw boater. 'She is dead I suppose. She must be dead. What was the name of the man she ran off with? I don't know.

'Funny this Herzheimer's woman having the same initials.

'Devlin says she's foreign. Wonder if he's really nice, that man. I can't help feeling he's not. I don't know why. I believe my feelings though. Hogley says it's sentimental to go by things like that.'

He twisted Cadwallader's hair and stared at his mother's photo which he held in the other hand. She had 'go.' She was superb in the way a panther is. 'Still. . . I don't know that I regret her. We wern't cut out for each other. I take after my father. Unusual that. That's probably why I'm abnormal.'

He put the photo carefully away in its drawer. Then he walked up and down the room; what a lovely room it was. Cadwallader looked at him and moaned. Of course, he had not had his dinner. 'Nor have I – Come on, darling; I'll give it you down in the basement.'

He went down, fed the dog, and asked Mrs. Frigate to make him an omelette. As he ate the omelette, he thought: 'So Hogley says one can't go by things like that. Well, let's put it to the test. I'll go round and see Herzheimer this evening. I'll bet to God he's a stinker.

CHAPTER EIGHTEEN

In June Janet and Devlin came back, having written and received no letters for three weeks. They turned up at Herzheimer's house according to contract; he had said, 'I give you three weeks from the day you are married; you needn't tell me when you begin, but come round when they're finished and we'll have a business talk.

So they came to see Herzheimer as soon as they arrived in London; before going to Mrs. Frigate's or seeing anyone. It was just tea-time. There were present several languid young Jewesses and Professor Shawes. Also Karl, and bulking over him a vast but well-brushed sheepdog. 'Good Lord!' said Devlin, 'It's just like Gabriel's beast; only not quite such a doormat.'

'It *is* Gabriel's beast,' said Herzheimer; Mella was attending to the Jewesses.

'It is?'

'Yes.' Herzheimer told them the few and astonishing facts. Gabriel had walked into his study at ten o'clock one night. He had said: 'May I introduce myself? I'm Gabriel Crash.' And there they were at once! Why hadn't Devlin told them Gabriel Crash was his name? Instead of just calling him 'the man who shares my digs.'

'I must have called him Gabriel, anyhow.'

'Perhaps. We hadn't noticed it.'

There they had been at once! Mella was Gabriel's mother. What Herzheimer had been urging her to contrive had happened of itself. Very curiously. For Gabriel did not know, till he saw her, who she was. Though he had known her initials.

'That was due to me,' said Janet.

'Yes, I know. And the odd thing is you would probably not have known she was Mrs. C. V. Edwards except for that letter.'

'No.'

'Do you know that is the only letter in two years addressed to her as Mrs. C. V. Edwards? She is always called Mella Herzheimer.'

Herzheimer gave them fuller explanations very calmly and clearly. No one else was listening. Mella had left Gabriel's father not violently or spitefully, but just to save herself from extinction – their rhythms killed each other. She had gone off with Edwards, an American, whom she married after Gabriel's father's suicide. After Edwards' death in India she had lived in various ways in various parts of Europe. Finally she lived for several years with Herzheimer in various parts of Europe. Owing to what might be called a complex she had made no attempt to learn anything of her son. But when they came to live in England last year, Herzheimer had urged her. . . . But it was no good. Till the son himself appeared out of the blue, the complex disappeared like smoke, and——

'Where's Gabriel now?'

'In America.'

'In——?'

'He was in an appalling state, my dear children. Mella could not imagine what to do. I told her he must be rushed. Save him from a lethargy. Send him to the States and make him a musical star. So that's what we've done.'

'But he's gone already?'

'Of course. He had to be rushed, I tell you. He was quite amenable.'

'Oh!'

'I am sorry you could not see him. Never mind, he admires you a great deal. And here is his dog.'

Herzheimer led them back to the general conversation; to the amazingly harem-like Jewesses pondering each other's ankles and eyelashes, Professor Shawes sitting silent like an image or an old monkey in a cage. Devlin did not learn till he got a letter from Gabriel that Mella had paid Gabriel's nine hundred pounds of debts; he never learnt of the full frantic melodrama caused by Gabriel's appearance.

Devlin anyhow was still incapacitated for thought; he could not take in what Gabriel's departure meant. Gabriel was almost irrelevant. Janet was his world even more than Mella was Herzheimer's. Other people were all in the background – flat, pale like figures on tapestry. There was no need to talk to other people. Just sit back and watch them bubble past.

Even Herzheimer was only a fairy Godfather, god out of the machine; delightful but not of the real world. The cottage they were going to was *their* cottage. Thanks to Herzheimer, yes. Thanks to him, certainly. The rain falls from heaven but it makes you and me wet. '*Our* cottage; that's where we're going.'

They went there. It was not a sham cottage; quite plain and simple. Electric light, gas cooker, decent-sized windows. Life became entirely practical. Janet was teaching herself to cook. One always had to be remembering things. Not like Mrs. Frigate's or Oxford or the Graylings'. Mrs. Grayling was fussy, but of course that didn't matter. But with little money and a wife——

It was very funny to remember one had a wife. One wouldn't have of course, unless it was just her. She was amazingly uniform and yet full of variety. Like light which can never be divided. To look at her and think of her tore him out of his rut. He could never get in a rut any more now.

Though there were disasters, rows. The time Devlin threw the plate on the floor and said: 'I'm damned if I will. Nothing but

fussing about things that don't matter. What sort of a life . . .?'
And the time Janet rowed him about the egg

For they had had breakfast late, about eleven. And Devlin was sitting content in the sun from the window when he sensed Janet being angry behind him; she was taking away the egg-cups, 'What's wrong?' he said.

'Why don't you finish your egg?'

'I have finished it.'

'No you haven't. You've left nearly all the white.'

'Oh, I didn't know I had. What does it matter, anyhow?'

'How can you talk like that? What does it matter? Can't you see it's disgusting? If you don't like boiled eggs, why not say so?'

'But I do like them.'

'Bosh!'

'But, darling, I certainly do like them. But I don't see the point of scraping the whole egg to bits.'

'Don't talk like a child, darling. Why, you've wasted half the egg.'

'Nonsense. Don't nag so.'

'Well, if you call that nagging!'

For in many ways she was much preciser, much more sensitive than Devlin. Just as she enjoyed things more fully.

In extreme moments they felt hopelessly out of harmony – Devlin was unfeeling, blundering, abstracted, always thinking about himself; Janet was all ups and downs, didn't understand one, didn't realise a man must get somewhere, must do something . . .

Devlin would just sit there thinking about himself, totting up his hard thoughts like metal, not understanding what it was like to be a female, to want things without asking for them. All these words that men had to use! Why couldn't they *feel* what one meant?

Janet was demoralising. It was all very well to do the cooking and then expect one to turn off one's mind like a tap and——

Oh, well!

For it was a very good life this. Flowing so fast, like water singing in the sun, and talking such utter nonsense – 'If your papa put a dictaphone in here he'd have us in the madhouse in no time.'

For firstly, one needn't say anything to an end or grammatically, or anything like that. Because the other one always knew what one wanted to say.

And secondly, one let oneself go in all sorts of extravagance, baby talk, swear-words, sing-song. For example there were all the names one called each other. From honey-love to pig-eyes. It was too balmy.

'After all,' Janet said, 'it's disgusting to hear two old women calling each other 'ducky', but it's quite a different thing with us.'

Other people made them laugh. They felt like conspirators. Other married people made them laugh a lot. They were all so incongruous. The Graylings, for instance, who came round and gave them a canteen of cutlery.

Sir Randal never came; nor invited them to his house. But he sent Janet one large cheque and an occasional kind but stilted letter; between the lines one could read his professional anxiety as to her happiness yoked to a psychotic. When this anxiety began to creep out in writing, Janet got bored and wrote back: 'I'm sorry you're still bothered by *that* little myth. If you're prepared to see straight, come and see for yourself. Otherwise wait and send us word when you are. We'll make allowances; my husband is extremely broad-minded. . . . Sorry to hear you're having the far greenhouse taken down. Why not tell Evans to leave it and remove the other one that's falling down, anyhow? . . . '

'I'm sorry for him,' she said to Devlin, 'but you know we're just as well without him being too genial. Just think what it would be like if he was always popping in and out.

Why, we'd always have to be putting a stopper on our language——'

'Elaine doesn't put much of a stopper.'

'Oh, she picks and chooses all right. There're lots of things she wouldn't mention in front: of him. Even lavatory. You'd never guess how prudish he is.'

'Oh, yes I would. My guardians are just the same.'

'But after all Dads is a doctor.'

'I know, darling. That doesn't save him from the tradition; ever since Cromwell——'

'My dear pet, don't start talking history; it means nothing to me. What I want to know is why can't people see things straight. All hypocrisy, that's what it is.'

'Not entirely, you know. People don't only pretend to be shocked. Certain things make them feel ill. When I was a little boy I really did feel ill when anyone talked about sex.'

'You? Rats!'

'Yes; right up till I went, to Hillbury. And after that, too. My first term in the house I was frightened out of my skin by the talk of everyone in dormitory. You see it was all so vague and innuendoish and I didn't know what it was about. And besides that I'd been terrified by my housemaster——'

'Your housemaster?'

'His warning talk. Didn't you ever have a warning talk?'

'Thank God, no. I wouldn't let any son of mine be warning talked to by a schoolmaster.'

'But they always do it. They have you in in a great atmosphere of gloom and secrecy and start off very very frowningly, saying, 'Have you ever heard any smutty talk?' That's the gambit; they go on to the dangers of sex and the need for knowing the facts. Then they tell you the facts very cloudily with lots of periphrases and in the end they send you away in a panic.'

'But do you mean to say you didn't know the facts at that age?'

'Fourteen or fifteen? No.'

'Good God!'

'I suppose you can't remember not knowing how the world worked?'

'No, I can't. It seems awfully funny to me the way you chaps grow up. Though as far as Dads was concerned, I'd never have learnt anything. My mother was French you see.'

'Yes, that must be an advantage. An English upbringing – '

'Don't talk about it, darling; it fair makes me boil. I believe one day I shall get bitter and mount up on a platform and tell everyone what silly boobs they are.'

Devlin laughed; he thought of the Graylings sitting in the audience. The Graylings who pretended to each other there was no illicit love in England and no you-know-what; while all the time their sons at Hillbury were smuggling the 'Pink 'Un' into dormitory or sneaking into the workmen's lavatory to look at the nude women on the walls (very well drawn, too.).

'It shows what a silly state the country's in,' Janet went on. 'Stopes has to sugar up her books with quotations from the poets and all that other high falutin stuff, and look at the things she has to suggest to people – *suggest*, I ask you, *tentatively*; as if it was a North Pole discovery. Is it feasible for husband and wife occasionally to see each other naked?' she looked at Devlin and they collapsed in laughter.

Shortly afterwards Janet was lying in the bath and Devlin brought in the gramophone and played her records. Then he powdered Janet and they both sang lustily Gabriel's song, 'Wenn der heilige Hogley macht Wasser.' Then he said, 'What is there for dinner?' and Janet said 'Haddock!' and they laughed.

For at the beginning, when Devlin still helped with the cooking, they had always been having haddock. Devlin would cheer it on as it sat in the frying-pan of water with its tail sticking out impertinently. And on the dish it was such a gorgeous colour.

And Devlin was privileged to gouge off for himself the narrow stratum of tasty flesh on the backbone.

Janet enjoyed cooking because of her sharp, humorous, enthusiastic senses. 'When she washed her first herrings she called Devlin before flouring them: 'Darling, do come at once, you've never known anything so deliciously sensual. Just hold them in your hand.'

And she wrote her recipes in different coloured inks into a neat little book with a red marbled cover. Mella gave her a lot of Viennese ones with lovely names like Nudeln and Kaiserschmarn. And she was very good at salads.

'We ought to have a cat you know,' she said, 'to eat up all the leavings. Especially the fish.'

'Of course we ought, darling. We ought to have a dog, too, for that matter.'

'Too expensive; besides, I know you, you wouldn't like it being sick.'

'Need it be sick?'

'That's a good one. Dogs never stop being sick; you have to be very nifty hurrying them out. No, darling, we can't have a dog till I've more time to spare to him.'

'Well, let's have a cat.'

'Yes, but I don't want a cat-like cat. I want something which will love me a lot.'

'Well, you've got that already, haven't you?'

'No. No one loves me. As for you, you rotten old pig-eyes, you're nothing but a blinking sham.'

'Nonsense.'

'All right then. Come here and abase yourself.'

Devlin came up and Janet tousled his hair at the back.

'There,' she said, 'now you look like a silly little boy. No, don't touch it. It's sweet like that.'

Thus they floated along, in perfect laziness. At least they both worked, but that was all. They took no notice at all of the problems which occupy everyone. Janet had no use for absolute law, for downright, sweeping generalisations. 'It's rats,' she said, 'the way people say red suits one type of girl and blue suits the other type, and then the wretched types of girl aren't allowed to wear anything else for the rest of their lives. What I say is, one thing one time and another thing another. Provided you're appropriate you're all right. I always think it so ridiculous on a slushy day in winter to see girls out shopping in silk stockings and thin shoes – it doesn't look well-dressed, it just looks silly. Just the same way when one's doing housework it's only sense to tie up one's head in a handkerchief; but to go on like Elaine and put on a handkerchief just in time for tea and sling glass beads round one's neck' – Janet waved her hands; she did half her talking with her hands.

They were very delicate hands; Devlin was terrified of her hurting them washing up. He gave her some rubber gloves from Woolworth's. But she wouldn't wear them. 'I like to feel what I'm doing,' she said.

For her fingers were very clever, they could draw out headaches – passing and passing over your forehead and then pausing, with a cool dream's pressure.

Headaches? Devlin had never before been so looked after. Sometimes it irritated him; sometimes he basked in it. Janet knew what to do for anything; she had a whole chest of bottles.

Devlin had, ever since he went to school, been accustomed to play the martyr whenever he cut himself, bruised himself, or felt in any way ill; play the martyr and do nothing about it. Janet said that was mucky nonsense. Even if he scratched his finger she would seize it at once and dab on hydrogen peroxide, saying 'You can thank your stars I don't give you iodine.'

Devlin laughed when he thought how at Oxford he had said: 'I'd rather die than fuss about with medicines.' But Janet didn't fuss.

Every night before going to bed she washed her eyes with a thing like a little glass egg-cup. Devlin was astonished but admired it. He admired everything she did going to bed. Though they said in the papers that wives put off their husbands by doing their teeth, etcetera. He supposed other people's wives did their teeth differently.

On the dressing-table stood Janet's heavy little bottles of scent, angular, elegant, green, yellow and brown. But she would not use them before going to bed; she said it kept her from sleeping.

She took off her dress and threw it on a chair. Devlin, if it was one that mattered, took it up and put it on a hanger in the great cupboard in the wall. In this fragrant dark Egyptian tomb of a cupboard hung many little Janets, Janets without faces. The summer Janets of gingham and flowered muslin, linen chiffon and silk, some of them like formal shepherdesses, some like young demure girls, all like ghosts in the velvet rustling gloom; next to these the tennis Janets, plain white; next to these the winter Janets, woollen and serge stuffs; then the smart afternoon Janets of flowered velvet, crêpe-de-Chine, black velvet; beyond these and inviting the fingers to stroke, the grand evening Janets, heavy red satin, black georgette and net, white with a cluster of flowers, blue with a yellow bow, nothing creeping or hissing (no purple, mauve, green); nothing trickling or stagnant, nothing oily or slimy; hanging there like coloured falls of water, all pretending to be Janet.

Whereas Janet was skipping into bed with a squeal, saying: 'How does linen contrive to be cold even in August?'

And Devlin was just going to turn out the light.

'Is the light out downstairs, pussy?' she said.

'Yes, pussy, dearest!'

With which trite remarks they closed the day's conversation, for in the dark they fell into coos and grunts like some furred or feathered couple.

CHAPTER NINETEEN

How people got on with those old iron saucepans Janet couldn't imagine. She gazed with delight at her shelves of aluminium, given by Herzheimer from his own factory. These were the wonders which Devlin wrote his blurbs for. Something which could be metal and at the same time so light – that was indeed wonderful. She cleaned them with a little wire scrubber.

For Devlin aluminium was a symbol of Herzheimer. Of the only man he knew who was both sane and cheerful. Of the only man he knew who could never be called a type. (Hogley had called him a typical Jew, but then Hogley didn't know Herzheimer, and knew nothing at all about Jews. He was, of course, beautifully Jewish, but that was not all.)

Devlin always respected Herzheimer's suggestions, but he had a shock when Herzheimer told him he ought to go back on his tracks ('back to my vomit'), i.e. back to the sphere of official intellect. 'You write me very nice advertisements,' he said, 'but it is really wasting your talents. Besides, it will never bring you much money. You should have gone on at Oxford.'

'I shouldn't be here if I had.'

'No, no. You would not. But you know, my dear young man, you have the mind of a pure don. You should not waste it. Why do you not still go through with your course?'

'I couldn't. It would be out of order.'

'Nonsense, my good man. Married men can take degrees.'

'But what's the good of a degree? I'm——'

'Use your imagination. First a degree, then a fellowship——'

'Well, supposing I was good enough for that, I've seen enough of the way dons live and the rut——'

'Nonsense. That may be all so but there is no reason why you should not be different. And I tell you you ought to be a scholar. You have got that sort of mind which puts things in boxes. And, besides that, you are lazy, you need to be able to work on your hearthrug. I know what you are going to say – that you get that with me. Very good, but it is really a sinecure you know; you want a whole-time job which will open out your brain. You can easily take a good degree and become a lecturer.'

'But that will mean residing in Oxford and paying fees.'

'Not necessarily. As for the fees they will not be much. And you must do my work at the same time. And if you need extra money, I can get you an occasional broadcasting job.'

Devlin gave in; he would return to his vomit; he would jettison the ideals which made him become a gardener.

Through Herzheimer's extraordinary influence he was allowed to read for an Oxford degree almost without visiting Oxford. It meant a great deal of work though. And was rather tedious for Janet. 'Shall we ever be gay again?' she said. Then she got a kitten from her greengrocer's wife, who had said to her: 'I don't know as how I can give you a *proper* cat, duck.'

Janet asked what a proper cat meant and learned it meant a Persian. Whereas this kitten was marmalade-coloured. Janet at once clapped her hands and cried: 'That will do for me.'

It was about six weeks old, small even for its age, very fluffy and with blue eyes. As soon as it arrived Janet prepared a little box full of bird-sand. It was not at all afraid, once it had got out of the basket. It ran about and even purred softly and took a little drink of milk diluted with water. Eventually it walked without faltering right into the sandbox. Which made them vastly proud.

Though Devlin said: 'But it hasn't dug a proper hole and why doesn't it cover it over?'

'Don't be so impatient,' Janet said. 'Besides – I suppose it only does that on the bigger occasions.'

It became very affectionate, especially to Janet, and would balance itself on the back of her neck as she moved about the house. All the time it sat on her neck it purred. And it was very soft like a little fur on the neck. 'It's not like a cat at all,' Janet would say. 'Whoever heard of a cat being so affectionate?' And, in return, she gave it a woollen shawl. 'Wool is the goods,' she said, 'and, besides, it will make it happy to smell its missus.'

And Devlin said: '*I* don't know what you'll be like when you have a baby.'

When the kitten was a little bigger, they gave it a pingpong ball with orange stripes and something rattly inside. It liked that well. The same day Devlin had his first broadcasting job, decanting the lecture of an old man who had suddenly found he was inaudible; not that it needed much finding.

Devlin's rendering was a success. They offered him more jobs and at last let him deputise for a month for an important announcer who was ill. It was soul-destroying but all the same he thought of making it his job. He consulted Herzheimer.

'No, no!' said Herzheimer. 'You don't want to become a machine; so many people are machines to start with. No, no, my good young man, you are losing your natural voice already. You go through with your degree.'

So Devlin went on, reading Aristotle and Kant, and swearing that philosophy was fatuous. 'Anyone could do it,' he said. 'It's merely a matter of words.'

The kitten became a cat, its blue eyes went yellow, shone topaz in the dark. But in the day the pupils were always dark, so that it seemed to have black eyes. 'My cat's got something to it,' said Janet. 'It's not a little minx like the ordinary cat which you see.' It lay on her breast reaching up to her neck, always trying to kiss it. As Devlin looked at them he wanted to yell his homage; instead he underlined a remark about the categories. 'I don't understand that' he thought, 'but I bet it's only words,' and he looked back at Janet. 'What one understands is beyond,' he thought, 'words.'

Janet would chop up raw meat for its lunch; two ounces of raw meat from her friend the butcher's daily. While she squandered on it nonsense-talk and baby-talk like bright jewels and sequins. Calling it puss-kitten and owl-cat and baboon and migs and pig-cat. And bumble-fur and fuzz-face and cat's whiskers. Sometimes she would cry to Devlin: 'Look, doesn't he look just like an owl?' And sometimes: 'Look, darling, hasn't he a face just like the moon?' And Janet laughed and the moon-face beamed, fuzzed out at the sides, long whiskers spraying like rays.

While Janet's own face was roundish, the sort of face that never gets old. A complexion showing the pink through the white; with long eyelashes, above and below, like a rather mischievous moon. But she encouraged Devlin to work.

When, however, she thought he was reading Aristotle, and found he was reading Tchehov, she was annoyed, and, as always, outspoken. 'What are you reading that stuff for?'

'Tchehov? Why, just for a change.'

'You don't mean to say you like it?'

'Well, I'm not sure. Yes, I suppose I like it.'

'You suppose? Well, I know downright I don't. It's so boring, darling. If anything happened or if only some of the chaps weren't half baked. And it's always the same story. A lot of poor creatures stuck in some dreary hole because they can't afford to go to Moscow——'

'Not always, darling.'

'Yes; stuck in some filthy backwater of a place because they can't afford to go to Moscow and all the time they keep telling you they can't afford to go there; first the uncle says it and then the old nurse says it, and then an old dotty creature off the farm says it and then the young man talks about his soul and then someone says they're going to shoot themselves and then the bullet gets stuck in the pistol.'

'Nonsense, pussy.'

'No, no, it's perfectly true. I tell you I've read lots of the stuff, and I've been to some of the plays. They give me the pip. They were all like that, every damned one. Only I left out the vodka – yes, they all keep drinking vodka and samovar, out of it I mean, and the old man keeps saying: 'If I only could go to Moscow, what fine vodka they have there——''

'No, no, darling; it's very funny what you say——'

'But it's true, you know it is. I don't say it's not like the Russians. All I say is I don't want to hear about them. . . .'

They talked on till they were both heated. Then Devlin went on reading his Tchehov, though with a sore and doubtful mind. After ten minutes' reading he put it away and took down his Aristotle's Ethics. His exam was to be next summer a year. After that a lightning thesis, and see if he could get: a University job.

'What a joke,' Janet said, 'I'll do well as a don's wife,' and she did a high lack, which nearly touched the beam in their bedroom.

'You'll have to give up your red trousers,' said Devlin.

'Not I,' said Janet. They both laughed and Devlin patted her haunches. There was a tinkle and they saw the yellow cat, who now wore a bell, uncurling himself on the bed. Janet examined him. 'He's still moulting badly,' she said. 'I must give him some condition powders.'

And an hour afterwards, as they lay in bed, she suddenly said: 'I do hope he's all right, our catty.'

'If ever we have a babe . . .!' said Devlin.

A fortnight later they found they were going to have one.

'I don't know how it happened,' said Janet.

'No. How *did* it happen?'

'Well, there it is anyhow. And it's all the wrong time with your work and everything. And we can't possibly afford it.'

'Oh, we'll afford it all right. A little more broadcasting——'

'Sixty pounds to bring it into the world and lots more afterwards——'

'Never mind, darling. . . .'

And soon they were caught up in the excitement of it, like people got on a wrong train going to a great city.

But, as the city drew near, the windows were full of chimneys, and there was a great noise and smoke. But Devlin's instinct had woken; he was thrilled by what was evolving.

It was not till the very event that he fell into a panic. Emotionally he was slow in the uptake. 'You like to sit in an armchair, to make marginal notes, to put things in boxes.' That's what Herzheimer had said. But Janet had begun to growl in a low way like a bear; doctor had come; Devlin retired to kitchen, where he now was. Kitchen was far from Janet, other end of the straggling thick-walled cottage.

For Janet wouldn't go into a nursing home; said economy could go rip; said she was damned if she wouldn't have her own baby in her own home.

But was this home? This little close house where the air in every room was a series of wires; wires with drops of sweat which ran up and down them. One could count them like balls on a ball-frame. But not coloured; nothing was properly coloured. Everything was dead like an engraving he remembered in an old magazine – an engraving called 'The Parlour,' an old couple with a family Bible.

Featuring an old couple with family bible.

Starring old couple with family Bible.

Why did he keep repeating things? Why not think about something?

'Think about – let us see – how Gabriel is getting on? Haven't heard from him – since when? About three months. Hertsy's friend seems to be doing well for him. Though his letters don't sound quite like the old Gabriel. But people don't come through in letters. Funny to think I never had more than four letters from Janet——

'No, no; think quickly of something else.'

Devlin sat in the kitchen, felt pinned to his chair, as if all the chairs and table had got pins and needles. The air was like sand-paper. It must be late now but the alarum clock had stopped. It was a blue alarum clock which Janet had bought in Selfridge's. He wished it was going because then it would overawe the silence; anything for a real ticking to over-ride the ticking and murmurs of the silence. Though the people upstairs made occasional noises, but far away because the kitchen was tacked on at the end of the straggly cottage.

The August day had been horribly long and hot. Thank God, it hadn't thundered; all day long the drum-sticks seemed poised ready, held like destroying rods in the swathes of heavy cloud; but they never – luckily – fell. Janet couldn't bear thunder or any sudden noises; gunshots on the stage or a car back-firing.

Corpses clotted the fly-paper, but many potential corpses were still walking and talking. Look at that fly on the table, on Janet's oil-cloth from Woolworth's, yellow and white check. Look how he rubbed his hands like an oily tailor. And what was that kept moving about on the ceiling, in petulant gauze circles? Like a ballet dancer in a stiff frilled skirt. When it stopped for a part of a second, he saw it was a daddy-longlegs.

All the legs and wings made a noise like sticks on his eardrum, a monotonous crashing tattoo on the taut parchment of mind. He must really get up and wind the clock. See if that drove them away – raising its hands like a policeman?

But he didn't get up.

Thought of being taken to church, when wan and little, by the Graylings. The smell of pew varnish, the marble skull opposite belonging to John Hogarth, the frightening intonations about, *sin, hell, death.* The monosyllables hung in the air, seemed plucked out on wires.

And in a cave of the sea, which was once Hillbury Chapel, seven hundred heads floated on green water; the organ-pipes like vast silver stalactites with growths of gilt lichen. Washing its yellow-white scum on the iron-echoing walls, dead starfish and strands of torn seaweed. But after all that was where Janet——

No. Quickly. What was that straight above his head? A spider making for another spider. Going to eat him. Approaching like a boxer, feinting with his hands. And the other spider, the male I suppose, backs away. What a racket they all make.

'I must really wind that clock.'

But now he fell into a stupor; instead of winding the clock, fancied he had wound it. When he looked at it again, he was surprised to see the hands still were where they were.

All the time the electric light went on, though it seemed to get sometimes very much brighter and sometimes almost dark. The silly bulb there, hanging still on the wire, like a silly crystal pear.

He relapsed into a quieter stupor, staring without blinking at the harsh grain of the air. Gradually his mind opened; he seemed to send something up out of him, which reached through the floor to hover around Janet; and just as this thing, like an angel but without any face or almost any body, just as it reached the bed, Janet's baby was born.

CHAPTER TWENTY

It was a little doll Janet had given birth to, painlessly and easily. It had a delicate fringe of hair, its face was neither flat nor red. All its limbs were neat and exact, it had ten toe-nails and ten finger-nails. But it made life very strenuous.

With a nurse running about always washing things and the little doll screaming which they said was only healthy, and this out-of-date exam hanging over his head.

In June he went up to Oxford for his exam. He took a first-class. Shortly afterwards Herzheimer suggested he should put in for a lecturership in London. Professor Shawes was told to recommend him highly, and so, as the two other candidates suffered respectively from scrumpox and aphasia, he got that job. At the same time he began a thesis 'on the reaction of the latest physical theories upon pure philosophy or metaphysics,' And now that he was a philosopher, he gave up his little commercial job with Herzheimer, who appointed in his place a young Scotsman in boots.

But Devlin's heart was not in philosophy. It seemed to him all a put-up job. A philosophic system was just an idol – a construction like a work of art, not a description, not science. And it fell between the two stools of science and art. 'But never mind, I can't follow my conscience. I've got to support this baby.'

Perhaps, he thought one day, there are such things as good philosophers. But then to be one of those one would have to be broad-minded to the extent of being empty; one would have to press out the sides of one's box till it was no longer a box, till everything was level with the ground.

Whereas he still had some of the bias, some of the erectnesses and angles of his father who governed Madras, some of the puritan stiffness which would not lie low and level. He still had some of the English puritan's craving to twist and shape his life, to fix his eyes on a goal Though he said to himself a goal was just a fallacy.

All the same it was difficult to live in the moment or even to think that being a good husband and father was everything. Or could one be a good husband and father if one was not a good something else? It was the man's job to be ambitious – to be abstract, 'cosmic.'

This thought made him irritable sometimes. When his nerves were bad he put it all down to Janet. Thinking that when he was just grown up, a young man in revolt, then he had been in the right. His setting off for a gardener had been quixotic but all the same logical. Then he had lived ministering to ideas, to his own and those of the world. All for creating himself and recreating the world. Whereas now he acquiesced, in the half-made un-made world. Because Janet was so strong, he had become like a woman. It was all right for a woman to be herself, herself plus her child; a man had to be, or at least pretend to be, the world; otherwise he lost his self-respect. All the men going up to the city in the morning and back from the city in the evening retained that self-respect; that was why they clasped the daily papers so fearlessly to their bosom – because they and the paper were different aspects of the same, the supreme thing, the World.

And many men had got right through their lives thinking they were the world. Napoleon and people like that. Though they had to be necessarily callous.

A Napoleon could not be a good husband. The Roman Catholic church was quite right to enforce its priests' celibacy.

For an artist must cut himself off, isolate himself, so as to be as free as humanly possible. Luckily many artists were born isolated – perverted somehow, like Gabriel. 'But I could never have been an artist, so what does it matter?'

Devlin looked at the little girl, who happened to be his daughter, and laughed a little sadly. She was pleasantly pouting, with a pencil in her fist, scrawling on a huge sheet of paper. Supposing one did write, one could never put her across. Nor Janet either. History and ideas were all one could put across; square hard entities, which travelled well, like biscuits. One couldn't put across the magnificent flux of experience. Janet and his daughter; or even the yellow cat.

The little girl, Anne, was very good. There she sat patiently, though her mother had been away all day. Away at Sir Randal's funeral. Devlin declined to go with her; said he didn't see how he could. For Sir Randal had never recognised him.

The thought of Sir Randal troubled him, made him feel, in spite of himself, guilty. He kept saying to himself there was no question of guilt. Sir Randal had died suddenly, believing implicitly in the country and Progress, in his four daughters and son. (Janet had married a rogue; that she managed to keep happy was all the more tribute to her. And Elaine rarely came home, and pretended strange standards; but that was all pose, just animal spirits; she would sober down in the end.)

For Sir Randal had, in the last year of his life, relaxed; he could not but make allowances where his instincts prompted him. He was very tired by his work for public causes and wanted to withdraw into his family. It would all turn out right, his family. Soon he might even have recognised Devlin. But on a May evening, when the gnats were high and promising a change of weather, he died of heart-failure.

The Reverend Bilbatrox preached his funeral sermon and *The Times* gave him a column and a half obituary. They all praised him without qualification. Yet the fact was he was not a great doctor; he had been very talented in his youth and very energetic and public-spirited afterwards.

And the *Church Times* got in a special boost for Bilbatrox, who would feel Sir Randal's loss greatly in his oncoming 'Campaign'; for all that, knowing his (Bilbatrox') qualities. . . . A paragraph followed on Bilbatrox' qualities.

But Devlin, as he waited for Janet to return, felt a curious remorse. He saw Sir Randal very plainly, sitting like a judge and judging by mythical laws. The young man, who had been judged, felt responsible for Sir Randal's deep conviction that these myths were truth.

And Sir Randal was, of his kind (as they say), a giant, a great man, a good work of the gods.

Devlin looked up and noticed his daughter crying. This call to action was a relief. He soon found out what was the matter; of course, yes, ever so long she'd been there; wouldn't Janet be angry? He led Anne away and saw to her.

Then Janet came home and swept away his sorrows (though she, too, was sad). First she asked about Anne and was duly indignant. Then she ran upstairs and changed her black clothes. Then she put Anne to bed. Then she set to work on the gas cooker – clank and bustle and warm smells. And there, suddenly, was dinner.

The yellow cat sat demurely by, waiting for its blue bowl to be filled; without mewing, staring into space like an owl. 'I saw Mrs. White today,' said Janet; 'she's just got a Siamese cat.'

And so she tattled away his sorrow.

After dinner Devlin went on with his thesis, writing it not because he thought it was valuable but solely for vulgar expediency – and perhaps to exercise his brain. He was habitually worried about his brain.

This thesis, when printed, was a surprising success. It won him an advanced degree and was shortly afterwards published in book-form. It was very well reviewed; it was even reviewed in *Mind.* The critics discovered in it (a) clarity, and (b) vigour. Devlin wondered how it could be so, when his ideas on philosophy were all so cloudy and cumbrous. Perhaps it was because his life proper was happy.

For he worshipped life. He almost agreed with Sir Randal that any suicide must be mad. Life meant the sun, flowers, food, Janet. Janet and Life were each other's warp and woof. Without Janet the world would be mere anatomy.

So when they offered him a fellowship at Oxford, he was not contemptuous. He ran out into the street with his face all over shaving lather and hallooed after Janet, who had just gone out shopping. He simmered with delight. He would go on playing the philosopher: they would pay him for it like any other actor.

Their last amusement before leaving their cottage and London was going to see Gabriel on the talkies. For Gabriel was now a member of New York's star band which had been enlisted to play in the new musical film 'Cut your Jonk.' Devlin was very excited and made Janet excited too. He hoped to see the real Gabriel again, instead of the dull topical Gabriel who sometimes wrote him letters.

The band appeared a good deal in the film but after its first appearance Devlin gave up hope; Gabriel wouldn't come across. There was indeed a man at the piano, accurately bohemianised with a big sloppy bow and his hair fuzzed to its fullest – though it seemed to have receded on his forehead. But his face was merely a mask. Occasionally there came a smile which the producer must have taught him. It was a great triumph for America.

Janet was amused by the film but soon sensed that Devlin was depressed. When they got home she sat on his knee and stroked his forehead and hair; smoothed away his disappointment, stopped him being tired, took away that feeling that he was now very old. Because wasn't it natural to feel old after seeing that man pretending to be Gabriel?

Fate was like the drawing-master at his prep school who snooped up behind one and suddenly altered one's drawing. He had planned to be a gardener and make his own life in the Tolstoy manner. Then Janet had appeared from nowhere and shifted his whole river – right out of its bed and into another country. They had decided not to have a baby for at least four years and then, shortly over a year – crash——

But that surprise was a good one. Still, who knows there mayn't be evil surprises too? It's all too good to go on. Suddenly a war, or disease. . . . One couldn't have believed Gabriel would fade to nothing, but so it was.

It would be Anne's birthday in a fortnight; they would move to their new Oxford house just in time for it. Hertsy and Mella were abroad; there was no one to say good-bye to. No one except the greengrocer and the fishmonger and the butcher. The greengrocer's wife would say 'Bye-bye, duck,' in her funny way like a gipsy.

Their furniture hardly filled the van they chartered to Oxford, and not one of the big vans. They themselves went up by train with many suitcases and packages and the yellow cat mewing in a basket. Anne was excited, sat inside herself, looking out of her vast long-lashed eyes. She said nothing; she was slow in saying if she liked things; 'chewing the cud' Devlin called it. She still looked just like a doll and Janet dressed her in stiff pretty little dresses.

Their new house was in North Oxford – not a bungalow, thank God, but something rather like one. Its outside was repellently stupid. All the houses on either side and across the road were similar; though they aspired to elaborate distinctiveness – to sudden gables of plaster and beam-work on the top of an otherwise brick house, to various textures of brickage (old and mellow mottled or new shiny hygienic); to bright little porches added like afterthoughts or built in in an ingenious way which hid the downstairs lavatory window.

Their house was not so offensive as some; while, talking of lavatories, it had a remarkably fine flush, the first thing Devlin noticed.

'Thank God for that!' shouted Janet, as she lugged a bundle through the hall.

The next moment the dining-room gas-fire lit with a pop and the house became their slave. The little polyps in the fire went hurriedly pink and obedient, all their little fingertips glowed, and through the holes below the gas welled blue and alive. Anne stood gaping at this unique coral island. At once they were far away from the house on the left called 'Capri,' and the house on the right, 'The Nook,' and all the other houses in Wellington and Victoria Avenue, Winchester Avenue and Nelson Crescent. All which other houses were clean, efficient and original, with sky-blue curtains and distempered walls – none of that frowsty Victorian stuff. The people who lived in them were all up to date, free from nonsense. Whereas Devlin and Janet were shockingly retarded, webbed in laughs and nonsense, dabbling for ever in pools of shining water. The families in 'The Nook' and 'Capri' walked high and dry; but civilisation hasn't, even as yet, managed to drain everywhere.

On Anne's birthday they took her in a punt on the Cherwell. It was morning and there was no one on the river. On this river Devlin, in a previous incarnation, had splashed about with an ordinary man called Gunter; amid a riot of gramophones and ugly girls in punts. Or perhaps they were all a book written by someone; the faint breeze of memory blew the pages, willow leaves bent backwards white. He had come one Sunday in a small canoe by himself; under that bridge had been a punt-load of young townees, gaping and giggling upwards under the skirts of the girls who stood leaning on the bridge.

Whack! Anne saw a water-rat. Very self-contained he stood on a broad leaf, eating something in his hands. He stood and he ate and, then, he slid suddenly away. Anne called it a 'tuddle-rat';

she was always coining words. When they got home, she made Devlin draw a tuddle-rat. Which he did very badly, so crossed it out and said 'Now I'll draw you Sal.' Sal was Hertsy's bright aluminium kettle with the round red blob on the lid – rather like a Chinaman's hat; when she boiled, she tilted her lid up and looked quite rakish.

Soon term would be upon them, and they would have young men to tea. Sal would be an official kettle boiling tea for pupils. How absurd. For all those half-existents who would attend one's lectures and talk a lot, all the time thinking of their new pipes and jumpers. Funny to have come back to it all.

'But before we return to that rather unreal vomit, let us go to St. Giles' fair; in the first week of September. It will be a treat for Anne.'

So Anne goes in the afternoon, and is overwhelmed by the disappearance of St. Giles' and the appearance of everything else. She rides on a little donkey in one of the tiny roundabouts which is worked by a handle, which is wound by a dirty man. Anne mustn't be bumped or hurt so Devlin and Janet see nothing of the fair. They trot Anne home and disinfect her. They ask Anne what she thinks of the fair, but she says nothing. They give her her monkey, which looks like Devlin, and leave her.

'Well?' said Janet, winking.

'You want to go back to the fair?'

'Of course I do. Don't I adore fairs more than anything almost in the world? Besides, I must win us a new pepper-castor because catty has cracked the old one.'

'All right. Let's go after dinner.'

It was dark. As they walked down from North Oxford, a glow greeted them like a whole city of pleasure. By the church was a batch of caravans, the gipsy women washing and cooking. Some pretty gipsy brats sat on the steps or leaned out of the doors.

Waves of sound crossing and re-crossing lapped foam on their faces. The fair swallowed them. Coarse grins floated in the air, showmen yelled their prices, cheap scent came clammy against the skin.

Devlin and Janet threw darts and rolled balls into holes. After spending three shillings Janet won a tiny china shoe with a pink and green bow. 'I love winning things,' she said, and pinched Devlin's arm.

So as not to spend too much they kept walking from place to place. Several times they walked the whole length of St. Giles'. Near the swing boats by St. John's they saw two well-dressed men in the squalid crowd of shop-boys. It was Cyril Hogley and a young man with model features. 'Look,' said Devlin.

'Oh! so that's your Hogley?' Janet wrinkled her nose.

'Why do you make a face?'

'I didn't mean to, darling. He looks so conceited.'

'So he is. Shall we go and greet him?'

'As you will.'

Devlin saw she didn't want to and they moved off. While Hogley and the young man went round the booths and won several prizes, Hogley aridly smiling, but every now and again feeling for a moment happy.

Devlin and Janet mounted a peacock chariot belonging to one Petronelli. At the back of the organ-pipes was a waterfall; classicalish figures stood on either side armed with swords and bosoms. The tune was eternally old. Going round this course was a whole life. Organ, waterfall, organ. The cars stopped before the tune did, and, though indignant, they descended and had another life on a dragon-car next door.

Coming again to a dart stall, Janet said she must just have another go. They waited in a crowd of potato-faces and potato-sack bodies; then squeezed their way to the barrier. Janet seized the darts and flung them with her whole arm. One of them missed the target——

'Damn!' said Janet, laughing. 'I'll be terribly stiff tomorrow.'

'You should throw more with your wrist, darling.'

'Rats! I like to have my money's worth.'

'Like another go?'

Janet grinned.

Devlin paid her twopence to the hard-mouthed showman.

As they pushed through the crowd again, 'I do hope,' Janet said, 'Anne will sleep all right. You know when she's excited she doesn't always.'

'Oh, Emily will see to her.'

'I don't know. I'm rather worried.'

Devlin had to hurry her on to a roundabout. This was a horse. This was the real goods.

Creakingly, slowly the iron rods rose, one horse in three put his head forward. Quickening into a surge that never withdrew its waves, always forward, never making contact, not falling to ground nor putting in to shore. The absurd piling and piling and never completing, bucking and rising to the roofs on the hoofs of triumphant, to the roofs that glittered on the hoofs that, but never, for ever, completing; repeating; luridly dipping and diving, soaring, never surfeiting, curvetting, ramping, snorting, cavorting, on high hoofs prancing to the roofs, to the clouds, to the full flamboyant moon, to the moon going round us and us going round, but never, never finding or ending the always replenished, the bright brim spilling, filling again the, always falling, filling. . . .

The horses dawdled to a stop. 'We can't get off,' said Janet. 'Pay him for another.'

Slowly the platform revolved, the horses gathered themselves, rose on their poles and sank, Devlin and Janet sat on one horse, Devlin behind Janet with one hand on the pole, and the other round her waist. They were on the outermost horse of the three; they seemed to swing outwards, over all the faces. They were on top now.

As they passed they swung towards the bedroom windows of the shocked elderly houses. As God might do, riding on a fiery cloud.

Around a round repeating. Till the horses dawdled down; again they paid and again the horse gathered them up, soared and tugged at his moorings. Each time he tugged something caught him sharp, drew his head downwards, but each time he reached the balanced top of his crest Devlin and Janet rose, almost off his back, screaming like mad gulls.

While Devlin's thoughts, quite distinct from his voice, were nothing but a shower of snow-flakes or the petals of a burst rose – unconnected, one by one, voluptuous. He no longer saw the crowd or any definite shapes, only a jangle of lights and the faint stars in the greenish milky sky – milky green like the sea at the mouth of a glacier. Against which vague background flashed imaginary faces: some for no reason at all like the maths, master at his prep school and some for very good reason like Anne, a jonquil, in her nightdress; each only caught for the least fraction of a second. Then he came back to Janet, felt her body against him, and her mind cloaking him. 'Darling,' she shouted, 'isn't it fun? Oh! isn't it fun?' She turned her face back to him, and he kissed it as the horse plunged downwards; and as the horse rose, his drowning kiss continued. As the sea rises and drowns the swooning sky.

'Isn't it fun?' she cried.

Down below there loitered the several thousand townees, taking their jaded amusement at the garish stalls of the coarse, faintly humorous salesmen. The showmen's faces were very hard and sensual – and their women's faces, though handsome, were hard too.

As the roundabout stopped, a crowd rushed up to mount it. But Devlin and Janet sat as if part of their horse; Devlin pulled another fourpence from his pocket and paid the bored face as it pushed between the horses. Then, as they moved forward again, he took his hand from the pole and slid both his arms round Janet, clasping her under her coat. In the crowd below young men were tweaking girls and hitting them with whips of coloured paper; while at the far end of the fair opposite St. John's a salvationist tent was pitched and a fat cockney was bawling about the wickedness of the world and how it was high time to take the road to Salvation. Careless of all which Devlin rode in the sky with Janet, his hands cupped round her breasts, and laughed at the world, its prudery and prurience.